I0761228

Nathan and His Wives

Judaic Traditions in Literature, Music, and Art
Ken Frieden *and* Harold Bloom, *Series Editors*

Other titles in Judaic Traditions in Literature, Music, and Art

Badenheim 1939. Aharon Appelfeld; Betsy Rosenberg, trans.

Contemporary Jewish American Writers and the Multicultural Dilemma: The Return of the Exiled. Andrew Furman

The Dybbuk and the Yiddish Imagination: A Haunted Reader
Joachim Neugroschel, trans. & ed.

H. N. Bialik and the Prophetic Mode in Modern Hebrew Poetry. Dan Miron

Hurban: Responses to Catastrophe in Hebrew Literature. Alan L. Mintz

The Image of the Shtetl and Other Studies of Modern Jewish Literary Imagination
Dan Miron

The Jewish Book of Fables: The Selected Works of Eliezer Shtaynbarg
Eliezer Shtaynbarg; Curt Leviant, trans. & ed.

Nineteen to the Dozen: Monologues and Bits and Bobs of Other Things
Sholem Aleichem; Ted Gorelick, trans.; Ken Frieden, ed.

Polish Jewish Literature in the Interwar Years
Eugenia Prokop-Janiec; Abe Shenitzer, trans.

A Room of His Own: In Search of the Feminine in the Novels of Saul Bellow
Gloria Cronin

The Stories of David Bergelson: Yiddish Short Fiction from Russia
Golda Werman, trans. and ed.

Translating Israel: Contemporary Hebrew Literature and Its Reception in America
Alan L. Mintz

A Traveler Disguised: The Rise of Modern Yiddish Fiction in the Nineteenth Century
Dan Miron

NATHAN
and His Wives

A NOVEL

Miron C. Izakson

Translated from the Hebrew by Betsy Rosenberg

Edited by Ken Frieden

SYRACUSE UNIVERSITY PRESS

First Edition 2003
03 04 05 06 07 08 6 5 4 3 2 1

Originally published in Hebrew as *Nashotav shel Natan* by Hakibbutz Hameuchad Publishing House, Ltd., in 1998.

Published by arrangement with the Institute for the Translation of Hebrew Literature.

The paper used in this publication meets the minimum requirements of American National Standard for Information Sciences—Permanence of Paper for Printed Library Materials, ANSI Z39.48–1984.∞™

Library of Congress Cataloging-in-Publication Data

Izakson, Meron H.
[Neshotav shel Natan. English]
Nathan and His Wives : a novel / Miron C. Izakson ; translated from the Hebrew by Betsy Rosenberg ; edited by Ken Frieden.—1st ed.
p. cm.—(Judaic traditions in literature, music, and art)
ISBN 0-8156-0788-1
I. Rozenberg, Betsi. II. Frieden, Ken, 1955– III. Title. IV. Series.
PJ5054.I88N4713 2003
892.4'6—dc21

2003006754

Manufactured in the United States of America

PART ONE

RINA

1

RINA WANTS to bring her husband Nathan a second wife. Not in order to leave him or to throw him out. Just to find him another woman.

"With two women at home, many new opportunities will arise," I heard Rina explain.

Usually Nathan is in no hurry to go along with Rina and would rather examine all the details closely before giving his consent. But this time he is eager to cooperate. Perhaps because the plan seems so interesting to him, even fascinating.

I've heard of cases in which a wife brought her husband another woman to keep him busy and to give herself a rest. Some people claim that a new woman may actually rejuvenate the marriage. In general, many conversations and activities that go on in a house with two women are not possible in a house with only one woman present. Then, of course, there have been instances of barren women who offered their husbands a second wife to give him children. Such things are mentioned in the Bible and, in any event, things that we haven't come across in the Bible are difficult to imagine.

Still, Rina's initiative seems strange to me. She gave birth to Nathan's two sons, and why shouldn't she have more children? At the office I heard someone claim that her real motive in bringing home a "rival" is to add zest to their lives. It's hard for me to grasp this claim. I mean, whenever my wife Rachel asks me for anything,

I try my best to satisfy her. But Nathan is shrewder and tougher than I am, and he doesn't forgive easily or go out of his way to make other people happy. He takes a hands-on approach to life and enjoys waving his hands in the air as if he were conducting a piano quartet—as he also likes sweeping big, sweet crumbs off the table and into his mouth. Nathan is meticulous about every fold he makes on a piece of paper, in particular when it comes to paper napkins; he keeps his fingernails long and clean but is never squeamish about touching slimy fluids or the inside of a banana peel.

I would have been wary of Rina's initiative. In general, I shrink from personal problems and legal complications. Moving from one apartment to another is enough to confuse me, not to mention having two women in the same home. And there's another essential difference between Nathan and me. As far as I'm concerned, a religious prohibition is law, and I am never lax about such things. Nathan, however, will accept no constraints at all. He likes to collect and keep for himself all options and objects.

This morning when I walk into Nathan's office I find that, instead of concentrating on his wife or at least on his work, he is busy drawing up a list.

"Come here, Meir," he almost roars in my direction. "Look at my new list. I'm writing down all of the essential questions—by which I mean every question that may be said to change everything."

I glance at Nathan's list and read the first few questions: Is existence possible without movement? Is it possible to forget a thing that we have never known? How much must go to waste (parts, letters) so that something will remain, in the end?

I'm not the only one Nathan subjects to such essential questions. One of his pastimes is to surprise his employees and business associates, right in the middle of meetings, with questions of this kind. He likes to ask about personal and business details that no one remembers.

"Now the essential question is whether I need to do everything at least once in order to find out whether doing it more is impossible." This is how he ends our brief meeting, during which I haven't said a word.

2

NATHAN AND RINA are going out to pick a second wife to bring home. I'm tempted to describe what's happening with them at this very moment. It's never been clear to me why, in reports, we place so much weight on past events. I value precisely what's happening now. The present, after all, is what determines thoughts and deeds.

Nathan smiles, puts a flower in his shirt pocket. He's uncomfortable in suits (too hot for a heavyset man like him), but there's nothing wrong with putting a flower in his shirt pocket. Rina is scantily dressed. Even if her husband takes a new wife, she still has to be attractive to him. Nothing Nathan does appears too extreme to her. He is the man she married and with him she will stay. It seems to me that there's no one fatter than he is in the street just now, and hardly anyone skinnier than his wife.

"It's important that you join us," Nathan says to me. "Sometimes you have very astute things to say. What are you worried about? Rina doesn't intend to break up our home, or to set up separate residences. She merely wants to add a new wife to our existing home. You know me, I wouldn't take on the extra expense of a second household."

He smiles and Rina punches him fondly in the belly. I could have replied that he probably needs several apartments just to store all the antique furniture he's accumulated, but I hold my tongue.

"I've drawn up this list of friends," Rina says, "who are gathering references for us."

"Generally speaking you can find anything you want among your personal acquaintances," Nathan says. "I set up most of my businesses through people I've known since my childhood." The friends sitting at the table prick up their ears and Rina watches closely. She and Nathan seem to be going about this in a very serious fashion.

My friendship with Nathan may sound a little confusing. I am thoroughly devoted to my wife, Rachel, whether she is devoted to me or not, whether I find her attractive or not. With Nathan you never know: all women are possible, all parts of the body are free to act as they wish. Nathan has no commitments other than preparing for the financial future of his sons, though he tends to disregard even their concerns. As for me, I sometimes speak with him about radical, even risqué things. I've never been good at curbing my tongue, though I'm fine when it comes to actions. I suppose that anyone who knows me from my words alone may form a pretty strange impression. The fact is that Nathan has chosen me of all people as his confidant in business, and even in some of his future planning. Then he reminds me of someone who's just composed a new melody and insists on talking about it to a friend who recoils from music.

We're sitting at a café together with Nathan and Rina's friends and, of course, Nathan's personal assistant, Uzzi. As usual, I order only a drink. The others are eating. I'd rather eat later, on my own. They all take out envelopes with photographs of available women (Rina, I gather, would prefer one who has never been married). Uzzi calls some other acquaintances and asks them to join us with more lists and information. It suddenly occurs to me that Nathan could choose any woman at all, even from some other country, though I still hope that he'll be satisfied with the local options. It looks to me as though they won't be able to finish the job today. So far they've only looked at pictures. Every so often Nathan makes an amusing remark and everyone whoops with laughter. Rina is taking notes, Uzzi begins sorting the photographs into piles (beginning with the girls who don't appeal to Nathan at all, up to those who seem possible), while I peruse them and read the information on the back.

3

LAST NIGHT I had an entirely new and different dream: in the apartment where my wife Rachel and I live, there was a small tiger. The tiger was waiting for me there before I came home from work. The presence of the tiger was evident to me, but it was not clear how I was supposed to live in peace with it under the same roof. Should I shut the door? Try to negotiate with it? I hoped it had been tamed and was not too fierce. In the dream, I wasn't especially surprised that I was expected to get along with it. I force myself to get along with all sorts of people, so why not with a tiger?

"You must have had an argument with Rachel, that's why you dreamed about a tiger," Nathan laughs the next morning at the office when I tell him about the dream. "Never underestimate the power of having a tiger in your very own home. I always knew you were a scoundrel, in spite of your meek demeanor." His words ring loud and strong. Who in the office would hint that he should whisper? His voice sounds steady, less hoarse than I used to think. He wears a pleasant smile, a cleaner shirt than my own. His bald spot is large and conspicuous. His fingers grasp the receipts for several of his more recent transactions, artistic and otherwise. Clearly I've succeeded in rousing his curiosity this time; perhaps I've even impressed him.

"Having a tiger of your own," he marvels, "would completely change your status. Think what you'd save on security, not to mention in business—who'd dare fight with someone who has a pet tiger at home?"

His enthusiasm pleases me to no end. Thanks to my tiger fantasy, I have actually aroused his interest. I always make an effort to impress people, especially Rachel and Nathan. Today I succeeded, and I didn't even have to take care of the tiger, didn't even have to feed it once. Incidentally, it makes perfect sense that the tiger appeared in my dream on a day when I was angry with my wife. One type of person, when he gets angry at his wife, dreams about a wild animal he needs to pacify. Other men who are angry at their wives want to exchange her for another.

NATHAN AND RINA have two sons, Shlomo and Shahar. Both were sent to study in select boarding schools in England.

"They're not missing much around here, are they? Well, maybe their mother will be sad for a couple of days," Nathan said to me at the time. I can't tell for sure whether he was stating this as a fact or trying to shock me. I don't know whether he is ever this outspoken with his sons. On the few occasions I met the boys, Shlomo seemed quiet or timid and Shahar (maybe because of his tender age) chatted nonstop with his mother. On these occasions Nathan would inquire about their schoolwork and set up a history contest between them. Now that they're abroad, he's back to his usual pursuits and amusements. Every so often I run into him with Rina and note that their exchanges are as brief and predictable as ever. He is still collecting antique furniture, which he arranges among his various homes and warehouses. He still lists the "essential" questions in his life—who knows how many by now? He spends much of his time verifying data about his childhood.

"Nothing is more important than my childhood," Nathan is fond of saying, "and my only worry is how much like my father I'm becoming. I never gave it much thought before, but now I see an uncanny resemblance. I loved my father, until he died. But I recoiled from some things about him, which I'm afraid I've started noticing in myself lately. His smell, for instance, when he'd get up in the morning, or the way he would doze off at meetings, or his tendency to put on weight, or the pointless anecdotes he told at meetings, like my inability to finish shaving completely, together with my love of smooth skin. He was afraid of remaining alone, at home or in life. So far that hasn't bothered me, but down the line, who knows?"

This growing resemblance to his father confuses Nathan, as though he'll have to start counting the years differently from now on. For the first time in his life (so far as I know), he talks about his fear of illnesses during business meetings. He used to joke about his health and his life, which he said, "is expected to be short," but his anxieties are mounting fast and he rarely fools around anymore. I also get the impression that he's spending more and more time with his wife. Occasionally he calls her from the office in the evening to arrange for them to meet. I haven't heard him mention the new woman even once over the past week. But Rina's mind is made up and she still thinks it's worth a try.

"Yes. It will do us good to have another woman around," she repeats. "Anyhow, I'm not running away. If we wish, we can always go back to the way we were—just you and me. But now, instead of buying one more property, you can invest in a second wife."

5

YESTERDAY A COMPANY EMPLOYEE passed away. This time Nathan was among the first to pay a condolence call at the home of the deceased. Few people were there, probably only a little more than had visited the man during his entire lifetime. A sentence occurred to me, perhaps befitting the man who passed away: "The master of the house has died, his house has died as well, and he who never had a house died long ago." I used to spend hours working out pithy sayings of this sort. I still have notebooks full of them at home, loose-leaf pages too. But now I worry about them, even if they have great power. I should concentrate on my current reports, not make sweeping generalizations. In any case, it is evident that the deceased had almost no family or acquaintances. He worked for a long time in Nathan's corporation, yet we knew next to nothing about where or how he lived. But can it be that, when someone dies, not many people come to his house, and not many people are informed? For this reason, I've noticed that when a person is not long for this world and immediately after his death, great efforts are made to locate relatives. They even managed to find his ex-wife and bring her to his deathbed. They hadn't seen each other in years, not since she'd left him. There wasn't any love or intimacy between them anymore, yet here she was at his deathbed (by then it was clear that he would never lie in another), and she stood watching and smiling as if she were his lover. When I heard about this, I thought it was strange, but maybe I'm mistaken. I mean, who else could they have brought to his bedside when he had almost no friends or relatives?

Nathan, as I said, has arrived to console the mourners. Or maybe there are no mourners upstairs, only a few acquaintances. I'm there too, and I see Nathan linger at the entrance with his assistant. Uzzi spreads a map out for him. They seem to be considering various locations in Africa. Uzzi tries to persuade him that a certain place is fascinating to visit, and Nathan asks him what's so special about the site. Uzzi takes two letters out of his briefcase and puts them on the map of Africa that is spread out before him. Suddenly Nathan turns away from him, looks at me, and says without so much as a greeting:

"I think I'll go upstairs with you, Meir. You know all these customs better than I do. It's good you're here. I don't think I would have gone very far with Uzzi here, maybe only as far as Africa," he jokes. "You, Meir, I've known since you were born. Your father and mine were even partners in something or other."

We enter the building and walk up the stairs (the elevator doesn't come). Nathan mops the sweat on his face with a special handkerchief as we enter the apartment. He makes the rounds, shakes hands with people, glances at a picture on the wall and asks when it was painted. Then he sits down, notices photographs on the coffee table, arranges them into a neat pile, picks one up, and tries to decide whether the deceased was an employee when the picture was taken. He asks the ex-wife some questions and is inclined to agree with most of her answers. He gets up to leaf through a book, wonders whether his help may be required.

"You can always call Uzzi or Meir if you need anything," he states.

Downstairs his driver, a young woman, is waiting for him. Nathan suggests that I go with them. On the way he dozes off, then suddenly wakes up and says to her and to me:

"These days people and countries no longer matter. The relationships between corporations are decisive. Once people worked so hard to establish states, but now companies are what count. Only they are worth fighting over and conquering. We've actually regressed to a prestate era."

I prefer not to respond, and I don't even mention certain problems at work that have been bothering me lately. I haven't sent him a single substantive report since he put me in charge of developing the firm's unutilized properties, nor has he asked me for any sort of information, which is not like him. Now they drop me off at home and continue on their way.

6

THEY DRIVE to Nathan's house. Waiting for him in front are some of his employees and associates; his wife Rina, wearing a short black dress; his son Shlomo; a brass quartet; and two singers in foreign garb. He observes all this and smiles. Surprises never frighten him.

What's wrong with throwing a big party in front of his house? Apparently he is tallying production costs versus the possible advantages of this event. Aloud he asks for plenty of snapshots. "So we'll have something left when this whole thing is over," he says to a veteran photojournalist who has arrived on the scene. Then he walks over to his wife and kisses her.

With her long, manicured fingernails, Rina combs his clean hair. Shlomo joins his parents and together they pose for a photograph. The musicians converge and everyone sings. Friends crowd around the refreshment table. They all praise Rina for her staging of this original street party and, of course, for the expensive food. Nathan helps himself to several rolls, asks Rina to fix him a platter, and scolds her for not serving any of that new vegetable he likes so much. Now I'm also at the party, having found a note on my door requesting my presence at Nathan and Rina's right away.

I hear Rina asking for silence. Some of the guests go on talking, mostly about work, but she ignores them and continues her speech, praising her husband and his thriving business, and, of course, her son Shlomo, who flew home especially for the occasion. She says that this is the first time she has initiated a party—during the day at any rate, and in the front yard no less—without consulting her husband.

"Yes, a momentous event has taken place today," she continues, "and I want all of you to know. Our Nathan, as you know, is a fascinating man. Several weeks ago I proposed to my Nathan that we bring a new wife into our home. He wasn't so enthusiastic, but finally he agreed." Rina's voice trembles yet she speaks at a moderate tempo. Although she is a talented woman, I have never been able to figure out her opinions on certain subjects, including her husband. Meanwhile, as Nathan moves closer to where she is standing, he exchanges whispers with Uzzi, apparently trying to clarify what his wife has done. For the moment she is the center of attention. The band has stopped playing, but the waiters continue serving food. Rina speaks:

"There are some who can only wish and dream, but our Nathan fulfills his every whim. This time I've followed his lead and acted quickly. At the home of family friends, I recently made the acquaintance of an attractive and talented young woman named Dana. I have spoken to her several times already and she is prepared to come live with us on a trial basis until she can get to know our family better, particularly Nathan, of course. The reason I didn't bring her here this afternoon is that I thought it would be more appropriate for Nathan to meet her before the rest of you. In any event, you'll all be joining us again in the not too distant future, for a special occasion of a business or family nature."

All eyes are on Nathan. He is standing very still, though it's hard to tell whether he's watching his wife or merely listening to her.

"And I have more interesting news for you," Rina continues. "Not long ago, Meir told us that he dreamed about a tiger. He dreamed, he said, that a tiger was living in his house. This dream of Meir's gave me an idea. From a French expert I have ordered a most beautiful and well-behaved little tiger. Yes, my friends, Nathan and I are going to raise a tiger in our home, all thanks to Meir's dream. It's possible to bring home whole worlds—antique furniture, art collections, women. Why not also a tiger? This is no joke, I have already ordered the tiger and many new and interesting possibilities will soon enter our life." Rina concludes her speech. Nathan takes a gulp from a large bottle of juice. He swallows a handful of cherry tomatoes like a hungry juggler, perhaps because he finds it difficult to respond immediately. Or maybe he already dreads the unfamiliar smell in the house and his wife's independent initiative. I don't think he has anything to worry about. He could always remove from their apartment whomever he chooses, or go off on his own for a few days, to relax in one of his other apartments. Why be frightened of a new wife, or of a tiger in the house?

7

IT'S HARD FOR ME to believe that Rina's initiative came from my dream, and I dread Nathan's expected reaction to me. I'm always fearful when it comes to conflict and I am only tough on myself. The next morning Nathan arrives at the office at the usual hour (around eleven). Presumably he has woken up late, gone over his private notes, checked through notices of forthcoming rare furniture auctions, and has planned his next trip abroad accordingly. Nathan would rather acquire complete sets of antique furniture than add to his collection one item at a time.

I hear him enter our floor. Boisterous as always, he must be talking about the tiger. He says some important people are coming from Europe to examine the animal. Employees walk into his office in groups, but I have not been sent for yet. He leaves the room and walks past my office accompanied by Uzzi and other staff members. I hear them exchanging opinions about the possibility of investing in the development of the hinterland. For some reason it cheers me up that Nathan's no longer content with high finance, and is interested in developing new enterprises and old family properties (with my assistance, as agreed). Suddenly Rachel phones:

"Rina called. She wants us to visit as soon as possible. Says we should be the first to see the innovations in their household." I tell her Nathan hasn't spoken to me all day and I doubt that he'll be home when we get there. Rachel says it should be interesting, with or without Nathan.

"A house with a live tiger is like no other."

A few days later we pay our visit. Nathan is still at the office. Half an hour later he arrives at home, calls out a few words in greeting and retreats to his study. Rina serves fruit.

"I know you're not a big eater like Nathan," she says to me, "though he did tell me that you two have similar appetites and that people would be astounded if they knew what you actually think about." I take an apple and study it. I hear a scratching noise. It's probably the tiger pawing at the door. Rina hurriedly explains the new rules—which doors can be opened and which have to remain shut. She also explains the new domestic traffic system. It seems they've had some serious professional advice. Rachel asks how they feed the tiger. Rina answers briefly, and Rachel says:

"But what happens if you run into him in the middle of the house, unprepared?"

"We always carry something in our pockets, to pacify him," Rina replies.

Nathan joins us, shows us an ancient Persian board game he managed to buy from a wealthy Iranian refugee. He explains the game to us. Rachel catches on quickly, while I have difficulty. The combination of dice and colored squares is baffling. Nathan coaxes Rina and Rachel to play a game and claims that in two moves he can predict which of them will win. Rina would rather talk than play now, but Nathan doesn't give up. He helps himself to a snack and starts playing by himself. For the first time this evening Rachel smiles at me, even whispers pleasant words, and especially wants to know whether I believe the tiger will be joining us soon. Nathan looks me over and remarks that my shirt is dirty. Rachel becomes embarrassed and falls silent.

Later the tiger finally comes in, around midnight. It is wearing a colorful light wrap and no leash. For the first time in my life I find myself gazing into the eyes of a tiger who is gazing back at me. He makes a gurgling sound. He pads around the room and it's hard to guess what will happen. Nathan urges Rachel to play the new game with him. Only now do I notice that Rina's outfit is longer than usual. Maybe she doesn't want to get scratched by the tiger. She stands up, leaves the room, returns with Nathan's supper, sits down on his lap, glances at his fingers, and tells him that it's time to plan their big event in honor of the tiger. Everyone will want to be there. I am extremely tense. I've adapted myself to many things, but I doubt that I will be able to share Nathan's latest preoccupation.

Rina asks if we want anything to eat or drink. Rachel would

like some more fruit. I am quite tempted to ask them whether the tiger is the only new arrival, or whether Dana has also joined the household. Rachel guesses what I'm about to ask and stops me with a whisper. The thought of Dana is thrilling. I yearn to see her. Nathan starts to doze off in his armchair, Rina continues chattering, perched on her husband's knees. The tiger, I assume, is searching for the exit. Rina tugs at a long electric cord, presses the button, and in response one door opens while another one shuts. It seems the tiger's movements have been carefully circumscribed. He runs around the room a couple of times and leaves. I can't tell how much bigger this tiger is than the average cat, but he is clearly a different breed. Rachel and I thank Rina for her hospitality, whisper good-bye to the slumbering Nathan, and leave the apartment.

In the weeks that follow, Nathan takes several trips abroad. Uzzi intimates that he's gone to some spectacular auction in England or France, though even he's not sure what the story is there. At Nathan's bidding, the firm's logo has been changed to include a picture of the tiger seated on a chair beside a bookshelf. I've heard talk that Nathan is trying to persuade some large foreign concerns to set up a joint venture based on the tiger. As for me, I think Nathan's interest in this tiger will be short-lived. Someday he'll trade it in for a rare art collection, though I wouldn't be surprised if he winds up selling it first—once he's sure he can control the animal without fear.

Rachel warns me to keep a distance from Nathan.

"Even though he's known you since were a kid and your livelihood depends on him. This time they've strayed too far from everything that truly matters to us!" She speaks critically of Rina, too: "You have to understand, Meir, that once you let a tiger into the house, you can never tell what else will get in. People are going to have all sorts of unpredictable reactions, and I don't believe Nathan is prepared for what's about to happen." I hold my tongue, neither agreeing nor disagreeing with what she has just said. But it's pretty obvious to me that she's right. I have decided not to ask yet why, during our visit to Nathan and Rina's, she showed such an interest in the tiger—an almost genuine enthusiasm, in fact.

8

NATHAN HAS CALLED me over urgently this afternoon. I'll be surprised if it turns out that he just wants to see me about some routine business matter. He rarely discusses that sort of thing with me, probably because he isn't really interested in what I do for the firm, or maybe because on the whole he trusts my judgment. Last time he summoned me to his office it was to ask about the relationship between my parents and his parents and to clear up something about his childhood. Although I'm younger than he is, Nathan figures there are certain details I must have heard from my family. If there's one thing he hates, it's forgetting, especially information concerning his family. Once again I find him sitting in the corner of the big office.

"Hello, Meir. How is Rachel's state of mind? She seemed a little flustered when you came over the other day. You'd better find out what's going on. But that's not why I called you in. I finally have an important assignment for you. Of course, what you would call important is not especially important to me, but I could use your assistance now," says Nathan, and for some reason his office looks bigger to me (maybe he's changed it around since I was here last).

Normally when he summons me to his office, there are other people present, staff members or various assistants. If possible, he conducts a number of meetings simultaneously: with me he'll talk about one subject, with somebody else, another. That way he gets a clear picture, and, of course, there are no secrets.

"You're always kibitzing, in any case," he once explained. "So at least when you're in my office together, none of you can claim you're any closer to me than the next guy." I think it gives Nathan a special satisfaction to hear people arguing in his office while he refrains from expressing an opinion.

But now it's just the two of us in his office. His eyes look tired although it is already afternoon, when Nathan has usually recovered completely from his slumber. On the desk before him are recent issues of scientific journals and art magazines. I also notice several impressive volumes dealing with the history of Anglo-French relations. Behind Nathan's chair hangs a portrait of his father, whom I still remember sitting—in a moment of rare intimacy—with my parents in their home. There are new gadgets and appliances strewn around the office, sound equipment and computers of different sorts. Experts have designed the layout, about which I understand nothing, marking the ideal location for each machine. Nathan has great respect for their calculations of the distances and the role of each appliance in the system as a whole. It seems to me that some of the machines are already operational, while some are still in their boxes waiting for Nathan to assemble them.

Different people walk in and promptly leave the room. Most of them are employees, though some are acquaintances of Nathan's on various errands. He doesn't respond when they speak to him and, as mentioned, they hurry to depart. Usually he greets everyone who enters with a smile that stays on his face for a few seconds.

I see the gleaming plate on which his previous meal was served, and nearby, a conspicuous area has been set aside for the next meal. Any minute now Uzzi will walk in and ask Nathan what he'd like to eat. I've heard that the cuisine in the building is much improved; apparently they've hired a professional cook.

Again Nathan speaks: "Meir, you're the only one of my friends, the only one of my employees, in fact, who has any distinctive ideas of his own. Like my favorite music—a successful piece always has a variety of themes, but until the composer finds one, he can't get anywhere." I assume that Nathan is getting ready to explain why he called me in, the way a story could open with the death of the hero, or a coronation ceremony with the line of succession. But I understand nothing. What he said about the difference between us didn't surprise me much, and was pretty obvious. But I'm still not clear on the sort of assistance he expects from me.

Nathan stands up. His legs are striking, not as heavy as the rest of him. They still project a kind of youthful vigor. He must be twice as heavy as I am, but my anxieties greatly outweigh his fears.

"I've got to protect myself," he continues, "If Rina succeeds in her plot to confuse me, I'll lose everything—all I inherited from my father, not to mention what I've built up for myself. I tell you, Meir, she's made up her mind, she wants to play havoc with our principles and boundaries. Can you imagine this world, or a street or a house in it, without fixed boundaries? It would be impossible even to forecast the weather that way. And she wants to try out her bizarre system in our house. Brings home a tiger, arranges a new wife for me, then invites over the employees without discussing it first, and throws everything into disorder. She opposes clear-cut distinctions of any sort, between the house and the street or between the family and the jungles of Africa."

Nathan always perspires a lot (he uses a special handkerchief to mop his face), but today he's perspiring nonstop and there's a weary expression in his eyes. He speaks to me in an unfamiliar way.

"Remember that poem we had to memorize in school, Meir, the one about the stalwart man: 'a stalwart face doth forge a stalwart man, a stalwart man doth grow a mighty brow.' Well, I'm not feeling exactly stalwart right now. It's true I'm stronger than you are, but I need your help all the same. For the first time in my life I'm afraid to go home. Not that someone like me has to put in an appearance every day in the same way as ordinary people who're there most of the time presumably, but even if I had a sudden urge to go home, I would avoid it. Because Rina's there with that tiger, in the house I bought us, the home I brought her into. You think she's ever had big, beautiful rooms like that, or anyone like me in her life before? No, and now she's succeeded in frightening me. Ever since that tiger came into the house I can smell him all over me. People have noticed, too, I can tell, and they're keeping a distance from me. They probably don't want to touch me either, with those ugly claw marks on my hands. I find I've been eating less than usual these past two weeks, especially sweets, and I haven't bought anything new for myself lately."

I listen to Nathan speaking in his gruff, uneasy way. His figure is imposing and canny, his fingers know how to get where they're going. What he says makes me think about myself and my wife

Rachel. She never uses harsh tactics with me. She enjoys typing for me, helping me out in various ways, and familiarizing herself with every aspect of my life. She almost always misses a letter or skips a line—which, I have come to believe, is her way of prolonging our collaboration indefinitely and making sure there'll always be something left to correct.

But now Nathan raises his voice, which is unusual. "Meir, will you concentrate on me for a second? You people make your living off my talents, isn't it time you helped me out for a change? Forget your humdrum thoughts for a minute and stop searching for comparisons." He has advanced to the stage of making demands, speaking to me like an ordinary employee. "I want you to take this key to my apartment, Meir"—he removes it from the large key-ring attached to his belt—"go in without telling Rina you're there, and lure that animal out to me. There's no way I'm going to let Rina control the tiger, I want him all to myself. Either I learn to live with him or I get rid of him. And while you're at it, bring me the items I've written down for you here (he hands me a typed list). I'll be needing them for my trip to Europe." He draws me a little map of the rooms in his apartment, with the precise location of the closets, and his special hiding-place. Why does he need this stuff from the apartment when I know he keeps spare clothes and equipment at his other homes around the world? I peek at the list and the names of certain books he wants from his very extensive library. A smartly tailored suit is also mentioned. "And, of course, I want you to keep an eye on Rina while I'm away. I still haven't gotten to the bottom of this latest scheme of hers, which is why I'm planning to use my new computer. For now, though, I want you to find some way of protecting me while I'm gone, that's your expertise, protecting everyone around you without getting into arguments. And one last thing: if Dana's arrived at our apartment, please ask her to leave and wait somewhere else. We'll reimburse her for any delays, but I don't want her to move into my house while I'm away. You can tell her that come what may, I will respect the agreement Rina made with her." Nathan neglects to mention what my payment is going to be. Apparently he regards these complicated tasks as part of my normal duties, or as a special type of personal service. I've been told by some of the senior employees that Nathan has trouble doling out large lump sums though he always pays a handsome salary. I leave his office to go phone Rachel and give her a whispered account of our discussion.

Her predictable advice is that I not go to Rina's: "You don't know for sure what Nathan is planning. Rina herself may be involved in the plan somehow, though it's possible there's some huge power struggle going on here. They're dangerous, they're stronger than you are, and they're not trustworthy. I think it would be best if you came home now. Anyway, I'm rearranging the furniture, and I want you to tell me your opinion. I don't want to be the one who decides when I know that you're going to walk in later, wondering whether to cheer or curse?"

All the same, I go directly to Rina's. I hope to avoid a quarrel with Nathan and to make it home on time. When I arrive at their door, for some reason I can't bring myself to ring the bell or even knock. So I call Rina's name instead. Something's fishy. Rina doesn't answer and I holler that I have a key. Still no answer. I try the lock, it's tricky, but the door finally opens, making a peculiar noise. I enter, turn on the lights, and look around. Perhaps only a skinny, anxious man like me can abduct a woman's tiger. I guess I'm best at things that are irrelevant to me. There are pleasant smells in the apartment. It's tidier by far than my own apartment in spite of all the bric-a-brac they have around.

I don't enter the closed rooms. If I have to, I'll get around to them later, but meanwhile I check the open ones. Nathan reckoned that the tiger spends most of the day in Shlomo's bedroom. It would stand to reason, since the boy is back at boarding school by now and the room is spacious enough for a medium-sized tiger. I imagine Rina is keeping the tiger where she and her husband agreed, she doesn't ordinarily quibble about things like that, though it's hard to know what's going on between them at present. I'm really scared. I never had much of a way with pets, let alone wild animals, even when they're muzzled and have eaten their fill. When I finish searching the open rooms I realize that this time I've failed in my mission. I'm used to getting fast results, though others may think differently. Anyway, why should a man like me stay in a strange apartment searching for a woman and a tiger? I have a wife of my own and a beloved son. And a decent income. True, my relationship with Nathan is getting closer and may yield big dividends later on, but that's hardly enough to justify this peculiar mission.

9

SUDDENLY RINA EMERGES from one of the closed rooms and, without showing the slightest interest in how I got in, asks if she can fix me a drink. Maybe she was busy when I called her name. I think I'd better not bring that up. I ask how she is. I'm usually good at drawing people out in a sincere sort of way. They feel they can confide in me and tell me things they've never told anyone else, in full detail. But this time Rina answers me tersely. Nathan is going to Europe for a few days, she explains, and in the meantime she would like to find out if she could resume her studies at the university.

I enjoy looking at her. I've never really understood the special quality of a woman's face. Rina's, I notice at once, has acquired a new air. Not only does she look prettier, her features are like isolated buildings that have finally been transformed into a city. Twenty years of marriage to Nathan have surely taken their toll, but there must have been a lot of excitement too. I seriously doubt whether Rina could have gotten this far, in her education and her ideas, without Nathan. I continue to enjoy looking at her face and find myself thinking: if I had to choose another wife, would I be more finicky about things that never seemed important before?

Rina brings me another drink but offers no other refreshments. She probably assumes I wouldn't want any. She asks briefly how Rachel is and when I don't answer she repeats the question, then looks through her diary to see whether she and Nathan have any social engagements or other plans today. While she searches she says:

"Nathan is a very big eater and he doesn't watch his diet. To put it in your language Meir, sleep and food get so mixed up inside him that he can't tell which is which any more." Again I don't answer. It's taken me years to figure out that I'm not obliged to answer every time.

Rachel calls. Rina hands me the phone with a smile that makes me feel terribly embarrassed. I don't believe Rina would check up on her husband this way. Rachel asks when I'm coming home. I explain again that Nathan has asked me to help him out. Rachel is angry. Her voice sounds weak and then suddenly strong again.

"Well, just see that you're home soon, I'm sick of waiting for you." I end the conversation and ask Rina where the tiger is. She says she's sent him out for a walk.

"He's already been tamed, and he can wander around the block all by himself. He doesn't touch anyone. I've walked him myself and checked a couple of times, and now I know I can trust him. Anyway, if anything happens, they can always find Nathan, or at least me."

It becomes apparent that I won't be able to sneak the tiger out of the house. Animals that come and go as they will are hard to get rid of. Nathan has waited too long, it seems. Besides, what am I doing here, dealing with the problems of another couple and their strange tiger when I should be thinking about myself, my ideas, and my own family. In the end there won't be any room left for me. Still I'm tempted to ask Rina about Nathan. All of a sudden I'm capable of asking a blunt question:

"What's going on between you and Nathan? You're driving me nuts."

"There are problems," Rina answers hoarsely, "Nathan is a very talented and very special man. But we women do better with someone more ordinary."

Again the telephone rings. This time Rina is informed that Nathan's plans have changed, he's flying out tonight. Rina asks his secretary whether he'll need anything from home. She's always practical, like a body that knows at every moment what one wants from it. Suddenly the tiger's back, rubbing up against the door. My entrance she ignores, but his she hears right away. She pats the tiger and leads him through the door. She rubs him down with an invigorating towel and offers him a bowl of water. The tiger laps it with a sidelong glance at me, and keeps his distance. I used to think people's eyes followed the objects they were thinking about. Then I discovered that lovers often look into each other's eyes when they're aroused. And lately I've noticed that people often look at each other in moments of weakness.

I remember the list Nathan handed me at the office. If I grope around for it in my pocket, the tiger may become upset. I could try to recall what was on the list without looking for it. There was a suit, I remember, but maybe I shouldn't bother about that. I'm not going to schlep a load of heavy stuff around. The books are probably more important to him. I ask Rina what she thinks. She says I shouldn't waste my energy. "Nathan's library is full of unsorted books. Just the other day he brought home a whole pile of them. Seems to me he's delving into some new field of research. If he needs anything, he can either tell me or come home himself." I wonder whether I should hand Rina the list or not and decide against it. I prefer just to leave.

10

MY WIFE RACHEL greets me with unanticipated joy. She may not be a great one for pampering, but she never forgets that we're husband and wife. Friends like Nathan and Rina seem superfluous to Rachel. In her view, the less we spend, the less dependent we'll be on my job at Nathan's, and then we won't have to bother about "their *meshugene* ideas." Quite spontaneously I blurt out to her that on my way home I noticed two or three couples walking hand in hand. After what seems like a long interval, one often sees men and women holding hands these days.

When I wash my face, I think I notice more black hair on my head than I saw there a few weeks ago. How could my hair turn white and then grow in black again? I stroke Rachel's hair, like a person preoccupied with one thing and talking about another subject altogether. Rachel limply strokes my hand and urges me to try getting some of my articles published in the paper again.

"Seriously, your writing is clear and persuasive. Maybe you could work on something to do with Bible studies in Israel, how some people have qualms about teaching children from primary sources." I find it odd that Rachel can be so involved with my activities yet so critical of my work at the office. Nevertheless, her interest is touching and means a great deal to me.

Since I married her, Rachel has gotten fatter, though her face still looks youthful. Her shyness has diminished in proportion to her contentment with me. She's slow to smile and to bicker. The way she can fall asleep at the drop of a hat reminds me of a schoolmistress earnestly teaching the same alphabet year after year. I have no doubt that she still finds me a little confusing. She used to admire me more, but now I've become possible and coherent in her eyes. I wouldn't be surprised if she sneaked a glance at these reports I write myself. It's a good thing she's refrained from commenting on them so far.

It's getting late but Rachel suggests that we go out for a walk. Before I can answer, a messenger girl arrives from the office. Nathan tends to employ women on his staff, whether as drivers or secretaries, though men are also acceptable. The messenger girl hands me an envelope in which, she says, I will find a cassette from Nathan. I hastily insert it in the appropriate machine and listen. It seems that Nathan has appointed me his "deputy in every sense." Apparently his trip will last longer than expected, which is why he wants me to sit in for him as director of his Israeli enterprises "and also to look after my home and everything in it." Rachel listens and grows very upset. She doesn't even wait for the messenger to leave. She bites her lip and almost at once starts to scream. She blames me for getting us into a mess.

"This has nothing whatsoever to do with our life. Who cares about Nathan and his plans? Look where this friendship is getting you." Rachel is crying and doesn't want my company. She leaves the room to read and be sad. Just then our son Yaron comes home. I stoop down a little to hug and kiss him. I feel more comfortable hugging a child when we are the same height. Rachel calls Yaron from the next room, suggests that he fix himself a snack, and tells him what there is in the refrigerator. I feel unhappy and sit down.

The messenger girl is still in the living room.

"Let me introduce myself," she says. "You're obviously the boss now, the one Nathan has appointed." She approaches me with an outstretched hand. "I'm Dana," she says. "Rina has probably told you all about my new position and the special arrangement between her and Nathan and me. As I understand it, Nathan has to fly out, which is why there's been a slight delay in the program. Anyway, officially I start today. Nathan wants me to sleep at their house starting tonight so that I'll get used to being there. Maybe you were given different information, but don't worry, I'll go straight to Rina's and make all the arrangements with her later." Dana is very attractive. She's younger than I am, I'm not sure by how much. So far, nothing about her is in any way repulsive, though who can tell what she'll look like a few years from now. I'm staring too hard. These moments are a strain on me. "It's good to see you, Dana. But I think I'd better take a nap. Maybe I'll spend a little time with my son Yaron now. My wife isn't feeling too well. Anyway, see you at the office tomorrow." Dana smiles. She's nearly as tall as I am, has a nice complexion. She thanks me and leaves. I sit down for a chat with Yaron and consider going in to stroke Rachel's hair, but when I do I find her already in bed, sound asleep with her back to me and all her clothes on.

11

IN THE MORNING I get a call from the office asking when I want to be picked up. Nathan, I realize, has put his entire staff at my disposal. A driver I've never seen before arrives at the door—Nathan must have laid off his regular driver until he gets back. The driver waits for me to finish saying my morning prayers. I wonder how many other employees of Nathan's say prayers in the morning. On our way out it seems a good idea to check in at Nathan and Rina's. It's my responsibility; after all, I mustn't neglect Rina and her affairs. When we arrive, she hears me calling and cheerfully opens the door.

I follow her to the kitchen where it seems she and Dana have been sitting for a while. On the table is a notebook full of lists. Rina dictates, Dana writes. I wonder whether they'll carry on in my presence. I'm pretty sure now that I could fall in love with Dana. I can't remember the last time I was really in love. Maybe it's easier to be married to a woman you don't entirely love. Dana looks at me with interest. In the first stages women find me exciting, even attractive. Later on, though, it wears off.

"We're preparing an outline under a few main headings," Dana explains, "Rina is filling me in on Nathan's routines and hers, and what the various rooms in the house are used for, and which is the most important one at any given time of day or year. Then we'll get down to the subject of travel, foreign and domestic, and where to order fruits and vegetables, and Nathan's favorite cuts of meat and then of course there's the matter of a wardrobe." This lovely young woman who has come to live with an older married couple is sitting here in their kitchen, and she will soon be capable of cooking meals for everyone. I wonder when Nathan will tell her about his hobbies and collections, or send her to check on furniture auctions in some faraway land. Dana is wearing slacks made of a fabric that looks pleasant to the touch and a soft, light blouse. Her hair is pulled back and is mostly brown. Rina looks mature, sitting upright, her body all in place.

"Do you have any information for us?" Rina asks. "I hear Nathan's put you in charge of us all." I had better not answer her. I'm not exactly sure what I'm supposed to be doing here.

Suddenly Rina jumps up and says: "Dana, it's time to go wake him." Dana follows her down the hall. "Wait, Meir," Rina says as she turns to me. "You don't have to get to the office so early. They're used to Nathan just before noon, so you're entitled to be late too. Stick around and see the tiger again. Last time you barely got a chance to see him." Of course I wait, though I can feel the tension mounting in me. My body resonates with it. I ask Rina if she knows how long Nathan's going to be away. She has no idea how long he'll be away this time or where he's gone. Rina and I are in the kitchen waiting for Dana, who is just returning.

I hear Dana in the corridor again. She's singing quietly to herself. She returns trailing a long, blue ribbon with a tiger at the end of it. He looks fairly clean and must have had a bath. There's a pleasant fragrance in the air, not just from Dana; it must be coming from the tiger too. I am reminded for some reason of a big tree. More than anything I love to look at trees, especially the type with branches that seem to turn into a separate little tree. I'm sure each tree has as much going on inside it as a woman does.

"What do you say, Meir?" Dana says to me. "Will you come a little closer to the tiger and me? No one's going to accuse you of illicit relations with a tiger, and I'm not going to hurt you either." She laughs at a pitch I haven't heard in a very long time. Again I feel pressure in my stomach. I can fight off my inner resistance. Dana and Rina won't notice my difficulties. I'd better leave right away. Maybe I should even go home first, and get to the office later.

"Time to go."

"Time for who to go?" Dana teases.

"Well, me. Just me. You two have all you need right here."

I leave and walk away, perhaps more clumsily than usual. At work I am greeted with affection. It seems Uzzi has been waiting for me all morning in the lobby with a bouquet of flowers.

"We're so glad you're here. Let me show you to your new office." We take the elevator up to Nathan's floor where my old office used to be. Nathan's door is locked, but a little way off they've fixed up a comfortable nook for me.

"Let's see how long it will take you to fill this desk up with your papers," says Uzzi with a smile. He is startled to see that I've been offended by his remark and hurriedly explains how to use some of the appliances they've installed for me.

"Nathan insisted we set you up with state-of-the-art equipment. From here you can communicate with any department, or any individual even, and get all the information you need. If you like, we'll put in a sound system too, so you can listen to music." I try to arrange the flowers I have received, and I find another gift inside: a small silver vase. I might have guessed that in Nathan's milieu they've learned to appreciate expensive articles.

I recall that on my way over I became a little tense, perhaps as I reflected on the meeting with Dana and Rina, so I didn't really pay any attention to the people in the street. I usually like to observe couples, comparing the way they look by night with their appearance the morning after. At night their faces tend to look more relaxed, and their arms swing closer as they walk, whereas if they walk together in the morning, all intimacy is gone, and they can barely stand to touch hands or even talk. If Nathan could hear these thoughts of mine, he would be amused and would laugh. My way of reckoning is alien to him. When Nathan approaches a woman, it has nothing to do with the time of day or even with his desire for caresses. He simply makes his move. All of a sudden I can't remember seeing him caress Rina, or how he usually touches her, and this despite my keen awareness of the importance of the physical side of their relationship.

It's inappropriate for me to continue with this line of thought. I am now in the executive office they set up for me, and that's what I have to focus on. As is not my wont, I sit down on the carpet and stretch my legs. Once again it has become clear that in order to succeed at one thing, I must busy myself with something entirely different. The whole time I've been working for Nathan, he's entrusted me with fairly trivial tasks, leaving me plenty of leisure to devote to my family and my thoughts, and yet I'm the one he's chosen to fill in for him. I'm like an artist suddenly abandoning his paintbrush to rule a country. I know Rachel disagrees. In her opinion the only way to achieve anything worthwhile is to concentrate on a single field. Some of Nathan's key people have arrived meanwhile, some of them wearing name tags so that I'll be able to identify them more easily. Behind me they put up a big sign: "BEST OF LUCK TO MEIR."

Naturally, I pick myself up off the carpet. It wouldn't look right for me to sit there now that all these department heads have arrived in my office. I have to start dressing better, too. The clothes I usually wear are sloppy and not very clean. I must tell Rachel to be more careful. I ask them all to take a seat and to brief me on the main developments of the past two days. I've worked for this firm long enough to know what goes on in most departments, though not in great detail. I'm acquainted with most of Nathan's original investments (and some of his father's as well), but it turns out there have been some impressive changes of late. I listen to what they're saying with a certain amount of concentration, though my mind wanders from time to time. After about an hour of this I suggest that we adjourn. They hurriedly leave the room. I jot down some notes in a special new pad—maybe I'll surprise them tomorrow with an intelligent question. I go to Nathan's office, open the door, observe that his armchair has been covered up and pushed aside, just as I move my regular chair out of the way during the week of Passover and use a clean, substitute chair instead. Other than this, the only thing different about Nathan's office is that he isn't in it. On his desk I see a pile of articles in English about art. I start to read one but I understand only the gist of it, never having excelled at foreign languages. The article seems to be about the relationship between French and English art during the Middle Ages.

12

MY STOMACH hurts again. I drink tea and decline everything Uzzi offers me to eat. To my surprise Nathan's secretaries rarely enter my room and it is Uzzi who acts as chief intermediary. In his opinion, it would be best to order a full dinner for me from a kosher restaurant.

"You're right not to depend on our kitchen being kosher." I explain that I'm not feeling at all well. Rachel calls up sounding weak, probably having her monthly weakness, like a body that keeps opening up and can no longer stand. By the time I get home I'll be sniffing blood here and there, even if I don't see it. Rachel asks over the phone how I am and then says:

"The only way you'll be able to do the work you've taken on is if I'm there with you." I realize that just about any answer I give now may humiliate her, so all I say in reply is: "You know you're always with me."

"No, I'm not talking in vague generalities," says Rachel. "You can't impress me with your whims anymore. I'm talking about being with you each and every minute, every meeting, every trip, every conversation." She falls silent. If I don't say something right away, our silence may go on and on. I tried this with Rachel once before, and in the end, I was the one who started talking first. Again I feel that her body is opening wider and that the sound of my voice might greatly distress her.

"Drop by whenever you like. I'll be here in any case."

But if she does, Nathan's people will look at her strangely. I can't imagine Rina parking herself in Nathan's office, if she ever comes here at all. Meanwhile more papers are brought in for me to look over and sign. I indicate that every document must be signed by a department head before it's sent here for my signature. Though I understand the main points, I'm becoming more and more confused. The investment figures are easy enough to understand but the balances and profit margins are too complicated for me to figure out. I try to clarify some of the numbers. Suddenly Rachel walks in, pale and plump, wearing a pleasant expression and a quaint loose-fitting dress. Book in hand, she sits down on a comfortable chair in the office, pours herself a glass of water, and locates a certain page in the book. She looks up at me. I don't like what she's wearing, but her modesty always pleases me.

Uzzi arrives and asks Rachel if she needs his help. Rachel thanks him briefly. She puts some things on my desk, cluttering it up, makes a phone call concerning Yaron, returns to the armchair to read, tells me I have to read this book, read it carefully, and asks if she might read a few paragraphs out loud to me. I prefer to keep working. She asks if I want to go out for lunch and if we could please turn down the air conditioner. I grope around for something new on my desk to keep me occupied so I won't appear to be loafing. An hour later Rachel gets up, says she's uncomfortable, and searches for somewhere new to sit. She approaches the window and looks out. Pulls a chair over, climbs up on the broad ledge and reclines upon it. Here I am, Nathan's acting deputy, and my wife has sprawled out by the window. She'll probably doze off in a little while. Uzzi says we're expecting a call from Nathan shortly, he probably wants a report, and this is a convenient time for him. Suddenly I remember that I haven't spoken to Rina or Dana since this morning. And there must be all kinds of things to take care of before I speak to Nathan. I prefer to put as much information as possible into my reports, even in summary form. It might actually be better for him to find me here at the office when he calls, otherwise he'll think I'm not discharging my duties, that I'm not up on the facts. I'm extremely tense about what Nathan will have to say.

Just then the switchboard transfers Nathan's call through to my room.

"Having fun, Meir?" he almost roars into the receiver.

"Your mood certainly seems to have improved," I answer him, amazed at myself.

"I hear you've taken charge of all important matters," says Nathan.

"Of course I'm not a man of your talents, but help is at hand," I joke, seeking Rachel's reaction.

"So how are the wives getting along at home?" asks Nathan and answers himself, "Just fine, I'm sure, better than us." With this quip, he ends our conversation.

I'm feeling worse now physically. I tell Rachel, and she gets up and smooths my brow. She goes out for a while and returns with a certain drink that's supposed to be refreshing. She claims I'm all mixed up inside.

"But this isn't the time to discuss it, I know. Soon you'll be saying it's my fault you can't work." For the first time since my childhood I feel a strong pressure inside. I'm always afraid I'll vomit, though I can usually control it because the aches and snags in my body go right to my head, where they build up and help me prevail over my other infirmities. But this time I am going to vomit. I run to the washroom, and there, just as in my childhood, things spew out of my mouth. The figures I have been trying to read and analyze whirl round and round my brain.

Rachel is standing behind me, pale and lucid. She asks Uzzi to bring the car around. I haven't been in hospital since I was a child and Rachel seems intent on taking me there. I did feel a certain relief after vomiting but now I'm terribly weak, all aquiver. I'm used to headaches and suffer them fearlessly, but my present symptoms are worrisome indeed. Uzzi asks whether to accompany us, and Rachel replies that she would prefer not. We get in the car and sit in the back, and the driver takes us where he has been instructed. Strange things keep happening inside me, some of which don't bear reporting yet; I mean, there are limits even to my candor.

When we arrive at the hospital Rachel asks to see a certain doctor. I assume she knows him, or at least someone else who knows him. As it happens, this doctor is busy, but he'll see us when he's free. They put me to bed and all my fears break loose. A few examinations later it is decided that I must stay in the hospital until a clearer diagnosis can be reached. They wheel me into a room with a number of other beds in it. Only a few of them are occupied. When Rachel returns, she tells me I've confused my own body, I have abandoned all we hold dear, and that I've endangered my health with strange, unnecessary schemes.

13

THE SMELL in the room is tolerable. It reminds me of the time I spent in the hospital as a child. I fell ill and then recovered, but now I'm sick again and I have no real strength. More than once over the past few months I've found myself wishing for some mild disease, or at least for a few weeks' sick leave. I didn't want to be mortally ill, I just wanted to be left alone by Nathan and Rachel and everyone else for a while. But this is serious.

Nearby is a boy (named Danny) who is playing cards with his big sister. There is a bandage covering his head, which has probably been shaven. The two of them are talking about their next game and about his return home, trying to decide when bedtime will be, when he'll do his homework, when he'll eat candy. And it seems they're planning a surprise party for their mother. The boy sounds nice but unstable, and I get the impression that his vocabulary is missing certain words.

"Now they know why I failed some of the tests, and they understand that I really did have a problem," says Danny.

"Right, and they'll stop getting angry with you," agrees his sister.

In the bed between the boy and me lies an older man wearing a robe and what looks like a green tie (or is that a crease in the sheet?). He's listening to music or perhaps to someone talking through his earphones. Beside him stands an empty chair which I would imagine is normally occupied. Then there's a little table with a cake on it (I think it must be a cheesecake) and a bottle with some kind of drink. My sense is that this man does most of the communicating with hospital staff, at least for our room.

A new bed is wheeled in. They shift me onto it, and convey me to the elevator that will take us to the floor where the labs are and where they do the tests. My body is sick. I'm vomiting less now but my temperature is really low and I'm dizzier than ever. They have to remove something to alleviate the pressure, I don't know what. The chief doctor gently and persistently examines my head all over. No doubt he can feel how weak I am with his hands. He leaves the room. Two nurses whisper that they haven't seen the doctor so tense in a very long time.

"You'd think it was his own son."

"And what are we doing here, with that boy from the car crash in the emergency room. I hear you can actually feel the crack in his skull. Why are we spending so much time with this patient? We should be hurrying to the boy and taking care of him." Meanwhile they draw my blood, from the vein in my arm that has been ready and waiting since the days of my childhood illness.

Back in the room. The boy is drowsing while his sister watches over him. The older man is sitting up, chewing his food. I feel I'm about to fall asleep. Someone comes to look at me. I don't look back, am not inspired to look back. I don't care if I fall asleep in front of him. The one thing that matters to me, and all I really want to do, is to cradle my son Yaron (especially his head). In fact I do fall asleep and dream the usual dreams, though they are strangely languid. In one of them, a friend who lost both his legs during the war offers me a car. But before he can give me the instructions for it a couple of kids get in with me and we drive away. One of the kids shows me how to brake and stop. I have no idea how to drive the cripple's custom made car. I guess you do everything with your hands. It's not clear where I'm supposed to be sitting either. The car reaches a steep incline, but if I follow a long stripe in the road, I might be able to make it without skidding backward. The fact that we're driving along the coast now seems perfectly logical. The fact that the sea has flooded the road, however, is rather strange. Be that as it may, the car speeds through the water.

I awaken with a sense of relief in most parts of my body, though I'm still having trouble with my eyes. Certain things look blurry to me. Rachel is at my bedside talking. I take her face in my hands and hold it directly in front of my eyes. This is the only way I can see her clearly. Rachel holds still so that I can focus on her face and her damp and wrinkled brow. The doctor she asked for will be coming in shortly. Rachel explains that he has a lot of experience. I don't close my eyes and ask her to read to me.

"I brought you the book you loved so much as a boy. You've told me that you read Dumas's *The Count of Monte Cristo* many times. I found it in Yaron's room at home." She begins to read aloud to me and meanwhile the new doctor walks in. He gives off an air of pleasantness and order. Asks what medications I've been taking over the past few months and whether I have anything special to tell him. I ask for a drink, and somebody brings me one, though not with the alacrity I expected. I thought they would be glad I was thirsty. This doctor's touch is firm and sensitive. I doubt he needs lab results to know what has happened to my body. Never before have I been so frightened, or felt so distant from my dear ones and myself.

Rachel and the doctor leave the room together. I sit up and also want to stand. My feet go limp as soon as they touch the floor. I tread with care, groping myopically at everything around me. A new voice has entered the room.

"What's happened to our boss? Scared of a little responsibility?" I assume it's Dana's voice. My head prepares to look at her. "Back to bed with you. I'm here to keep you company now, to laugh at both of us." Now I see Dana. I wonder whether my body is capable of falling in love in its present state. She reaches out, to shake my hand first, and then to pat my shoulder. "They told me you were seriously ill, but I think you just look a little tired. Nathan and Rina send their best. He calls every morning to ask how you are. Talks to Rina. She may fly out to join him for a while."

I lie down again. For months now I've had an urge to suck my thumb. If Dana weren't around, I would do just that. How much longer can I resist the temptation? Is it so unheard of for a man to suck his thumb, and why should the simple act of sucking my thumb invariably lead to trouble? Dana sits down on my bed, facing me. I know that her body has its own offensive moments, that her stomach too secretes strange fluids, but I don't really care just now.

"What shall I bring you to eat?" she asks.

"How about some grapes?" I suggest with a wobble in my voice. She leaves the room and returns a while later carrying a bunch of red grapes and maybe a couple of green ones. Who needs a full meal with grapes like these?

"It's hard to know what exhausted you more, Nathan's assignments or me," says Dana, and both of us nearly start to laugh.

"Would you mind if I dozed off?" I ask, and Dana seems delighted. I turn around, focus inside my eyeballs and try to rest. From my corner I ask her, "How's your tiger?" and she tells me about the behavior course Rina has found for the animal.

"He'll be better trained than any of us, you'll see. You have no idea how excited Rina is about him. She likes him to sit still and look at her as much as possible. She goes around telling people that the tiger's in love with her." I fall asleep again. Who would have imagined that I could lie here so unabashedly, sick and nearly blind, beside a woman I hardly know. In my dream this time I return to the car that was driving through the water, only now it's sliding down a steep incline. To my surprise I manage to regain control of it during the steep descent. Other drivers avoid descending there, but I'm doing fine. I have nothing more to fear, because once you skid, or fall, what else can happen?

I wake up feeling relieved. I'd like to get some exercise before they bring in my food. Again I try to stand up, and Dana offers me her delectable hand. She is stronger than I thought. My eyes still see only what's in front of them and even that not too clearly. We go out to the balcony and I approach the railing. I climb up on it and teeter there. This is one of the lower hospital floors; what could happen? I slide around and maneuver my hands and feet from hold to hold with a boldness that would have terrified me even as a child. There are several people watching me with interest, and Dana is gasping. I believe someone has run off to call a doctor. I manage to climb as high as the drainpipe between the balconies. Only a short distance, it's true, but I am definitely climbing. Rachel appears at the window and calls me. She is quite alarmed, asks me to get down at once and come back to the room. Ten minutes later I stop my climbing and swinging routine and return to the balcony. A stiffly agreeable lethargy pervades most of my body. I drink a large amount of juice and consider a snooze.

Rachel and Dana are chatting together. Rachel gesticulates a lot, while Dana's hands rest comfortably on the back of the chair. I curl up and rest. A new doctor walks in and explains to me that they're going to have to shave my head.

"Hair grows back in no time. But we wanted to tell you ahead of time." The doctor enjoys his little pun on "head." I would like to know whether Dana and Rachel are smiling too. They're standing at my bedside but my eyes don't see them. The attendants are ready for me now. Again they lift me onto the gurney, wheel me to the elevator, to the ward, to surgery. When I wake up I'm not sure I can see at all. I let out a terrible scream. The doctor comes over, asks me how many fingers I see.

"Three," I answer, but maybe I don't really see any. They explain that my blindness is due to some ointment they put in my eyes to protect them from some other guck they had to rub on my head.

"The effects are temporary and you'll soon be able to see again." They give me some tea with sugar to drink through a straw. They wheel me back to the room, put me in my bed, or maybe it's a different bed. The boy cries out in his sleep. They wake him, harshly but also comfortingly. My head burns.

"Where does it burn?" asks Dana.

"On top."

"If it's just on the surface there's nothing to worry about. It's normal to feel a burning sensation where the knife touched you, or where they rubbed in that stuff," says Dana, pulling up a comfortable chair for herself. "I can sleep here; it's more comfortable than a bed. I'll just rest beside you until morning when Rachel comes."

Of all the staff, I like Dimitri best. He immigrated to Israel a few years ago. He's strong and straightforward. He pours a vile-tasting medicine into my mouth with no fuss or nonsense. Sometimes he brings me an ice cube to numb my sore tongue, but it doesn't help much.

Someone passes me a mobile phone for an urgent call.

"Pick it up and find out who it is," says Dana, patting my hand.

"Hello there, Meir," Nathan says cheerfully from afar. "I let you run the show and you escape to the hospital. They tell me you'll be back at work fairly soon."

"And when are you coming back, Nathan?" I ask.

"I've got a whole bunch of meetings here yet; it's a good thing we didn't sell the tiger meanwhile, we're sure to get plenty of use out of him. Maybe I'll ask Rina to join me for the remainder of the trip. If you need any money, they'll know where to find me."

Days go by. They don't yet know for sure what brought on my affliction. Was it the medications I was taking a few months prior, or some type of infection that got into my stomach? Perhaps I'm sensitive to soporifics (which have only aggravated my condition since I was hospitalized). The ointment they apply every day relieves the pressure in my eyes. It's always my eyes that have to bear the brunt, either because of what goes on in my head or what they see. Apparently I'll be required to do eye exercises for a while, but my vision is improving.

Rachel arrives to take me home. Dana has already packed my few belongings. It seems Rachel is driving one of the company cars. She asks if I'd be more comfortable resting at Nathan's for a couple of days.

"At home Yaron and his friends can be awfully boisterous, and there you'd have Dana around all day to look after you. Rina's probably on her way to join Nathan by now, so I'm sure you'll be very comfortable."

"But what about food? Their dishes aren't kosher—I never eat there.

"Don't worry about keeping kosher, you think I'd forget something like that? Dana's already brushing up on the rules."

14

THE DAYS at Nathan's are strange. The big question is what, from these days, to take note of for myself. I'm the kind of man whose faith is central to his life, yet his descriptions almost never mention it, as with those biblical accounts of eras that give no sense of how Judaism was practiced at the time, or what rituals were observed. I've been rereading my favorite books, some my childhood favorites and some philosophical works. From time to time people from the office come over to have me sign, as Nathan's deputy, sizeable bank transfers. Rina isn't home; at least, I never run into her. Dana occupies her room, the tiger wanders in and out, and Rachel drops by to visit us nearly every day.

Dana usually brings me breakfast in bed.

"I'm sure you're allowed to eat before your morning prayers," she says. Later she helps me with my toilette—she's especially fond of combing my hair with her own comb and squeezing the toothpaste onto my brush. Then she asks whether she should go out or stay home with me. When she goes out she calls me several times to ask how I'm doing and then hurries home. She nearly always brings me a surprise, the sweets I like or an amusing story, some new delight. It seems that Dana is getting more and more intimate with me, is sensitive to my every remark. How can it happen that this young woman, who was brought here by Nathan and Rina, winds up pampering me? I'm clearly attracted to her, but I never do more than stroke her hair or hold her hand for a while. My vision is improving. Every day Rachel arrives with a special therapist who's supposed to help me increase my field of vision by improving my focus. I believe this therapist is the daughter of a famous ophthalmologist, not very talkative though she often smiles with some of her features. As my vision improves, my body strengthens. I could never have a strong body unless my eyes could see. Dana leads me on farther-reaching tours of Nathan and Rina's, to the rooms I haven't yet seen. The furniture is unquestionably charming and comfortable, and there are many more books here than I imagined. As for art, I think Nathan keeps his more important paintings at the office. The tiger has been placed in the charge of a special young trainer from Africa, I am told. Sometimes I watch Henri (the trainer's name, Dana has informed me) washing the tiger with a special apparatus. Once he tried to put him into Nathan's bathtub and Dana was furious. Henri eats with the tiger, tends to his claws and walks him at least three times a day. He takes him out, I gather, to a special training field Nathan had someone buy for him, where they probably run and frolic. Fortunately for me, Dana tries to keep the tiger out of my way in the apartment, except when I choose to stand and watch him. I wouldn't be surprised if, one day, Dana persuades Nathan to send the tiger off to a special lair.

Rina, it seems, actually did go abroad to join Nathan. When Dana calls Nathan—to brief him, pass on requests, and ask for instructions—she in fact confers with both of them. I gather that Nathan was unexpectedly detained, which is why he asked Rina to join him. Maybe he realized that her motives were innocent, or perhaps for some reason he needs her there with him. I amuse myself with strange notions, such as maybe Nathan and Rina planned to push Dana and me together by leaving us alone in their apartment. Still, it does seem odd that only a few weeks after Nathan was furious with Rina, he asked her to join him.

Important material from the office is apparently still reaching Nathan by special delivery. Dana tells me that, when in doubt, they consult her about whether or not to send him documents. Just how she's supposed to understand all these complicated transactions is not entirely clear to me, but the fact is that in a matter of hours every other day she gets the job done. In addition, more and more department heads are meeting with her to review new material. The conferences take place in Nathan's study, and every half hour or so she comes out to see if I need anything. Perhaps the department heads think she's going to confer with me as Nathan's deputy, but Dana avoids involving me in business complications. On particularly hectic days she calls my wife Rachel and asks her to help look after me. So far, Rachel has only come over once or twice for such an emergency.

I ask Dana if Nathan knows about the new work arrangements, and that I'm barely involved. Dana says he's been informed and that naturally as soon as I'm stronger I can attend to business again.

"And if you miss going to the office, that's probably a good sign." This being so, I had better hurry up and get well. I ask Dana if we might take a long walk tonight. Dana responds enthusiastically, takes me by the hand and pulls me outside. Henri follows us, ever alert. Dana gently loads the bag with the medication and the drinks on his shoulder. I wouldn't be surprised if she's stashed some of the candies I like there too. We stroll through the neighborhood and Dana tries to choose streets with trees for me.

"I remember your telling me once that trees are what you love most in nature," she says. "Other than people, I hope you meant," she adds with a satisfied laugh. It's a good thing that there's still some light and I can look at the trees and relax. I very much want to see Yaron right now, but for some reason I refrain from saying so to Dana. I don't understand why Rachel doesn't bring him over to see me every day. Maybe she's worried about him seeing me so weak and thin. I don't believe my appearance would harm my son in any way. Dana and I are walking hand in hand as we have been since we left the apartment. Whether she's holding my hand in order to lead me, or whether we're simply enjoying this intimacy, I cannot say.

Dana points out that the doctor has warned me against too much sun ("so you should walk only in the evening") and losing my temper ("so no one's allowed to make you angry"). I am trying to follow the doctor's advice, at least until I return to my normal activities.

"Anyway, it's time to start making plans," she says. "You have no more obligations. This is your chance to re-enter life in a new and truly different way." I am amazed, even moved by Dana's lovely idea.

"You know how many people would be overjoyed to have such an opportunity?"

"Yes, Dana, but I'm not well yet."

"No problem, Meir. I can wait. I've got plenty of patience. Besides, you and I are together already." We try to figure out how long it's been since we first met ("I walked into your house like it was *Mission Impossible,* and I even brought you a videocassette with instructions"), how long I stayed in the hospital, and how many days I've been living at Nathan's.

"Who knows, Meir, maybe it was you who tricked Nathan and Rina into taking me on, and then devised this trip for them?" she asks with a giggle and a pat on my head.

15

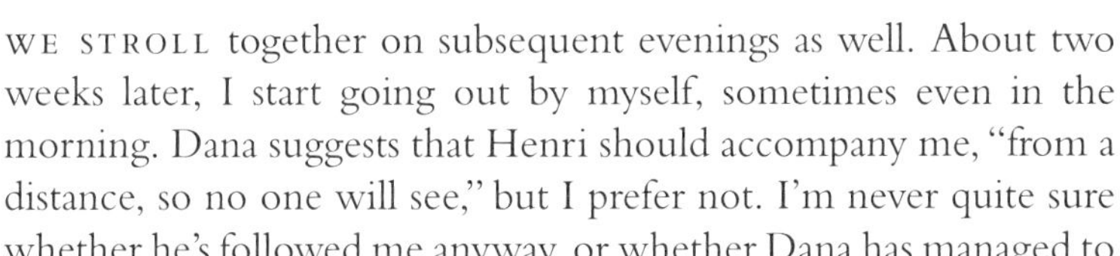

WE STROLL together on subsequent evenings as well. About two weeks later, I start going out by myself, sometimes even in the morning. Dana suggests that Henri should accompany me, "from a distance, so no one will see," but I prefer not. I'm never quite sure whether he's followed me anyway, or whether Dana has managed to stop him.

Today I happen to meet Uzzi, Nathan's personal assistant. He gives me a big warm hug.

"Hey, Meir! When are you coming back? We miss you. No one thinks of new ideas the way you do." I thank him and want to continue walking but Uzzi holds me back. "Now that we've run into each other, what's your hurry? You know that raise I asked you about, have you had a chance to think it over?" I'm not sure what to say. It seems to me that he got a raise from Nathan just recently, and in any case, I don't really know what he contributes to the firm. It's true he performs various personal services for Nathan, but these bear little relation to ongoing business.

"As I recall, you were given a raise not long ago, you and nobody else. We can't be making changes all the time. What about the other employees? You of all people should show a little consideration with Nathan away. But if it means so much to you, go ahead, call him, ask him yourself." Uzzi is still holding onto me, but he seems to be calming down. I walk away, surprised at myself and at the turn of our conversation, wondering what made me speak to him so harshly, and whether I should perhaps go home to Dana now.

Suddenly I remember that I neglected to pray this morning. It's probably too late by now to recite the *Sh'ma Yisrael.* I try to hurry, maybe I'll find a shortcut back to Nathan's. When I get there, the door is open and people are wandering around the entrance. Some of them look familiar, from the firm, while some are strangers. I ask a man in the corridor if I can go rest in my room.

"What, you just got here?" he asks.

"No, I've been convalescing here for several weeks now, but it looks as if you've changed something around, I hardly remember where my room is." He looks through his notes, finds my name, and hands me a new key and a sheet of instructions that are more suitable for a hotel than a home. In my room people are sitting about, some on the bed and others on the floor. They eat peanuts and joke and throw pillows at each other.

"I think maybe I'd like to rest for a while," I tell them. But they continue playing around, thoroughly enjoying themselves. Maybe they expect me to join in.

"Where's Dana?" I ask.

"Better ask the doorman. Don't worry, though, she'll be here soon and we're leaving in just a few minutes."

I wait, sitting on the edge of my bed. I see my trousers folded on the chair with my wallet in the pocket. I don't suppose they've gone through the wallet—luckily I didn't leave it in the drawer or they might have thought it was full of money.

Slowly and boisterously people start leaving the room. I want to rest now, but suddenly Henri walks in and asks (in English) whether I feel like taking a walk with him or playing ball. I am persuaded and accompany him downstairs to the garden. I ask him who all those people were and he explains that Nathan left orders for them to make certain alterations in the apartment.

"Dana said he urgently needed more storage space for his new research. I think they're installing a whole new communication system with London, too." I'm amazed that I haven't been told anything about this new preoccupation of Nathan's. Again I remember that I haven't prayed yet, so I go back upstairs and call Rachel, asking her to bring my other prayer book because the one I had here has disappeared from my desk.

16

DANA WAKES ME UP exultantly:

"Rina and Nathan called. They're coming home soon."

"Why so happy?" I ask.

"Oh, I just love it when everyone's here," she answers.

"Who were those people wandering around the apartment yesterday?"

"Sorry about that. They came to do some jobs here and didn't check with me first. Nathan asked Uzzi to make a few structural changes."

"And you pretty much neglected me most of the day," I say.

"Well, I'm sure I have a good answer to that, only I can't remember what it is just now." Dana is the only one laughing as she punches me lightly in the belly and goes off to bathe.

About an hour later she informs me that Rachel has arrived with Yaron. Finally they've remembered to pay me a visit. Yaron wanders around the spacious apartment, discovers Nathan's train set in my room, and starts playing. Suddenly I realize that I'm wasting my time here. I'd be better off resting all day, gazing at Yaron, watching his activities, even touching him. What am I doing in this strange apartment? Yaron emerges from my room and goes off to explore some more. I decide that if I can drink something before he returns, it means I'll get healthy. If not, it's possible that my condition will take a turn for the worse. Now there's a strange idea—what's the connection between my health and how fast Yaron or I may be? The old anxieties are back, with the illusions that overwhelm my mind. There's nothing to them, I know, yet I'm relieved just the same to have finished drinking before Yaron returns.

He's in good spirits and that makes me happy. He gives me a kiss on the forehead, moves away, and a minute later comes back and kisses me on the cheeks as well. I cry in his arms. A sixteen-year-old boy is holding me, and I am crying. But what if I still had poor eyesight and I couldn't see him? And why am I so involved with Nathan and his follies when I could be talking to my Yaron all day?

"I'm really good at soccer now," he says, "I'm not the fastest kid in the class but I score a lot of goals. When I run with the ball I always score; the rough part is getting the ball. And you know what, Dad? I'm doing okay in the subjects you're interested in, too: my grades are pretty good and I've learned to be more organized. Would you believe there are kids in class who ask to copy my notes?"

"So why stay here?" he asks suddenly. "We could just as easily let you have peace and quiet at home. I've learned to keep still like Mom." Yaron's words are painful to me. I can't let myself drift further and further away, no matter how good I feel with Dana. It's possible that I'm actually in love with her now, and in my mind I can almost call her "my love." With Rachel there were always terms of endearment, but never "my love." Maybe with Dana I could say the words. But Yaron is here and he speaks to me again.

"Come back, Dad. I mean it. When will we have a chance to play together again? Last time you won, thanks to me—I played so badly. How about tomorrow, can we play? Say yes. You know you have as much fun as I do. And don't keep pretending that you're happy all the time. I've seen you cry before, and Mom. You made me sad for a minute, and Mom made me sad for a really long time. Anyway Dad, sooner or later you and Mom are going to have to talk about it. You can't go on hiding out here forever. I mean, what is this, am I the only one in the family who knows how to talk?"

I prefer to answer Yaron regarding soccer. I ask if it's that important for him to beat me. If I lost, would he no longer be able to take me seriously?

"Not too many things are important to me, Dad, and beating you isn't one of them. But promise me you'll try to win—no cheating this time. Only don't promise too hard, because that'll mean you're lying, and I'll know. I'm kind of tired now and you're not well yet. Mom's waiting with Dana and she's ready to go home. You stay here and rest a while longer and then come back to us. You know, Dad, every time I come home I feel as if I'm there for the first time."

Yaron leaves the room and I try to fall asleep. Dana comes in and looks at me (I think). She whispers something and changes her mind. Speaking aloud to herself she says she'll just sit down and read a new book she received. I wouldn't be surprised if Rachel brought her some interesting reading material—nothing too weird, I hope, the kind of stuff Rachel occasionally goes in for. Dana has a very pleasant smell and her voice makes me happy. Yaron's last words have merged in my mind with Dana's whispers. Suddenly I find it a little strange that Rachel didn't bother looking in on me. Maybe she hoped I would come out to greet her.

17

IT'S A GOOD THING that no one reads my reports. I'm not required to consult anyone. I may just let Yaron have a look, though—maybe Dana and Rachel too. They would read them right away and point out any inaccuracies. Rachel would no doubt wonder how I managed to put together such a hodgepodge of vital information and trivial details.

"In your reports you mix everything up, just as you do in the life you've made for yourself," she'd say.

Dana would merely smile and Yaron would offer factual comments. Yet despite this new readiness of mine to expose myself, I would really prefer not to show my reports to anyone. I must find myself another pastime. I can't stay on at Nathan's indefinitely, but I don't want to be parted from Dana either. Maybe I should consider some sort of activity that would bring me in contact with new people. Things that once seemed strange to me about Nathan and Rina's way of life (like the idea of a second wife) are quite possibly applicable to me now. It's fairly clear that this prolonged stay in their apartment is detrimental to my thoughts. I talk to Dana and ask her how to make things easier.

"I think you've made a pretty good recovery, actually," she says. "Why hurry? We're happy together, you have no obligations toward me, and I take care of you. I told you, I've got plenty of patience."

"But I'm so confused," I answer her, "I want to be with you and yet I'm homesick."

Two days later, Dana walks into my room in the morning, pulls the covers down, looks at my body (good thing I'm wearing something), smiles and asks what I want, pulls the covers up again, and kisses my forehead. She says someone's made the interesting proposal that we all take a trip to the Galilee together. "You, me, Rachel, and Yaron, too, if he likes. What could be nicer than all of us hiking together and seeing the sights?"

"I'm sure the doctor will be pleased," I tell her. "He'll be glad to know that I'm finally out of the city and walking about."

"There is that problem with the sun," she reminds me. "The doctor warned us about your sensitive head and the possible dangers of too much sun."

I think it will be nice to take a trip. Lately I've been struggling with my internal difficulties and my exhaustingly obsessive thoughts. I force myself to look at the clock even when it sickens me. I force myself to open certain doors at Nathan's house and walk through rooms I used to avoid. It's interesting that even at Nathan's I have found some places that seem friendly and others that put me off. I must get used to opening all the doors and walking through all the passages, and this trip to the country might make it easier.

Nathan calls from Europe and insists on speaking to me. Dana cheerfully hands me the phone and says, "It's a good thing Nathan understands that you're the real head of his business." Awkwardly I say hello to Nathan,

"Hope you're taking good care of Dana for me," he roars, and I hear Rina laughing beside him. "I won't take her back if she's flawed. Anyway, I'm sure you've recovered by now and you'll be able to return to work. I imagine you'll be going home to Rachel soon, too." Again, hilarious laughter. Dana takes the phone from me and continues the conversation. She tells Nathan about the plans for our trip, and points out that, in fact, the idea was his originally. Nathan confirms this and tells her that he and Rina may join us at some point if they return in time.

The trip is set for the beginning of the week. The night before I have insomnia (more than usual), like a kid before the first day of school. What do this trip and the strange house I'm living in have to do with me? I've never been great at travel or travel-related activities. Over the past few days I've overheard some phone conversations between Dana and Rachel about food. They were coordinating their respective duties.

"I want the food to be right for Meir, so I'll do what I can to make it tasty as well as kosher."

This morning our organized tour of the Galilee is supposed to set out. I'm ready to leave. Rachel calls up from the parking lot outside (it's been a while since I heard her yell).

"It's good we made an effort to fit Rachel in too," Dana says to me. I remember promising Rachel after we were married that some day we'd go hiking in the Galilee. She used to go up there with her father and wanted to revisit their favorite places with me. She said something very touching: "Once we've been there together, we won't be strangers any more." But we never did go on the long-awaited journey, and Rachel avoided the subject of my erstwhile promise.

But I'm not ready yet, so Rachel will have to wait. Even things I used to be able to do quickly take forever these days. I've always had sweaty palms but my hands never used to tremble like this. Lately I've developed the ways of a bachelor, it seems: I attribute great importance to everything I do; I warm up my own food (when Dana doesn't have time); and I open one pack of sweets after another. But now I lift the heavy suitcase Dana packed for me. On top she has put my prayer book and a Bible, "Which I know you like to read, and will probably want on this trip." Finally we're walking down the stairs. The hallway is not dark but I turn the lights on nevertheless because there are certain actions I must perform. Rachel is still waiting for us below and suddenly Yaron jumps out of the car as well.

"It isn't easy being alone," says Rachel, "and that doesn't change very fast." I look at my child and am filled with love for him. I wonder whether other fathers love their sons so ardently, almost the way a man loves a woman.

We drive to the meeting place where the others are waiting. Among them I recognize certain friends of Nathan and Rina's and a number of employees from the firm. They tell me Nathan and Rina have also made reservations for this trip and they'll be joining us soon if they're back from Europe in time. I look around at the group; familiar faces nearly always have a soothing effect on me. It's strange that I haven't thought about such things since my army service—questions like who else will be joining us along the way and who will decide whether to let them into the group or not. Meanwhile I hope I'll be fit enough to keep up with the general pace. Dana seems much amused. She's glad to be going on a trip, all packed up like brand new gear.

"Why so grim?" she asks me with a wink at Rachel. "We're not setting off to conquer the land, or hunt for buried treasure. It's only a little trip to the country. You're here, your wife Rachel is here, and I'm here too. So what if a few more friends will be joining us? That's nothing to worry about. Most of the group is from our region, they all had the same sort of education as you, and I'm sure you'll eventually get used to their smells." She laughs aloud. Rachel turns very red. She is still my wife after all, close to me with her ample figure. Stiffly and abrasively she strokes Yaron's head, and he stifles a cry of pain.

Uzzi is also here at the meeting place. Nathan has asked him to supervise and report. He approaches me with a newspaper in hand.

"Look at this, Meir. You're a celebrity. This organized tour of ours was mentioned in the paper. They say the Galilean settlements are worried that we're up to something, that we plan to buy up their land and destroy the countryside once we're there."

"You'd think we were conquistadors," I say.

"Try to be more understanding," Rachel answers. "People are easily scared."

"Eventually they'll see that we're perfectly friendly, sensible folks who pose no threat whatsoever," says Dana reassuringly, still in great high spirits.

"One thing's for sure," Uzzi chimes in, "when they find out that we're not as good looking as the picture in the paper made us out to be, they'll be less impressed. Dana, of course, is extremely beautiful, but this isn't the first time a beautiful woman has gone camping." Uzzi nods at me with satisfaction, and returns to his post at the registration booth.

Everyone who signed up for the trip has arrived by now. Our guide Hagai goes over the list. A crowd has gathered—they've come to see us off for some reason. Some of them may want to join us, only they haven't registered and paid in time. You can see how eager they are, the way they whisper and look especially at Dana, Rachel, and me. They seem to be tallying the number of people in our group, like children counting their toys over and over. Rachel appears to be somewhat calmer. Maybe she's even beginning to enjoy herself. We haven't spoken much lately, certainly not about her unhappiness. I'm glad to see her smiling now. It's kind of girlish, her smile, and kind of like a wrinkle. With a lively step she approaches me and lays both palms on the back of my hand.

"Isn't it wonderful that we're going to the Galilee at last! Remember when I asked you years ago? And it even looks like a pretty nice group." Hagai finishes calling the roll and asks (almost harshly) for silence. He makes a strange little speech:

"We are an ordinary group. From now on you are not responsible for anyone but yourself. There's no need to interfere in matters of general concern: leave them to me. Remember that as soon as we leave, none of us will have any advantage over the others. Neither Nathan nor his money nor all your ideas will make any difference whatsoever. Get used to the fact that on this trip there is no escaping hardship, no defense against the rain and sand or even the hostility of passersby."

I don't believe anyone really understood what Hagai just said, but maybe such a speech is a necessary part of this trip. We begin to walk. The pace is reasonable. It's a good thing I used to go jogging around the block sometimes before the war. Yaron runs ahead, leading the ranks. Rachel and Dana walk beside me, more or less chatting together. It was announced on the radio that several villages in the Galilee region are getting ready to meet us. Each settlement is convinced that theirs is the one we'll visit. I wonder how they've prepared for our arrival. What could they possibly do? Drink, dress up, have fun, make special gestures? I really don't know. Hagai says their fears are both understandable and justified.

"What if we want to spoil the landscape when we get there, or torment the animals? I may even have a mind to rename some of the inhabitants. They're well aware that the moment we arrive their lives will be thrown into turmoil." Again Hagai's words sound strange to me. Next thing you know he'll be suggesting that they set up flags around their villages or some such colorful idea.

"If I were in their shoes," Rachel interrupts, "I wouldn't wait for people to show up. What are they waiting for anyway? They should come out and meet us from another direction. Why wait like sitting ducks? They could turn the tables and foil our plans—that way they could chase us while we're chasing them." Rachel sips in silence from a large bottle, and smiles at me like someone capable of handing out extraordinary advice. Dana comes closer and whispers: "What nonsense. You'd think we were fighting a sophisticated war. This is nothing but a little jaunt in the hills. Rachel and Hagai are talking as if we were engaged in some historic campaign." Dana's right, but I'm afraid Rachel was alluding to something entirely different.

18

I SEE there's no way I'll be able to write a full report on this trip. I am taking notes, on quite diverse matters generally, great and small, but these will have to be kept to a minimum while I'm hiking. And then I must confess that I have never been crazy about sleeping away from home. As a child I was always eager to get home from any trip, back to my parents—and later, to my wife Rachel. Yet for the past few months, since my illness, I've been sleeping at Nathan and Rina's, where I feel cozy and comfortable, with Dana's diligent pampering. But tonight we're camping, and it's obvious that we have to sleep away from home. At an army base, as it happens. Men and women have been assigned to separate quarters (according to base regulations), so I'm far away from Rachel and Dana tonight. Since we set off on this trip I've noticed that even my prayers have changed—they're more precise, but also more anxious. I haven't had a chance to compare my dreams yet; I'll need a few more nights out to discern any differences.

Just as we sit down for a drink a car drives up. They've apparently brought me some urgent documents from the office, perhaps even new instructions from Nathan. I wonder whether he'll be back in time to join our trip. The driver hands me a large envelope with my name written across it. The car speeds off before I've had a chance to look over the papers. I have no idea who's been left in charge at the office, with both Dana and me on this trip. Dana suggests that we get in touch with Nathan—maybe he's forgotten and thinks we're still at the office. Meanwhile she helps me look over the papers that have just arrived and scribbles some notes with a black pen. I wouldn't be surprised if she's crossing things out. There are five places where I'm supposed to sign. One page deals with the acquisition of an old building in Tel Aviv, another contains instructions for employees. There is also an order to transfer money to

London "for the purchase of official government documents." I have not been consulted about any of these matters, but if I don't sign, it may hurt Nathan's business. I hear a loud exchange, maybe shouting. Dana and I go out to find an argument in progress.

"Nice of you to show up," says Rachel to me. "This is just the sort of dispute you like." I assume they're arguing about our route. Hagai, who is standing next to Rachel, leans over a folding table, and keeps pointing at the map. But they're arguing about something else.

"Hagai won't let us carry our own bags," Rachel reports. Hagai refers to these vehemently as "our supplies." I happen to know they're only our personal backpacks plus a few containers of food and drink. Dana suggests a compromise solution to me in a whisper, but I don't repeat it out loud. My wife's whispering is quite enough for me, I don't need any more prompting here. Hagai turns red, explains the hazards that lie ahead, and insists that we let him decide how and where to carry the supplies. Rachel appears to find his arguments more and more persuasive, and she draws even closer, gazing at him with admiration.

I'm fed up with this conversation. I want to go rest now, eat a few cookies and a whole lot of candy I've been saving in my pocket for tonight. This trip is disturbing me. There's something a little too breezy about it. I wish Yaron would come over and play in my room. I think I may have brought a game of checkers along. Suddenly Hagai steps away from Rachel and announces loudly.

"At this point, now that everyone's calmer and cooler, I would like to consult you about an important issue. Many people who'd like to join our expedition have approached me. They're constantly sending me reminders or accosting me along the route. I don't get it—why couldn't they have registered on time, or simply waited for the next tour? Anyway, there's a lot of pressure on me and I've decided to share this with you. As I see it, we have to be very selective. We can't accept just anyone. We should hold a vote on every candidate and run a thorough background check."

Now Hagai has really succeeded in mixing me up. We're only taking a little trip through the Galilee, but to hear him, you'd think something really major were going on. Maybe I should drop out now. A man like me with a beloved son needn't join in such strange conversations. From what they're saying, I gather some of them plan to have another meeting later tonight. This is difficult for me: there's tension with Rachel, Dana's here, Nathan wants me to run his household as well as his business, and I miss the good old days.

19

HEADING BACK to the room for a nap. It'll be good to rest my weary head, to dream or just relax. A little time off from Rachel and Dana. I suck my thumb, stretch my legs again (the way my old gym teacher showed me), and try to remember my childhood. Outside a whistle blows. I go outside. Hagai's whistle is still in his mouth. More people gather around; some look sleepy, others wide awake. The campers sit down in (quite orderly) formation, with Hagai and his whistle and a new guy in the center. I understand from what is said that this new person wants to join our trip. Let him. Once as a child I walked into class to take a test, and couldn't remember what subject it was in—that's how I feel now. Pens and paper are passed around. Dana suddenly stands up and beckons me in a loud, clear whisper. Hagai and Rachel (at his side) look up. I signal Dana that I'm fine where I am, but she cries out: "Hagai will not begin until you're here beside me." I make my way over and sit down. Hagai starts off:

"Good evening. You've probably all had a good rest by now. Hope you'll learn how to breathe right and to make the most of your opportunities here. Okay, down to business. We have here the new candidate, Menachem. He arrived tonight after calling a couple of times and sending me a few letters before we left. First we'll hear what he has to offer and then we'll decide whether to accept him."

Menachem begins in a quiet voice, speaks of his childhood and his physical attributes. He does look pretty strong. Someone like him will probably be useful. All of a sudden Rachel stands up and interrupts him with a few questions. The whole procedure is confusing to me, I would even say profoundly troubling. I mumble something to Dana and slink away. Rachel is just asking Menachem to tell about his fears and failures. "We don't want to hear only about your virtues." I get back to my room hoping to have a rest from these people. Their voices still ring in the distance, questions and answers, perhaps even some sort of performance (Menachem's?), and then more voices and bickering, and finally what sounds like a vote.

About an hour later I hear loud talk outside my room, the voices of Hagai, Rachel, and Dana. Rachel is upset.

"You spoiled everything, Dana. I was trying to ask Menachem serious questions and you kept joking around. As if what you're doing to Meir isn't enough, now you have to ruin the trip for me too?"

"Calm down, Rachel," Dana replies quietly. "You aren't even capable of nursing Meir back to health, so don't you dare underestimate me."

"I've held my tongue," shouts Rachel, "I've kept out of your business, even where my husband was concerned."

"Don't force us to kick you out," Hagai addresses Dana now. "We're tired. It's been a long day. Let's all go to sleep, shall we? If you like, you can come and talk to me in the morning, but make it early, so we won't start off too late." Now a few more people walk in, apparently assigned to my cabin.

"We should all get as much sleep as possible," I inform them, before they can say anything.

20

IN THE MORNING Dana brings me some bread with jam. I like the taste. Hagai blows his whistle and we continue our hike. I used to enjoy running more than walking, particularly walking like this where you stop every minute. Along the way Hagai points out the flora and fauna but I'm not interested. I like the scenery, I just don't need all those details about every species. Rachel walks over. She wants to know if I have any special requests to pass on to Hagai. "Through me you can send him any message you like."

Again Hagai stops to point out various plants and explain the different breeds and their resistance to the vicissitudes of nature.

"Maybe we'll be able to add to the variety of plant life in the Galilee, but we should think twice before embarking on anything major." I think Hagai has decided to do less talking himself from now on (in front of the group) and to leave the explanations and instructions to Rachel.

A few days later we arrive at the outskirts of the first village on our route. I see a pleasant place with only a few houses. The inhabitants all stand around, smiling at us warily. I have absolutely no idea what the plans are. I hope Hagai has no sinister intentions and will merely pass through the village. But what if I myself speak rudely to one of the villagers? What if I ask why they were so frantic about our coming here and tell them off for going to the press about it? It's their fault we're being followed everywhere we go. They forget that in this country you don't need anyone's permission to go from village to village. But why do I have to decide what to say? It's possible to just stand here quietly and watch. I hope Hagai isn't planning to give them another of his weird lectures. He's capable of trying to threaten them one minute and plead with them the next. I'll be embarrassed if it's like that.

Our group stops at the entrance to the village. From here you can see the signboards of various craftsmen, scattered placards advertising natural remedies, and a notice about someone who teaches an ancient martial art. I read the signs, I observe the little village, and wait. I always feel strange after a few days away from home. What I'm not sure about is whether I'm homesick for my own home or for Nathan's, where I've been living for several months by now. Dana approaches, offering me a flower and a sip from a small bottle. She dabs my eyes with a moist towel, prim and clean as ever. Hagai and Rachel head on into the village. We wait for them vacuously. A sensitive-looking woman approaches, her name embroidered clearly on her blouse: "Tamar." As if to confirm this she says:

"I'm Tamar. You must be that group we heard about."

"I'm Hagai. This is Rachel. She's married and her husband's here too. My group would like to visit you."

"People always find us somehow," explains Tamar. "We're unusual that way. Anyone who wants to visit has no trouble getting here."

I have to interrupt. This trip was not my idea, it's true, but there's something I want to add. Tamar is going to hear my explanation too. I start to walk toward her but Dana holds me back. She has amazingly strong hands for a woman.

"What do you say we stay here a couple of days?" she whispers in my ear.

"What about Rachel?"

"I think she's enjoying herself. She's more familiar with the itinerary than we are. Let her have some fun." I don't answer. This is the first time she has ever suggested openly that I stay with her rather than my wife. Dana and I step forward and join Tamar, who guides the four of us through the village. It seems there are several streets and several dozen houses here after all. I assume she won't show us everything. Perhaps she wants to keep certain parts of their village for herself.

Dana walks beside me, sweet and lovely. No one is more faithful to his wife than I am, and no one is more in love with Dana. Not since the days of my early youth have I been in love; with Rachel there was only a great sense of intimacy. I think Dana may have put on a little weight, but her body still looks very attractive to me.

There's a delicate strength and clarity about it. The few moments allotted me to be in love this lifetime are quickly passing; I mean, how long can someone like me remain preoccupied with love? Dana is very near and tall. Maybe even too tall, she reaches almost to the top of my head. Her hair and complexion are darker than mine, and her arms are even stronger than I realized. She engrosses me more than I ever dreamed possible. I don't know how many hours a day she devotes to improving her appearance. Maybe it's just a few moments, but her vitality and goodness conquer all.

It looks like we're inside the village now ("Still Waters," I believe the place is called). As usual I didn't notice how we got here. Rachel says all of a sudden that she wants to rest.

"You go on to the other villages. I feel like staying here a while. If Meir wants, he can join me, and we'll let Nathan and Rina know we've arrived. Maybe the tiger will like it here, too," she adds in a new and irritating voice. Hagai says we'll all stay here for a couple of days. We have to establish a base of operations in the Galilee so that we'll be able to plan the rest of the trip at our leisure. He asks Rachel to tell the other hikers they should find rooms to rent in the village and make suitable arrangements with the landlords.

"They know who we are, and they know we have power. I think we can arrive at a comfortable understanding with them."

I call Rachel over. She actually comes to me a few moments later. I try to hold her hand and succeed with difficulty. I ask if she's enjoying the trip and she says yes, very much. I ask if she wants to stay here a few days more and she says she'll have to think about it. I'd rather go home now. I want to be at home with the beloved head of my son. Here I fear the situation will become more and more bewildering. Nothing's familiar. There may be people waiting for me in Nathan's office, and it's possible that something extremely urgent has come up. Rachel says she'll decide in the morning whether to go back with me or not. She says it's too bad I didn't tell Hagai about my hesitations right away.

"He might have accepted other applicants. They're constantly hounding him to let them join. It's a shame you didn't say you wanted to leave the trip with me."

21

HAGAI AND TAMAR are planning where to put us up. (In the end they preferred that we not make private arrangements with the villagers.) Hagai reads his list aloud. It seems Dana and I have been assigned to separate rooms in the same house. I didn't quite hear where Yaron will be staying, and I have no idea where Rachel's room is. The fact that Dana and I will be sharing a house again comes as a bit of a surprise (both confusing and exciting). We've simply transferred our city status to the country. Separate rooms, but still under the same roof. I wonder where else I'll wind up with Dana.

We go into a small house. Dana asks which room I prefer and what I'd like to eat and drink. About a quarter of an hour later she returns from the store carrying several bags. Even here, after all the exertions, she has a pleasant smell. Someone raps lightly on the door. As Rachel enters with Hagai, looking pale and speaking in a whisper, she says:

"Have a nice day. You may not be sick of all this, Meir, but we are. I never thought Dana would have to look after you here too. I was under the impression that you're at least as healthy as the rest of us by now. Be that as it may, in a little while I want you to go see Yaron and talk to him about your behavior—he's extremely confused and very angry. I think you should explain your arrangement with Dana to him." Now Rachel looks at Dana (who is standing in the kitchenette) and turns even paler. I go over to hug her shoulders but she recoils toward Hagai.

"Now to business," says Hagai quietly and clearly. "We can come back to your problems later. Meanwhile, though, we've had a message from Nathan. He and Rina will be arriving shortly, maybe even by private plane."

"And of course we have to get ready, that's what Hagai means to say," adds Rachel, and I sense that her identification with him and his role here is becoming stronger. Hagai looks at her for a moment and together they walk out of the house.

Dana asks me in the morning if I want to help her tidy up "our little apartment. I'm sure you want everything ready by the time Nathan gets here. I'm not surprised he's coming directly to the Galilee, he probably wants you as his deputy to brief him."

"I see you haven't forgotten who our employer is," I say with a smile, not entirely certain what I mean.

"Happy, Meir?" Dana approaches and strokes my cheek. "I was sure I loved you very much and now I may start hesitating. What are you waiting for? If you're worried about a scene with Rachel, leave it all to me, I always work things out."

"You know that I'm worried. And my precious Yaron. Anyway Dana, there'll be an awful lot of confusion afterward. Let's go away for a few days, maybe even back to the city."

"We're waiting for Nathan and Rina now," Dana reminds me. "We can't leave yet. There will always be time later. So what's the problem? We'll spend a couple of days here, then go somewhere else, and hear what Nathan has to say. With me you can always relax."

Now Dana hugs me tightly, and whispers in my ear with a little nibble.

"If you really want us to be together some day, and even get married, that's nothing to worry about either. I mean, how much time do couples spend together? How many of them really stay close? You don't have to get so upset." I don't quite understand what Dana means, but now we have to tidy up our rooms and this is the first time she's ever asked for my help.

An hour or so later we hear the loud rumble of approaching vehicles. Dana calls me outside and there is Nathan at the center of a motorcade. In the lead is a van with all sorts of gear piled on the roof (it's more than a communications system, I would guess), followed by Nathan, Rina, and their two sons in the new family car, driven by Uzzi this time. From here it looks as though Uzzi has chosen to wear a tie and a funny hat for the occasion, perhaps in an attempt to give himself a holiday air. Behind them arrive still more of the firm's employees followed by the tiger in a special cage. The procession comes to a halt nearby and everyone crowds around—both our people and the villagers. Hagai approaches Nathan and Rina with Tamar and Rachel, who give them a hug and present them with large tumblers of water "from our wonderful village spring."

I continue to watch from a distance. I see that Nathan is having difficulty getting out of the car. Someone brings him a wheelchair. Uzzi and another employee lift him and set him down on the chair. I think his legs are covered. Maybe he's been in a serious accident and I wasn't even told. I walk over to Nathan and shake his hand, while Rina stands beside him smiling pleasantly.

"Didn't you hear that Nathan suffered a fall? It's not so bad, he'll be up and about in a couple of months. Meanwhile, this is a good opportunity for me to take care of him properly and make him lose some weight." Nathan grumbles and Rina quickly caresses the back of his neck.

"So, you're having a good time at my expense," he says. "You, Meir, and the rest of this entertaining bunch."

"Hello, Nathan," I answer, amazed at my own responses. "It's good to see you again."

"Sure it's good. I understand you didn't much like being boss. From the business you escaped to the hospital, and from my place to the Galilee." He watches me with a silent smile. Rachel looks downcast. "Luckily I made a couple of big deals abroad," Nathan continues. "Otherwise it would have been a waste of time. I'll show you what I bought later, I'm sure no one else in Israel has such a historical artifact. Fine, we'll come back to that. Now bring Dana to me. Let's have a look at my investment."

Rina interrupts. She asks him to put off his meetings "so we can rest a while." She turns around and there's Henri, their African helper from home. It seems his responsibilities have been greatly increased. He is not only in charge of the tiger (and conveying him from the city to the little airport where Nathan and Rina landed) but from now on it is his job to push Nathan around in the wheelchair. For some reason this makes me think of a ninety-year-old man I happened to see recently. He was so lucid, I knew he would never get sick, he would just die one day.

Yaron appears suddenly and stands beside me. He hasn't approached me like this since we set off on the trip. For the first time I notice that he's started shaving regularly. I also notice something mature about his body, like an archeological site that has just been excavated, altering the lay of the land. We hug each other; he's almost as tall as I am, so there's no point stooping anymore. The people watching us are no doubt surprised.

Before dusk there's an assembly on the big playing field in the village. By the time I go out, Dana has left the house, presumably to meet Nathan at long last. On the field there is a lectern and standing beside it are Nathan and Hagai. Uzzi is in charge of the amplifiers. Nathan begins:

"Good to have you here. Until further notice you are all my guests. For a long time now I've wanted to take a trip like this to the Galilee, and it's not so terrible if I pay through the nose. As you see, Rina and I have returned directly from our own trip to yours; we landed not far from here. I had a little accident while we were abroad, but I'm sure I'll recover. And, well, there have been several important developments in my businesses so there's no point getting upset over a few small fractures. Anyhow, I'm happy. At my age my father used to sit around most of the day, and he wasn't interested in anything outside the office. For days on end he would have only the most trivial conversations. He did succeed in business, but only to a limited extent, whereas I have my own activities—all interests converge in me." Rina walks up to Nathan, wearing a bright new dress—she always used to wear somber colors; nice to see that she's changing too. She leans over her husband's wheelchair, kisses him on the head and whispers a few words to him. Nathan grabs her by the waist and sits her on his lap.

"Yes, Rina. What Rina just said is absolutely true. The news is that I'm buying this village. That's right, all the houses, all the streets, the surrounding fields, everything. I think it will be fitting and proper to go hiking from here. And of course I have several other interesting projects in mind." (Uzzi nods vigorously.) Some of the people seem astounded, but Nathan continues in the same tone. "You've met Hagai. From now on he will not only be our guide on this trip, but my permanent adviser on village matters."

I watch as several villagers approach Tamar, and then there are shrill whispers and frantic gestures. Hagai calls for silence and tells us that we should all have fun now. He appoints Uzzi and Henri to divide us up into teams and organize games and matches. My son Yaron and Nathan's son Shahar are appointed the soccer captains and they will now choose players. I'm very eager to be on Yaron's team; together we can win. Yaron doesn't choose me until his third pick and this hurts my feelings somewhat. Maybe he's afraid that Shahar will get all the good players and clobber us.

Dana sits down on the ground and watches the game. I wouldn't be surprised if she joined in at some point and turned out to be a star player. Henri pushes Nathan's wheelchair as Rina instructed him to. Nathan cheers for the players, hands out candy and looks a little less fat than I remember. I'm still not sure what happened in that accident. My hunch is that there's something mysterious between Rina and Nathan's body: maybe she's rearranged his energies for him. Dana approaches me during the game.

"What do you think?" she says. "Do we move on or stay around here a few more weeks?" She seems to have drawn into herself, like someone who has gone out into the cold. "I suppose Nathan's buying up this village as part of a larger strategy. We'll probably know more in time." Dana is still upset, though she's succeeding in disrupting the soccer game for me. "What does Hagai have to do with this? I thought his thing was nature hikes and giving those weird lectures. He doesn't seem the type to stay in a remote village working on a regional development plan."

22

I WAKE UP with a burning face and when I look I see strange colors in the mirror. Yaron must have painted my face during the night. I hope he didn't paint anyone else's. He's suddenly acting like a boy on a school trip. It would be highly embarrassing if it turns out that he has painted other people. I go outside and call Yaron. Dana appears, pulls me inside again.

"Leave Yaron alone. It's hard enough for him as it is. Come in and relax a while." I go back inside with her because if I do yell at Yaron, I'll only end up apologizing right away.

Dana washes my face with water and a special kind of lotion she has, and my face feels cleansed and refreshed. She stands facing me quietly.

"As you see, I'm here now. Come lie down beside me. You'd be scared to do more than that, so let's just lie in bed together for a while with our clothes on." If I weren't so shy, I would tell her that she reminds me of Potiphar's wife. At one point I think she too despaired of ever sleeping with Joseph and had to make do with asking him to "lie beside her." How often have I dreamed of this and longed for this moment? I'm so attracted to Dana. I take her hand and kiss it. I never desired to kiss Rachel's hand, but with Dana it actually feels good. Now we embrace without moving from our places. I'm happy with Dana, yet I start to cry. I suppose I want her to see me crying so she'll gently let go without pressuring me. But she ignores my eyes and caresses my back with warm emotion and with a pleasing vigor.

"This is hard for me, Dana. It's pretty obvious that I love you, but it's hard for me. Don't leave, but let's just sit here quietly a while. Maybe we can listen to some pretty music."

"You're crying."

"Yes."

"You're also trembling."

"Right," I say, laying my head on her shoulder.

I feel a little calmer. Dana gets up, brings me a glass of orange juice. She sits down without touching me. A firm, fixed distance. I offer to tell her something interesting about work, or about a book she hasn't read. She seems to agree with anything I suggest. I'd like to take a little nap right now but that's liable to insult her even more. Anyway, I'm going to have to say my morning prayers and then eat. The awful weakness is returning and I don't want to fall ill again with some terrible disease. Dana strokes my hair and watches me with a clear look. I don't know whether she's angry or merely disappointed with me.

23

THE NEXT DAY Dana leaves the house carrying a small bag and I'm suddenly afraid she won't come back. I follow her out a little later but can't seem to find her—she walks so fast. A new organizational style in the village has become apparent—from the energetic work being done in one of the houses, for instance. The foreman tells me they're building an office for Nathan here. Various employees from the firm (mostly from Organization and Properties) greet me as they stroll through the village. Some of them stop, point at the beautiful scenery, and speak to me.

"We know you're happier now that Nathan's back and the responsibility is off your shoulders. One could say that you pretty much succeeded in your role, Meir. Congratulations."

The regular villagers seem less and less conspicuous. I wonder what kind of deal they made with Nathan. I wouldn't be surprised if he's paying them a salary too. On the notice board I see a new map of the region under the heading "Development Plan," marked with different areas: "new industrial zone," "land cleared for cultivation," and a large "entertainment complex." Several times over the coming days I run into Henri, wheeling Nathan around. Rina has worked out a new eating plan for him, and I haven't seen him look so relaxed and healthy in ages. I wouldn't be surprised if he slims down even more. Too bad he has to sit in a wheelchair, though Rina intimates that there's no cause for despair.

In just two weeks Nathan has managed to convert several village huts into guest houses for VIPs. He has also brought in a number of experts, for instance, a chess master from Germany to practice with him and two antiques dealers (he pores over notebooks full of sketches with them and draws up lists of acquisitions). I believe he's also recruited a natural healer from one of the neighboring villages. At times I detect an unfamiliar smell (from the direction of the healer's house) and rather thick smoke. Dana and Rachel (each on her own) recommend that I try out the new techniques, but I don't want to.

To my surprise Rina has a nearly independent routine each day. She does supervise Nathan's diet, it's true, but mostly she roams around the village and the surrounding area with the chauffeur (or with Uzzi), sometimes by car and sometimes on foot. She's always back early, though, in plenty of time to prepare dinner, chat with her two sons (I believe she and Nathan are considering having the boys enrolled at a nearby school), and pamper her husband.

Dana did not come back to sleep in our house. She shows up every morning and leaves at night.

"If you really want me sometime," she says before going out, "don't forget to ask." And then she smiles and blushes simultaneously. I can't tell if she's actually in love and still interested. For me it's also difficult to respond unambiguously and I regret the additional pressure now. That's why I stay alone in the house most of the day and read in bed. Sometimes I like to stroll through the village, especially past a long row of trees nearby. I don't go far, for fear of the stray dogs. I eat meals (vegetables, milk products, and chocolate), either in the dining hall Nathan set up or alone in my room.

Yaron comes to visit at least once a day. Uzzi likes to talk and consult with me, and he arrives bearing what he calls "surprise packages." Sometimes either Rachel or Dana invites me to her room for a drink, a short conversation, or mutual silence. I realize they expect something from me, but I can't seem to mobilize myself properly. I'm very much surprised at the active role Rachel has taken in village life. She tells me about the lectures she attends, about her involvement in Nathan's enterprises, and, in particular, about her long conversations with Hagai.

24

THIS MORNING I feel an urge to see Nathan, maybe because I miss him in a strange sort of way, or because I'm simply bored. I reach his home (which towers over the other village houses), hear loud voices inside, and delay my entrance. But I can't resist the temptation to eavesdrop. Once upon a time I would have left right away and forced myself to assume indifference, but today I want to hear what they're saying. Rina is speaking loudly, Nathan barely answers her, and when he does it's even harder for me to comprehend what he's saying.

"What more do you want?" Rina says. "I bought you a tiger, I bought you a gorgeous girl like Dana, I followed you to England, and I returned with you to this peculiar village—I'm sick of your demands."

"You talk as if you're lacking something," it seems to me that he answers her. "Uzzi takes excellent care of you, you look attractive, almost like a young girl again. Haven't you noticed the way everyone admires you? Even Meir peeks at you sometimes."

"Enough Nathan," Rina screams. "You're intolerable! You meddle in everyone's life. You've even managed to spoil Meir and Rachel's marriage. And now this stupid wheelchair. You had to see how people would treat you as an invalid. How long will you go on with this charade?"

"Be quiet. Go back to the city if you've had enough. I have

work to do here. Anyway, what good are Dana and the tiger to me? I've never really used the tiger, and until now Dana's been busy with somebody else."

I turn away from their house and go looking for Yaron. I find him on a hilltop taking in the view and calculating the distance to the horizon. We give each other a hug and sit down. I kiss his cheek and then his lips.

"When will we go home with Mom?"

"Soon, I hope."

"But what about Dana? Is she still your girlfriend?"

"She's just a friend, nothing more."

"A friend is a lot. I don't have a single female friend."

"Come, Yaron, let's go buy something nice."

"Maybe later, Dad. I want to think over what we were just talking about." That's how Yaron ends our conversation. A few minutes later he comes jogging after me and asks me to wait.

"Hey Dad, did something special happen, or is everything still the same?"

"Everything's almost the same," I say, and want to leave.

"Let's go see the tiger soon," he requests. "I've barely seen him since we got to the village. I tried asking Mom and Hagai but they didn't know anything about it, or else they didn't want to tell me."

"I think the tiger is being looked after in a special stall somewhere. I haven't taken much interest in him lately."

25

THIS EVENING I'm going to rest. Maybe I'll be able to unwind a little. Even in the army there were times when I managed to relax. Let me enjoy what's going on around me, even the unfamiliar smells. Anyway, what's so terrible about a vacation in a Galilee village, where I can lie on my bed, propped up on a few pillows, sucking candy while I wait for Yaron? Maybe he'll come by and read a book that used to be a favorite of mine. But I can't stop thinking about Nathan. Why did he want to make everyone think he was an invalid? On the other hand, I'm not at all surprised that Rina is playing along with him, since she obviously wants to prove that her initiative with the tiger (and maybe Dana too) was one-of-a-kind, and that she has no more ideas of her own. Still, I'd better think about other things until I fall asleep so that I'll have a relatively peaceful night.

I fall asleep faster than intended and find myself in a dream about the afternoon of Yom Kippur, apparently during the intermission between the morning Musaf prayers and the afternoon service. For some reason I realize that I should eat something, as though it were just an ordinary Sabbath afternoon. I drink some water and eat part of a banana. Suddenly I realize that I've just eaten during the Yom Kippur fast. Big panic. Then the dream itself tries to reassure me, to convince me that I didn't actually swallow the food, I was merely considering it. I check my teeth to find out for sure.

In the morning I realize that I'm lonely. Because of this, a brief note that arrives from Rachel—while it doesn't surprise me—makes things much more difficult for me.

"Hello, Meir. Our love was once very beautiful, or so I believe. But it's over now between us. Let's decide what to do about Yaron. The separation has already taken place. Rachel." I cry, of course. I could never leave anyone. It's others who move me from one place to another. I'd better go now—at least I should get out of this room, and the time has come to talk to Nathan. The closeness between us may have created certain problems, but I think it would be worthwhile now to have a serious talk with him about my situation. On the way over to his house I am still crying and for the first time in my life I don't feel like interacting with anyone I meet. In the past I would have explained all my business to them, spoken at length about my fears and accomplishments, and answered every question I was asked, even by recent acquaintances. Presently the crying stops and the miscellaneous pressures in my stomach begin.

I enter the house. Rina, in a long white dress, smiles at me.

Nathan sits in an armchair and, facing him on a high stool that looks like a draftsman's chair, is Hagai.

"Hello, hello," says Nathan (who often doubles his hello). "Finally you've got yourself into something interesting: I hear you're all mixed up between your wife and Dana. That isn't like you. Leave such things to me. And don't forget that Dana was supposed to live at our house."

"Nathan," I say to him, "I'm going through hard times, and as you know I'm alone now."

"I don't get it, what's so hard?" he continues. "It's not as if anyone expected great things from you. I, on the other hand, have many salaries to worry about. Instead of getting rich myself and exploring interesting places, I'm busy with all of you."

Now Hagai turns toward me. "It's high time you made up your mind. I can't stand indecision, I've never liked cowards, dilly-dalliers, or softies in my groups." I turn red, and to my surprise Rina signals Hagai to shut up and asks if I'd like to stay in their house a while longer.

Nathan answers before I do. "Sure he does, where else could he go?" Still standing in place, I can't figure out why Nathan is more aggressive than usual—it's not as if I were the actual source of his problems.

Hagai asks Nathan to continue their conversation.

"We have to make good use of the time, Nathan," he says in his peculiar way. "Tell me again what you have in mind." Nathan shifts in his seat and starts talking in a fairly loud voice about medieval European history. He asks Rina to fetch a few books, takes a notepad from a nearby table, and shows Hagai (and me too, perhaps) a list of details about population, borders, languages, and cities. He asks us which cities in Europe are situated on the banks of rivers and which city names have a known origin. He promptly answers himself with a number of examples. He asks Rina for something to eat and she brings him a plate of chocolate cookies and a glass of lemonade. He continues talking, sipping, and especially eating.

"Why are you so interested in that?" Hagai stops him. "We have an amazing plan right here in the Galilee. Forget your history books and help me out." Nathan looks at him with an expression I've never seen before. Rina looks fixedly at Nathan.

"Hagai," says Nathan, " don't forget that I'm the one who's financing your strange ideas, and don't bother me too often." Hagai smiles, takes a sip from a big glass of cold water. He adjusts his precisely rolled-up sleeves.

"Fine, no problem. I'm going out to visit your tiger."

Now Nathan tells me he's interested in getting ahold of some rare medieval documents. "My antique collecting won't stop, but I've made some surprising moves. I may need your help, Meir. Only this time don't get sick on us."

"Great," I say to Nathan. "I'd be glad to help you out with something interesting." I get up and leave. They may have intended that I stay a while longer, but they didn't say anything.

26

IT'S INTERESTING that I have no desire to see the tiger anymore. Only a short while ago I was sharing a large apartment with him and now I feel inclined to keep my distance. I think I'll take a nap and maybe later go see Yaron and propose that he come live with me for a couple of days. It's time I learned to enjoy this village, to make the most of its simple possibilities. I'll probably feel stronger in a couple of weeks and then I'll be able to make my plans.

A few hours later I'm clearly about to fall asleep. All of a sudden I hear shouting outside. Yaron is calling me. I get up right away and hurry out to him. I'm relatively calm, like someone who's slept at least half the night. Yaron, wearing shorts (long pants would be more appropriate at his age) whispers something in my ear. I ask him to repeat himself and he says aloud:

"There are strange noises in the village, and I can't find Mom." I'm frightened. Maybe there's been some sort of trouble involving Rachel. Maybe she's run out of patience. "Let's go to Nathan's," he says, and though I don't see why I should go back to Nathan's when I was already there today, I don't want to argue with Yaron.

Sure enough, there is shouting and a commotion in front of Nathan's house. Someone asks me what I'm doing here.

"You'd better stay away." I see Uzzi running up the road.

"Hey, Meir! Come quick, we need you." He leads me off to a nearby house. I see Rachel, Tamar, and several others there.

"We've got a problem," says Tamar. "That Hagai fellow you brought up here is inside fighting with Nathan. He says Nathan's ruined everything—the trip and his plans to transform the region. Claims Nathan's been stalling him and doesn't want to leave our village. I wouldn't be surprised if they actually come to blows; at any rate he's not letting him out of the house. 'Preventive detention' he calls it, in his peculiar language."

"I'm fed up!" Rachel exclaims. Uzzi shouts back with something of a stammer:

"Wha-wha-what exactly are you fed up with? Freeloading off Nathan or indulging yourselves in quarrels? We have to get Nathan out of there: that's all that matters now."

"Who says we have to get involved?" asks someone from the village. "What does any of this have to do with us? You people are like guests at a hotel here. Since when is a hotel manager supposed to interfere in the guests' quarrels?" Tamar tells him to shut up and says:

"We can discuss our private business later. I have my own opinions about this."

Uzzi turns to me: "It's important for you to be here, Meir. You're someone we can all rely on. You have to take charge now. There's no one else around."

"Where's Dana?" I ask. "I haven't seen her since yesterday morning. Maybe she's locked in there with Nathan and Rina. And who helped Hagai with the kidnapping, anyway?" I ask, and this time Rachel answers me quietly, in a near whisper.

"What does it matter who it was? The important thing is that this is a serious crime, kidnapping. This is completely insane. We should call the police, maybe even the army." There's a sound of scampering. Someone's run into the room. It's Henri, who has changed his clothes and is now wearing a suit and tie. The suit is torn and dirty.

"I managed to escape," shouts Henri, "But they've caught the tiger. Hagai's taken over. The tiger won't obey anyone else. It's in love with him."

"What about Dana?" I ask Henri.

"I haven't seen her," he replies, "I only know that Nathan, Rina, and the tiger are all in there. Hagai tied Nathan and Rina up together and he's running the show with some equipment he brought along. I think a few people came over to help him guard the place." I turn to Rachel and suggest that we go off somewhere and talk. Outside I try to reason with her very cautiously, but she is adamant.

"What I wrote you still stands. There's nothing more to say. First you have to free Nathan and Rina. There are some people around here who, for some reason, think you can do it."

"But Rachel, why this obstinacy? You're my wife."

"Forget it, Meir, I'm not afraid anymore. There's no point talking, it won't make any difference what you say."

Uzzi looks at me (when we go back inside) and hushes the others. He hopes my discussion with Rachel is over. At my suggestion he calls the police. Their first reaction is alarm.

"We'll send some people over right away." Then they phone back and ask if we happen to be "that city bunch" because, if so, we should try to settle things among ourselves first. "We've heard some strange stories about you people—maybe you're playing tricks again. Your boss is notorious for his tricks. Still, if anything serious should come up, give us another call."

Uzzi is tense. He suggests that we get in touch with a government minister. Rachel isn't keen on the idea; she doesn't like politicians meddling with "personal" problems. I suggest that we start by finding out who is against us. Meanwhile there are cries from the street. An unknown man asks to come in.

"Hagai sent me. He wants you out of the village. He'd rather we worked things out with Nathan directly, without your intervention. In any case, you haven't done very well on this trip so far; we've all seen how limited you are. Rachel is the only one Hagai is willing to talk to, and if she wants to she can go back in with me. But before you make any radical plans, you'd better decide whether Nathan is even interested. We're taking good care of him, and Hagai is about to draw up some important plans with him which you wouldn't want to jeopardize."

"Tell Hagai I want to talk to him," I suddenly say, to my surprise.

"I'm not sure he'll agree to that. I told you, Rachel's the only one he'll let inside."

"Rachel's staying here, for the time being," I answer the messenger and Rachel doesn't argue. "Okay, I'm going in now to Hagai, Nathan, and the others. If you want anything, call. But it would be best for you to return to your homes in the city."

NATHAN TELEPHONES and asks to speak with me.

"Most of what you've heard is true. Hagai beat me up and tied me and Rina together for about an hour. But things have calmed down now. He made certain demands and a few proposals. I have to figure out what is worth doing. Physically I'm not in great shape, but my strength won't run out so fast. I only ask you not to bother us. If possible, just go home, all of you. I need to think a little, to discuss things with Hagai," he says, and hangs up before I have a chance to answer him.

I report to everyone what Nathan has just told me. Uzzi looks pale. I think he's trembling.

"We're not going anywhere," he says. "It's too dangerous. Maybe Hagai has mesmerized them in there."

"Oh really, now!" Rachel says, astounded. "In my opinion we should simply get up and leave."

Henri is crying. He claims this mess is all his fault. "I can't believe the tiger has turned against me and that now he's obeying Hagai. For an animal to behave like that, I must have really failed in some way, I must have done something terrible." Rachel goes over to comfort him. This time I don't feel like getting involved. In the past I could never have stood idly by; if someone started crying, I would immediately have gone over to offer comfort. Henri is not the main problem. What should I do in this complicated situation Hagai has created? I want Yaron—it's urgent that I see him. Everyone seems agitated about my request, as though our fate depended on it. They send a person to call him urgently. No one can find him at first and I hear loud shouting from various directions. But finally he turns up, bouncing a ball, perspiring, his belly peeking out. It's not exactly clear to me where he's been for the past few hours. I look at Rachel and get angry. At least she should make sure our son keeps himself clean. Who knows when he last had a shower.

I suddenly think of Menachem, who came to the village with us. I ask where he is. Everyone in the room starts talking about him now and they all set off to search for him. I haven't spoken to him once since he joined our group. Maybe I was wrong to be so indifferent. Naturally I'm suspicious of him at a time like this. To my surprise Menachem soon arrives. He shakes my hand and kisses Rachel's.

"What's happening?" he asks, and continues: "There's a huge fight going on. It's not a good idea to have fights when you're on a trip."

"Menachem, do you know anything about Hagai's plans?" I ask. Menachem draws closer, puts his mouth to my ear and whispers:

"Not a thing. I haven't done a thing."

"And did you know that Hagai has grabbed a couple of our people and that he's holding them captive in a locked room?"

"But Hagai is our leader. He must have had a pretty good reason to do a thing like that. Just wait a while. Don't be angry with him."

Menachem's words astound and infuriate me. I'm sick of this discussion. I call Nathan's hut. Hagai answers promptly:

"Hello, Meir. I hope you've calmed down by now. Nathan and I have been having some interesting talks here. You know Nathan, there's hardly anything you can't discuss with him. At the moment we're arguing about the Roman Empire. Nathan claims it declined because the people wanted it to. They were fed up with being strong. They wanted even their downfall to be the result of their own free choice. What do you say, Meir?"

"Hagai," I shout, "you're holding Nathan and Rina captive. You're in big trouble. Why don't you drop the historical questions now and release my friends?"

"Meir, my friend, mind your own business. Decide for example whether Rachel will be joining our side or staying with you. Decide when you're going home with your son. Forget the other stuff; it has nothing to do with you."

Rachel draws closer and asks me to stop the conversation.

"You'll see, Nathan is strong. He can stay locked up in there for weeks and he'll never give up on what's important to him. All that self-indulgence has actually fortified him for this struggle. He won't break down now."

"I don't know, Rachel. You're mixing me up."

"Meir, it's time we found ourselves again. You and I have to make up our minds. You can't just keep writing reports to yourself about what's going on with you and others; you and I have to pull together and come to some genuine agreements, for a change. Meanwhile I'm taking Yaron to my hut. I think it would be best for him to go home with me now, but I'll hang around here a few more days and let you know whether you can come with us."

28

MY THOUGHTS are in turmoil. Some of Rachel's more distinctive odors as she goes about her business—her surroundings generally not so clean—come back to me. She even leaves the shower without rinsing it out. And she just drops her clothes on top of mine. I lay my clothes out neatly on a chair in the evening and the next morning I have to look for them under Rachel's pile. Inside me are harsh thoughts—something to do with the four directions. Again I recall the peculiar words: henceforth I will have only south and east; I wish to live without north and west. If I collected aphorisms, the way Nathan used to, I'd definitely write this one down.

Uzzi asks what's new. Are there any decisions he should pass on to the others? Should the workers go back to the office now? How will we compensate the villagers? What about the operation Nathan set up at a nearby lot? I keep quiet and look at Uzzi. I smile at him, trembling. I don't want to fall ill again, to get that pressure in my stomach and the visual disturbances.

"What were you saying, Uzzi? It's not easy to break up, but when it happens, it happens, like a sedative that gradually dissolves, so it'll last a whole day, not a couple of minutes. I never understood whether those pills dissolve little by little, or all at once and then circulate slowly through the body." I'm not sure what Uzzi's thinking about my thoughts just now. He wants for us to go visit Nathan. We can't just leave him all alone. And we have to find out what's going on with Rina, too. I agree. A coward like me agrees. Several guards halt us on our way. Some of them look familiar. They call out to Hagai and ask whether to let us approach. He emerges slowly from the house, leading the tiger by a heavy rope. I don't believe the tiger has ever been tied to such a strong rope before.

Hagai approaches and signals for me to come alone. I follow him into the house. Nathan, sitting in an armchair, seems a little drowsy to me. Rina looks pale, lying partially hidden in the corner of the room. There's a strong animal scent in the air. It seems to me there's a kitten on Nathan's lap. I remember his aversion to the tiger, and now they've stuck him with a kitten too. No doubt he finds this animal rubbing against him hard to take. Suddenly Rina gets up, walks over to him with effort, picks up the kitten and brushes the hairs off Nathan's lap. Nathan does not respond.

Hagai takes out a notebook and shows it to me.

"At my request, Nathan has copied out a whole list of questions here. You know how he collects important questions, in the style of 'the essential question is . . .'? I rather enjoy reading the notebooks. Down below (he points to the exact spot) I've added one question of my own: supposing two cars meet briefly at an intersection. Does it matter then what either of them was doing a moment before? Does it matter that one of them has just driven out of the parking lot, while the other is about to park after a long drive? In the end, does it make any difference where each of them started off? This is my big question and it requires a lot of thought."

I look at Hagai and he looks back. The tiger is dozing beside him. Hagai has strong arms; he is wearing a visor cap even though we are indoors. He sips quite often from a nearby bottle of water. His clean fingernails and neat clothing impress me. It's almost as if the whole village were his large and comfortable office and he had nothing to worry about.

"So tell me, did you people intend to ruin my project here?" he starts in again. "I planned this trip down to the last detail. I planned to buy up vast regions of the Galilee. What did you think, that I was just some strange tour guide? Nathan promised he would join in and help finance the enterprise. But from the moment he arrived, I saw that to him this was no more than a vacation. That's why I had to stop everything from falling apart. There's no reason why Nathan and I shouldn't get along perfectly well from now on. He needed someone like me around to restrain him. If everyone were as weak as you, Meir, Nathan would just keep playing his games, and the hell with everything else."

I see Nathan blush and smile simultaneously. He looks at me and Hagai, avoids looking at his wife.

"What are you so excited about?" he asks Hagai. "It's no big deal for me to keep buying up land here so we can develop it according to your ideas. You don't have to go on a rampage to get me to change my mind about business." Nathan smiles again. He gets up and starts walking around. I haven't seen him walk unaided in a long time. He approaches Rina and strokes her hair. She cries quietly. I am amazed by the stamina of a self-indulgent guy like Nathan. As for me, it makes me nervous just to hear their conversation.

Dana walks into the room. She didn't go anywhere else after all. She's been to the grocery store.

"I brought you what you asked for." Hagai and Nathan run over and peek inside the bags. They grunt with satisfaction.

"Hurry, we're starving," says Nathan.

"We all know our roles around here," says Dana, and sets the food out. Rina gets up and goes to the kitchen to cook. Her face looks haggard; there are deep scratches, maybe gashes. Once I knew a woman with scratches like that whose son married a girl just like her. He never realized he'd chosen the girl because her face was scratched like his mother's.

The odors are more pleasant now. To me even the tiger looks drowsy and content. Rina sets the table. At the head she places a card with "Nathan" written on it. At the other end she places another card with the name "Hagai." Rina and Dana take their seats on the remaining two sides. Dana asks me if I'm hungry.

"Never mind. I think I'd better just sit off to the side and talk from here." Hagai says I'm welcome to eat with them.

"This is all health food here. We had the whole thing planned out."

"Would you mind telling me what you've decided?" I ask. Dana looks away. She clears the table, rubs the stains off and serves the next course. Rina ties an apron around her waist and warms up the side dishes. Nathan and Hagai pour water for each other and, I think, red wine as well.

"In effect, from now on there will be two centers," says Nathan, perhaps by way of an answer to my question. "Both in the village and back at the office. We'll staff both locations and expand our old enterprises along with the new ones."

"Rina and Dana can choose where they prefer to be," adds Hagai.

"Not a good idea," says Nathan. "They should always be with me."

It hardly seems appropriate to argue now. Nor do I know for certain which point of view I'm supposed to affirm. I walk away, for the first time in my life without saying goodbye to those in the room. The guards watch me angrily. I saunter off so that they won't be tempted to chase after me. It seems advisable to leave the village. I wouldn't be surprised if Rachel and Yaron have already gone home. If they agree, I want to live with them again.

29

YARON IS WAITING in my room.

"I asked Mom if we could all live together again. I'd rather go home, but for now it's okay here, too. I don't much care how you and she get along, or that your friends have loused up our life. We can still be here together for a while." I ask whether Rachel is willing and he calls her right away. Rachel says things are "confusing enough as it is" and that we ought to get out of the village. Meanwhile, she says, we can live in her hut. "We'll all have a fair amount of space." This heartens me and I caress Yaron, who is standing at my side. He asks if I need any help, and together we round up some of the things I'll need. I no longer remember precisely what I packed for this trip, but I seem to have fewer and fewer belongings with me.

About two hours later Yaron and I arrive at Rachel's. It isn't a real homecoming, of course, but even this much togetherness is not easy. Rachel barely speaks and Yaron keeps hugging her and kissing her. I hope he'll be prompted to hug me too from time to time. Rachel hands me an envelope from Nathan. It's a brief note requesting that I regularly keep in touch with the firm's city office. I'm to send him reports of our current transactions, any major deals that fall through, and forward appeals for donations and letters of particular interest.

"And it won't hurt if you keep me informed about any pretty new female employees," he adds. I assume he's appointed others to inform him about other matters like art and antique furniture. I'm not quite sure how I'm supposed to acquire this information for him, unless he means for me to commute between the city and the village.

During the first few days of the changed arrangements I'm not sure whether Rachel is busy with something new or what she's up to really. In the evenings she usually puts food out for me, talks to Yaron a while, and shuts herself in her room. At first I thought I'd sleep in the room assigned to Yaron but he probably wouldn't be too happy about that and Rachel too might be offended (even though she's the one who secludes herself in her room). This is why at night I sleep in a comfortable armchair in the hallway, and during the day I rest on Yaron's bed (when he's out, of course.)

Nathan, Rina, and Dana share the house in the village. Next door, as I understand it, lives Hagai, who is busy planning some new project in collaboration with Nathan. I'm not sure he has an official position yet, but it seems he and Nathan are on better working terms. Until I see Nathan, though, I won't know for certain whether he's regained his strength. It is a little odd that Nathan didn't throw him out after the scene he made; apparently Hagai has some special influence. Uzzi works a few days a week at the new branch in the Galilee and the rest of the time he's at the main office in the city. There are rumors that he's about to be promoted company director, but putting a personal assistant in charge of such a complicated business doesn't make sense.

Then there's the matter of Hagai's relationship with Rachel. I have the impression that he sends her letters and also calls her from time to time. It seems they're discussing various philosophies. Surprisingly, I am interested neither in their letters nor their conversations. Rachel dawdles over the replies, adding a line here, a line there, as she continues to ponder. She also clips various items from the newspaper, entire articles even, and puts them in an envelope. I wouldn't be surprised if someday she announced she was going on yet another trip with Hagai as her guide.

30

RACHEL TELLS ME that Rina's condition has deteriorated. She seems to be alluding to a serious illness, for some reason not yet specified.

"I think she'll be needing me more now," says Rachel, as though in conclusion. Just how Rachel can help her is not at all clear to me and it would be rather upsetting if instead of looking after Yaron (and me too for that matter) at such a sensitive juncture she busied herself with Rina's health. I haven't seen either Rina or Nathan for several weeks now. I spend the hours reading in my armchair, wandering around the village, playing soccer with Yaron, and going over the massive envelopes of things for Nathan that I get every evening from the main office. Uzzi announces that there's going to be a special ceremony in a couple of days, and then we'll all have a chance to see each other again. Preparations are indeed under way—they've set up benches and a small podium and there's an almost festive air in the village. At the appointed hour Yaron and I go out to the assembly grounds (Rachel left the house earlier this morning to bring Rina some homeopathic medicines). Almost everyone from our group is there and so are most of the villagers. Uzzi asks for absolute silence, and Henri pulls over the cage on wheels with the tiger inside. I haven't seen him for ages. He doesn't look any different, really; I ought to find out sometime whether animal faces change with age. Now Nathan arrives with Rina and Dana. Rina is leaning on a slender cane, looking pale and wan. Wearing a new suit, the lovely Dana (once I might have said "my lovely Dana") smiles at her audience but doesn't say a word. Hagai is the last to arrive, in shorts as usual, but this time with a dressy-looking shirt.

To my surprise, Hagai gives the opening remarks. He praises the weather, says that at long last Nathan is beginning to keep his promises, and that the combination of "Nathan's money and know-how and my planning will ultimately have a tremendous influence on a great many people." Now Nathan speaks briefly, says that happily he is back on his feet, only now Rina is sick and this problem too must be overcome.

"As long as she's sick I won't be able to inform you about new developments here; even Dana's status is unclear at this point. I used to think we'd form an interesting triangle, Rina, Dana, and myself, but now we'll have to wait for Rina to recover." Dana blushes deeply at these remarks while Rina seems unruffled. Now Uzzi explains the purpose of the assembly. "Nathan has given Hagai the go-ahead to set the tiger free. We amused ourselves with him for a long time, but we have no further use for him now. There's nothing to worry about, folks, we've taken every precaution. The tiger has received all his shots and sedatives, and we're quite sure he won't harm anyone." I am much alarmed. I approach Dana and ask her to do something. Dana is happy to see me, she kisses my cheeks, but hushes me too.

"This is the wrong time for your remarks," she says.

Henri halts in front of Nathan and asks whether he can start now. Nathan says yes, and Rina sits down on a chair that was brought from the house. Henri picks up a colorful rope, approaches the cage, whispers something to the tiger and proudly faces the audience. The tiger walks toward him (still in his cage); Henri manages to tie one end of the rope to the tiger's collar through the bars. Now he takes a small key from his pocket and opens the cage door. The tiger emerges, surprisingly apathetic. Hagai advances and stands before the tiger as though waiting to pet him. Henri asks him a question, and they amble off at the tiger's leisurely pace. Hagai asks for a loudspeaker, says that in just a few minutes the tiger will be free of humans again. I'm still hopeful that they're not going to free him. I can't believe Nathan has been persuaded to trust this animal. Now Hagai and Henri lead the tiger off together, the colorful rope uncoiling to its full length, much longer than I imagined it.

Henri pets the tiger's head, which from this distance looks pretty small. Hagai picks up the loudspeaker and asks everyone to concentrate.

"Keep quiet and, if you must speak to share your words with others, don't waste these moments on trifles." He hands the end of the rope to Henri and addresses the audience. "The tiger will go his own way and Henri will shortly return to us. Anyway, who needs a tiger when we have among us here a man as strong and singular as Henri?" I don't quite understand what Hagai means by this and whether it is a compliment or an insult to Henri. A few people wave at the tiger, and he continues to trudge along after Henri until we lose sight of them. Nathan requests that we all have fun now.

"After the tension of the past few weeks, and until Henri comes back, we have time to enjoy the special food we've had catered from the city."

I'd be interested to ask Dana why they set the tiger free and whether this had anything to do with Rina's sudden illness. But Yaron approaches and asks if we could go back to our hut now.

"I think the main event is over," he says, "and I want to spend some quiet time with you—maybe play or talk, or we could even rest if you like."

31

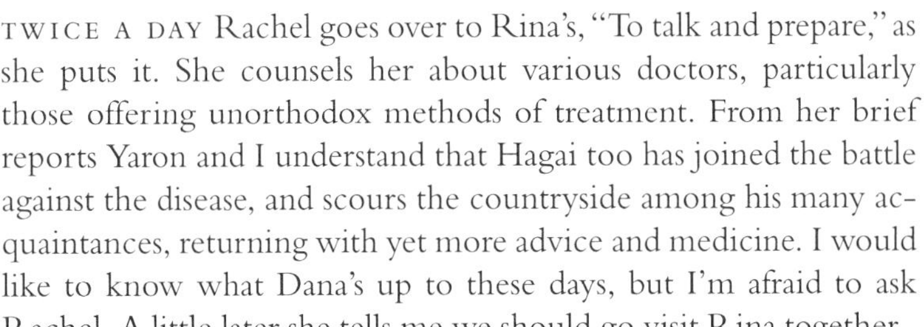

TWICE A DAY Rachel goes over to Rina's, "To talk and prepare," as she puts it. She counsels her about various doctors, particularly those offering unorthodox methods of treatment. From her brief reports Yaron and I understand that Hagai too has joined the battle against the disease, and scours the countryside among his many acquaintances, returning with yet more advice and medicine. I would like to know what Dana's up to these days, but I'm afraid to ask Rachel. A little later she tells me we should go visit Rina together.

"I'm glad you've finally asked me to come along," I whisper and immediately regret it. Rachel glances at me without a word. Yaron decides that he will not join us but concentrate instead on making up the school lessons he's missed. It seems Uzzi installed an effective computer linkup with his school until we go home.

As we draw closer to Nathan and Rina's house I am struck by certain changes. Most of the houses in the area seem to have been rebuilt or at least expanded. There are signs announcing the imminent development of resort facilities, businesses, riding trails, and playgrounds. From the large blueprints, we understand that the houses will be built in the American suburban style. Rachel leads me to a hut next door to Nathan and Rina's. I notice the sophisticated hospital equipment there, complete with medical staff. This is where Rina is now and where we are meant to visit her.

We are given permission to enter. Inside the room sits Dana, reading a newspaper (she seems to be working on a quiz or crossword puzzle). She immediately comes to greet us, almost at a run, caresses my shoulders and hugs Rachel (who blushes as she did the day she told me some twenty years ago that we had to get married).

"Where have you been?" Dana whispers to me. "Why did you disappear? Anyway, the important thing is that you're here at last. She's really sick, you know," she points at Rina, who is asleep. "It's hard to know if she'll ever recover now." Suddenly the two sons, Shlomo and Shahar, walk in. They're dressed identically, perhaps in school uniforms. They are now attending a local school instead of their old boarding school in Europe. They greet me, give Dana a brief hug, and go to their mother. Each in turn takes out a notebook, strokes Rina's hand, searches for signs of vitality, and tries to read aloud to her interesting things learned at school. Rina opens her eyes, tries to put on makeup, and Dana and Rachel rush to help. Dana even suggests a wash and a change of clothes, "Because you have company and Nathan will probably be here soon."

"Come on over, Meir, it's wonderful that you've joined Rachel today. What a wife you've got, you have no idea! It's only over the past few weeks that I've realized what fine qualities she has. Such intelligence and devotion. Our conversations give me strength." Rina speaks in an almost normal voice. "I'm so happy you're living together again," she continues. Rachel is shocked and I giggle strangely. "Come, you can sit together on my bed, there's nothing contagious here. If Nathan had any fears about that, he would have put me in quarantine by now. I think he suspected the tiger, some nasty microorganism he may have been carrying—that's why they set him free. At least he's keeping me," she jokes in a feeble voice that turns into a cough. "You saw that village life agrees with my sons. Instead of freezing to death in Europe, they're having fun. So where's Yaron? It wouldn't hurt you to bring him over, too. Or maybe you didn't want your darling Yaron to see such a sick woman, Meir?"

We sit down on the bedside chairs. Dana asks if we want anything to drink and Rachel says we don't. Dana informs me that Rachel occasionally brings over some of her delicious homemade pies.

"Even Nathan enjoys them. He says he never knew kosher food could be so tasty." Everyone laughs and I look at Rina.

"My life is probably over now," she suddenly says, "and Nathan hasn't taken full advantage of our life with Dana yet. Still, some things have worked out all right. My sons are doing well, Nathan has managed to lose a little weight, Dana will be perfectly capable of looking after him, and they'll probably open a new wing at the museum in my name." Now Rina sits up and heaves a sigh and, so far as I can judge, things are looking bad here.

Dana says Nathan's health is fine now. They brought a well-known nutritionist to see him in the village: he's been fairly disciplined, and he's sleeping reasonably well—better than he used to, at any rate.

"He spends part of the day working on the plans with Hagai and the rest of the time he's absorbed in his research on medieval European history. I think he's concentrating on Anglo-French relations."

Hagai calls, asks to speak to Rina, and wants to know how she is. I think he's telling her about some new medication he's come across. Rina ends the conversation and turns back to us.

"Hagai is a good man. As soon as I got used to his way of talking, we became friends. He's promised me a new, surefire cure. 'We're tired of losing'—that's what he just said to me."

"He sure seems to have calmed down since they let the tiger

go," says Rachel, much to my surprise. "Suddenly he has no reason to argue with anyone; it used to be all-important for him to prove he was the one the tiger obeyed."

Nathan enters the room. Shlomo and Shahar turn from their mother and walk over to greet him, each in turn giving Nathan a kiss on the cheek, as though the spot were marked. Nathan approaches Rina's bed (still without a word), kisses her broad and tired brow, again and again wipes the sweat from his face, asks Uzzi (who walked in with him) what there is to drink. Asks Dana if everything's all right. Finally turns to me:

"Hello, hello, Meir. Good to see you together. Are you pleased with your new quarters? We could find you a bigger place, if you like. There's been a ber-illiant improvement in living conditions"—he emphasizes the "r" as though we might otherwise mistake it for a different consonant. "You see this, Rina's gotten sick on us. She finally persuaded me to bring Dana home, and then she had to get sick. You never know what their real intentions are."

I cross over to Nathan. As usual these days I give him a warm pat on the shoulder. I find myself doing this to more and more people and it seems to embarrass them a little.

"Is there anything I can do, Nathan, anything I can . . ."

"Don't be silly," he interrupts. "I have plenty of helpers already and more than enough partners here. Don't forget, Hagai sees himself as a full partner in our 'Project Galilee,' as he calls it in his funny lingo."

"But Nathan, I've been extremely close to you for years."

"Very nice of you to say so, Meir. If I need you, I'll let you know. Now go solve your own problems with Rachel."

In light of this remark I call for Rachel, who has meanwhile left the room. Not only did she leave; she was whisked off to see the house next door, which has been fixed up for us. Dana reports that Rachel started working on the new place several days ago. What's this? What helped Rachel to do so much on her own, without whispering a single request in my ear? I hurry off to search for her. I find her cleaning the new hut.

"If you like, Meir, you can set up a little study for yourself in the hallway; I don't need that space. I've asked them to move your things to the bedroom and you can decide where you want to sleep, next to me if you like. And of course, don't forget to call Yaron and tell him that we've moved into a nice new house, so that we can be close to Rina."

32

RACHEL'S MAIN ACTIVITIES have to do with Rina. In the morning she hurries off to her with a freshly baked cake (after years of not baking) or casserole.

"You have no idea how delighted she is with my food," she says. And sometimes she sits beside her and reads aloud. I don't think there was ever any real closeness between them before Rina took ill.

Dana seems disoriented. She rarely speaks to me and spends much of her time at Nathan's local office, dealing with London, filling out the forms they send in the mail, and returning them with Nathan's signature. She and Nathan spend several hours a day at the office together, but it isn't yet clear to me how close their relationship has become. Apparently Nathan visits Rina's sickbed every evening, either on his own or with his sons. Every time I try to talk to Dana she answers that not everything that was appropriate before is still appropriate, and that she's busy with other matters now.

Hagai brings in a number of specialists (oddballs, if you ask me) to attend to Rina. She's willing to let almost anyone examine her. I wonder whether she's undergoing some kind of conventional treatment. She's losing her hair and she's skinnier than I've ever seen her. And yet her conversation sounds almost normal. This evening she says to me that maybe the tiger transmitted some deadly African disease to her.

"How can I complain when I'm the one who brought him home to us in the first place?" I ask her whether we know how the liberated tiger is doing, and she answers in a whisper that it's no concern of hers. Then she says: "I bet Nathan and Hagai put a homing device on the tiger so they'll be able to retrieve him after I die."

I believe Nathan's got the business under control now. The surveys that pass under my scrutiny show handsome profits for his investments, although substantial sums have been diverted to a European venture about which I have not been told. I wouldn't be surprised if it has something to do with the purchase of rare antiques. Dana intimates that the objective is far more surprising, but Nathan forbids her to go into details. Now he's also on sounder terms with Hagai, who is developing large parcels of land around the village, naturally with Nathan's backing, to supply produce and raise experimental crops.

33

WHEN RINA DIES I feel awful. Not that we were ever very close, but I can't stop trembling. Uzzi called us from outside this morning and said she'd passed away during the night.

"We decided to wait until now to break the news. You know, Meir, he just put me in charge without explaining what he wants me to do. If I forget something, I'll get all the blame, as usual." He's carrying a long checklist—people to contact, places to post notices, and plans and schedules for the city and village branches. The original villagers (what's left of them) hurry around fetching whatever is needed. They tell me Nathan's at home and I go over to see him.

He and Hagai are sitting in front of a map, quizzing each other like schoolchildren to show who knows more.

"How many riverside cities are there in the world?"

"Name some artists who died in the country where they were born. What areas have been conquered most often? Now list all the great inventors and scientists with places named after them," and so on and so forth. Nathan is wearing a white shirt and suit trousers; Hagai is wearing shorts and a light sweater. "I only get cold around the middle," he once explained to Rachel.

"So she's dead," says Nathan to me. "It's always harder for those who are left behind. She herself simply died."

"Where are the boys?"

"They will come to the funeral, stay on here a couple of days, and after that we'll see. I may send them back to boarding school in England, and maybe I'll even go with them."

"Listen to me," says Hagai, "Don't take them away. They suit the scenery here. Those boys aren't quitters."

"We'll see, we'll see," answers Nathan. As usual he has a pleasant smell, but his body is heavy, cumbersome. He may have lost a little weight but the clumsiness remains. "We were married for so many years. She was a pretty good wife to me, all in all. You know that I'm not the easiest man to be around, but at least it was interesting for her."

Nathan crosses to another chair. I believe I see tears. Uzzi hurries over with the latest science and art journals. "I didn't bring you the usual things from the office today. There's a lot of news here about upcoming auctions and the latest prices." Nathan thanks him quietly, laying the brochures down in front of him and then suddenly turns to me.

"Which do you like better, Meir, symphonies or concerti? Someone as neurotic as yourself probably likes it better when all the instruments are trying to get along."

"I don't know, Nathan. It's hard for me to think about music just now."

"But why? Why?" Nathan wonders. "Uzzi, go bring those new recordings we bought. Let's give Meir some idea of what's happening outside his house."

The two boys arrive. This time Shlomo is dressed in a suit and tie. Shahar is wearing long trousers and a white shirt; the heaviness about him is reminiscent of his father's, though he has agile legs.

Nathan approaches Shlomo and adjusts his tie. He asks Shlomo if he's careful to shave every day. Shlomo blushes and doesn't answer. Shahar remarks that he too has started shaving. He asks his father how long they'll be staying in the village. Nathan says they can talk it over. Shlomo asks him why their mother died—no one told them she was so seriously ill, and people don't usually die from just any disease. Nathan starts to answer but Hagai interrupts and suggests that the boys go horseback riding with him "Until everyone arrives for the ceremony." Nathan looks at Hagai, stands up, gives one hand to Shlomo and the other to Shahar and leads them to another room where they sequester themselves.

I sit down and want to think. What should I do with Rachel? Should I continue working for Nathan? Why do I have only one son? When did I begin to neglect my studies? Why have I practically stopped reading the Bible and making annotations? Hagai looks out the window, then shines his shoes (I guess he's getting ready for the funeral), takes a sip from his bottle, inspects something on the wall (a spot of mildew perhaps), and goes out the door. I bet he's off to visit Rachel. It's been a while since they saw each other, although they've been in touch by phone and mail.

THERE'S A BIG CROWD at the funeral. I've never been in such a big crowd before. All Nathan's employees are here, as well as his customers, his agents, friends, and partners in various enterprises (antique dealers, chess players) and, of course, family members. Rachel is walking primly beside me; I change my pace from time to time but always find her at my side. I wonder if anyone will give a eulogy. We are near the grave, while Nathan stands over the pit with

Shlomo and Shahar, who sob uncontrollably. Dana strokes their heads and Uzzi keeps offering them drinks ("or have a lemon drop"). From here it's hard to see Hagai, who has probably found himself a comfortable place with a good view. The cantor faithfully recites verses from the Psalms, including "A Woman of Valor"—this is probably the first time it has ever been read in Rina's honor, and now she's dead.

Dana takes a folded sheet of paper out of her coat pocket and hands it to Shlomo. He reads the typewritten farewell to his mother and twice repeats that he is also speaking for "my father and Shahar." People start talking about a wide range of subjects—there are a great many connections between them, after all. Uzzi calls for silence and Shlomo continues reading aloud. He recalls two times when his mother comforted him or his brother. Once when he wanted to run away from boarding school and once when he was in the hospital and she slept at his bedside every night. When Shlomo goes on a little too long, Nathan looks at Dana. Maybe he's annoyed with her for writing such a lengthy speech for his sons, or maybe he's worried that Shlomo has tacked on something of his own. When Shlomo finishes reading he adds, in a broken voice: "Shahar and I love you very much, Mother. I know there were all sorts of problems, but I'm going to take care of everything now." Nathan must be flabbergasted. Uzzi starts walking over to Shlomo but he's almost through in any case.

RACHEL AND I return to our hut. We're not sure where Nathan is going to stay for the next few days. It seems rather strange that he chose to bury his wife here in the village rather than close to their home in the city. Maybe that was Rina's request. Why should I interfere or burden myself with more questions? No wonder I often mix up the letters when I write, with the middle letter before the first letter; there's always some part I have to finish before I've even begun.

I propose to Rachel that we not stay the night here, but instead hurry home to the city. (In the past I would have used a different tack, avoiding words like "hurry home," so as not to emphasize how little time we have. Nowadays I can speak more freely with her.) Rachel is willing, if it's so important to me, but she thinks it would be best for us to stay over another night or two.

"At least another three days here. That would be more considerate toward Nathan. What's so bad about staying another few days in such peaceful surroundings? It won't do us any harm." We do indeed stay until the following evening. Last night we shared a bed for the first time in quite a while. Rachel held me for part of the night, but she kept her nightgown on. I remained dressed and had trouble falling asleep in such an intimate position.

We call on Nathan the following morning and in the afternoon as well. It's not clear to me whether prayers have been organized at his house, but I don't try to find out about this either. In the evening we bid farewell to Nathan and the houseful of friends and employees. Secretaries are serving drinks and cookies. Nathan sits in his armchair—talking, dozing, reading newspapers. Shlomo stays in his room most of the time and Shahar sticks close to Dana. He helps her with various tasks and seems happy to fill her every request.

Rachel and I hurry off to load the car. I feel a little weak, but Rachel has packed fruit for the trip. Here we are, driving home together, and our son Yaron is with us in the car. On the way we sing Hebrew songs, including several liturgical pieces. Rachel is wearing, for the first time in quite a while, a pair of soft-hued, almost dainty-looking trousers.

"If you promise not to laugh at me," I say to Rachel, "I'll make a beautiful comparison."

"Say it, say it. Here you go again, saying something and not saying it."

"I only wanted to say that we used to be too slippery for each other."

"Slippery?" Rachel laughs and blushes. "What does that have to do with anything?"

"You know, when you get too wet nothing sticks together. Things get all smeared and they slip away. So even your body, when it gets too slippery, can't connect and stay joined with another body." Rachel turns to me with an old-fashioned look. Not since we met, not since she was first excited by my imagination, do I remember her giving such a look. Later she turns away, dozes off, and wakes up in fear that I'm driving too fast. She opens her purse and sorts through various letters. Yaron speaks very little and says he wants to rest now.

PART TWO

DANA

36

TEN DAYS LATER Nathan returns to his home in the city, together with his two sons and Dana. It's Dana who gets in touch and tells us they're back.

"We'll be close to you again now, Meir." A few days later she calls once more, for Rachel, and reports that things are definitely improving.

"The children are getting along together really well, with me too—especially Shahar, but I know that Shlomo will also calm down. Nathan wants us to go away for a while, but first he has to get his business sorted out. I think he's planning a turnover in personnel. He probably intends to find a suitable position for Shlomo with the firm." Rachel surprises me with her improved spirits. I was concerned that Rina's death would bring her down, and she isn't the most cheerful person to start with. Since our return she has been talking to Yaron quite a bit, asking me about my doings from time to time, discussing things with Dana over the phone, and looking around for interesting groups to join. Every few days she suggests that we all go out for the evening. I nearly always agree, even though I still need a lot of rest. I couldn't bear to say no and then have to deal with her sadness.

One evening we're invited to Nathan's; Rachel says Dana did her best to coordinate with everyone. I haven't been at the house for almost a year now, not since we took the trip to the Galilee. It's hard to believe I actually lived there for so long. I wonder, for instance, whether the bed I used to sleep in is in the same condition now. Dana greets us with kisses (I become more excited than I expected) and leads us quickly through to a large and tidy room. It's very possible that the furniture there is new. She seats us on comfortable floor cushions and says that Nathan will join us shortly. And a little while later, when he actually turns up, he looks happy to see us, and settles down in the only armchair in the room.

"I can't get used to Dana's cushions," he tells us. "Maybe she's trying to keep me young—you can never tell what her motives are," he jokes, and Dana smiles. When Dana asks whether he wants to change into lighter clothes, he answers that he doesn't and that he might just doze off in his armchair for a while, "but you're used to seeing me fall asleep while everyone around me is talking."

Shahar walks into the room. He asks Dana if she needs him for anything. Maybe to serve drinks or something. He talks to her, stands close to her, practically turns his back on his father. Dana asks him about his homework, asks if he wants to join us and if the meal she prepared for him was enough. Nathan wakes up for a moment, asks whether he missed anything.

"I actually heard everything," he says, and he begins to tell us about a new kind of painting he's come upon. "Paintings on mirrors, which makes the mirrors precious—they show you who lives in the house as well as what they painted."

Dana asks Nathan if he has any interesting news to tell Rachel and me, but Nathan doesn't respond. A little later he says he'd like to do some work in his study, but we can go out somewhere and have fun together without him. Rachel and I decide we may as well leave now, though it feels strange to be walking out so abruptly.

37

IN MY JOB at the office a significant change has taken place. I doubt that I'm still considered management, and I'm no longer kept informed about current business. I've been transferred to a nearby annex, recently purchased at Uzzi's initiative. The building itself is nice, though a bit old and shabby. Nathan is planning some major renovations there and wants me to supervise them.

"Try to set up a new business for us while you're at it, you won't be too busy. If you come up with any interesting ideas, I'll even make you a partner—you won't be a mere employee anymore." I'm not quite sure what he means by this. He's either trying to bolster my confidence or to keep me busy doing trivial things. I had better consult Rachel and proceed with caution.

Reports from the village are nebulous. It seems Hagai's plans are both costly and complicated. He is setting up various trial businesses and resort facilities, and he's also cultivating vast tracts of land with crops imported from Africa. He's taken out substantial bank loans and has also been using up more and more of the company's assets. I decide to warn Nathan about Hagai's plans to expand. When I arrive at his office, he listens a moment, then turns on his new computer, loads an enormous graph, and tries out several alternatives.

"What are you worried about, Meir? According to my calculations, the worst that can happen is that we'll lose what Hagai has already earned us. Consider the amount of property he's acquired for me, and you'll understand how limited the risk is here. Not to mention the profits we'll make on agricultural breakthroughs, if his experiments pay off." I disagree with Nathan, but as usual I am not able to persuade him.

"Nothing's going to stop where you think it will. The losses might be greater than all the Galilee properties and they'll affect your whole business. What you have here is the convergence of a brand new enterprise and a strange fellow like Hagai. Each of these factors on its own may seem reasonable enough, but you're laying yourself wide open here." Nathan argues that I'm overwrought and suggests that the two of us go for a tour of Hagai's latest installations. Miffed, I return to my office. Rachel calls and tells me that Dana is coming over for supper.

"She said she'd like to join us for one of our nice, home-cooked meals with Yaron."

At home I find Rachel all astir. It's been a while since we had guests for dinner. Though Dana is coming on her own, apparently, there's still plenty to do in preparation. Rachel asks me to set the table and I regret having to help even with this. The house looks tidier than usual, Yaron is dressed up and in high spirits. Dana arrives early with a gift of books for us. She kisses Rachel (I'm a little surprised), caresses Yaron (who is as tall as she is now), and shakes my hand twice.

"This is really exciting. Here I am, a guest in the home of my special friends. There's so much I can learn from you. Nathan admires you a great deal, I want you to know that. I see how right he is." Rachel blushes contentedly, enjoying every word. Yaron glances at me in wonder and I smile back at him.

"Shall we hurry in to supper now?" asks Dana in a loud voice, "I haven't eaten since last night. Nathan takes me out to eat at the craziest hours. He's completely messed up my inner mechanisms." She suddenly falls silent and looks as though she's mulling over what she just said or trying to analyze something she never thought of before.

We sit down to eat. Dana asks to sit next to Yaron.

"I want to enjoy looking at him. Maybe I'll have a son of my own some day." Rachel says she had a different seating arrangement in mind, but no matter. I can't figure out what they're talking about.

"And now I have some really big news to tell you," Dana says. "Nathan and I are getting married. That's right, a big wedding with all the works. We want everything to be just so, that's very important to us. Maybe you can suggest a nice rabbi to officiate." Rachel gets up and kisses her. She's always able (despite her lethargy) to share in the joy of others, even when it barely shows. Yaron listens in silence, and meanwhile I have nothing to add.

"Fine, after dinner we'll talk about the details," Dana continues.

"It may come as a surprise to you that Nathan wants to marry me and isn't content for us just to live together. To me it all makes perfect sense. But now let's eat the delicious meal Rachel's cooked for us. We can go on talking afterward. There's so much to consider—Shlomo and Shahar, for instance, and any other children Nathan and I may have some day. Or where we'll live and what sort of job Nathan is planning to give me with the firm. You see why I need to be with you this evening."

Finally Rachel gets up to serve the vegetable soup. Yaron says he's going to his room for a minute. By the time Rachel brings in the soup I'm very hungry. I have been alone for too long in this room with Dana, who was so close to me once and who is now about to marry Nathan. Suddenly she starts asking me questions about Nathan's childhood.

"You know a lot more about him than I do. You knew his parents, after all, and you even know which one of them he resembles more." Rachel returns from the kitchen with the soup pot and four bowls. I call out to Yaron and he returns to the table, though only for a while. Rachel barely sits down, she keeps running in and out, but doesn't stay in or out for any length of time. "You have Yaron and Rachel," says Dana. "Isn't it time you had more children?"

"What's that got to do with you?" I say, surprised.

"Don't take it the wrong way, Meir. You're an extremely sensitive and intelligent man. All four of us can be together. As long as I'm with Nathan, he'll never hurt you, rest assured. Think about it. And remember that Nathan will have to behave like a real husband. I've already informed him that anytime he goes abroad for more than three days, he has to take me with him."

Yaron returns to the table for dessert. Now Rachel also sits down for a while. It isn't clear to me why she keeps leaving Dana and me alone, and stays with us only when Yaron is present. Dana offers to serve the dessert and Rachel agrees, to my regret, whether out of generosity or laziness. Dana serves Yaron first ("Sweets for the sweet"), and next Rachel ("the hostess with the mostest"), and then me ("Meir who needs some calming down"), and finally herself ("last but not least, darling Dana who is about to marry a big fat guy"). Yaron laughs and enjoys her patter, and so do I, though mostly my thoughts are taken up with Dana's face and figure.

38

ONE MORNING Nathan calls me to his office. "He says to drop everything and come over right away," his secretary informs me. I'm in great suspense, maybe I should call Rachel first and consult with her, but I have to hurry off to see Nathan (luckily the annex under construction is very near the firm's main building). Nathan, who is in the midst of a meeting, looks exhausted, keeps swallowing little cubes of sugar. Dana sits apart and looks mainly at him.

"Uzzi has totally messed up," says Nathan, and the employees in the room rustle through their computer printouts. "He didn't supervise Hagai properly. We're heavily in debt and I want precise information from each and every one of you." I sit down. Nathan hasn't greeted me yet, and I'm not sure what I can do to help him here. Dana approaches Nathan and whispers something in his ear but he dismisses her with a wave of his hand. He calls for silence.

The secretary pokes her head in and asks if anyone's hungry. Nathan tells her just to bring in "whatever's there" rather than hold things up with a choice of refreshments.

"Don't forget the fruit for Meir," Dana adds, and I feel shy and happy. It seems the food had been stored next door, because the trays are brought in right away, and some of the staff members pass out plates and silverware. Who needs all this food now? I don't understand. Nathan starts eating immediately and Dana keeps serving him more and more. He eats and talks, asks questions, makes comments, and argues with almost everyone.

"Why can't you people ever give me an explanation that makes sense? The only time I get straight answers around here is when I explain things and lose my temper."

The empty trays (with the remains of stuffed vegetables) are cleared away and platters of cold cuts are brought in. Nathan just keeps talking.

"I'm firing Uzzi," he announces all of a sudden. "But that's the easy part. The big question is how much we really owe and how to pay it back. But don't you dare suggest that I sell a single one of my antiques! Think of practical solutions. Whoever's finished eating can leave. I want you all back this evening with your suggestions. Think for yourselves, I'm not looking for teamwork here."

People stop eating and hurry away. Dana gazes at me in silence. Nathan does not ask me to stick around for a private conversation. The room is full of dishes, Nathan fiddles with the scraps, asks Dana for a napkin, wipes his fingers, checks his nails, and opens the new art book that lay all wrapped up on the table. Since the others have left, I too get up and slowly make my way to the door. I half expect Nathan to ask me to stay, but I hear no voice address me. Why did he want me there as a participant if I wasn't allowed to speak my mind? Only after I shut the door does he call me back for a moment.

"I hear Dana had a lovely dinner at your house. I hope you didn't put any weird ideas into her head before the wedding. Don't forget to come back this evening with ideas—it's a tough situation and this is your chance to help me out, for once."

I GO BACK to the house and recall that I haven't really had the time yet to enjoy my homecoming, after my illness, the convalescence at Nathan's, and the long stay in the Galilee. I'm happy when Yaron opens the door. "Mom's gone out for one of her checkups," he announces. It's true that Rachel has been preoccupied with her body of late, claiming that now is the time to find her proper balance. "Whenever I get tense, I can't take good care of myself," she explained to us.

Yaron is the one who brings up the subject of Rachel's health and asks whether the tension between her and me has eased. He's certainly done some growing up; it's been a while since I last checked his face and physique for signs of maturity. I know very little about his activities and his conversations with others. I tell him that his mother is well and that we're pretty relaxed with each other now.

"If she were really healthy, you would have more children. There aren't many families like ours, families with an only child."

"What do you mean?"

"I'm sure you understand, Dad. Religious people like us are supposed to live differently. We never talk about it, but Mom and especially you, Dad, are confusing me with your way of life."

I'm glad when Rachel comes home. She finds Yaron and me sitting close together, talking, and lapsing into silence. I tell her what happened at Nathan's office today. She sits down and says nothing for a while. Then she offers to go with me this evening.

"Now that we're together again, it's important to show Nathan that you're getting better. He could hurt you if he figures that you've failed. I sense some real complication here." I answer that none of this seems especially serious or dangerous to me. Rachel stands her ground. "Maybe I'll call Dana and find out," she says, and surprises me. I go off to rest. That chronic weakness in me is getting worse again. I need a few minutes to rest my head. Fortunately I am able to persuade my head that it's lying on the pillow alone now and resting.

In the evening we go out together. Yaron wants to come along, but Rachel asks him (somewhat tactlessly, in my opinion) if he thinks he has a practical contribution to make and he says he was just hoping to check on Nathan for himself. Rachel decides that won't be necessary, but we'll call him later and fill him in.

Rachel drives and I sit beside her. It's better this way, whether because of my physical weakness or Rachel's concern about my driving ability today. Most offices are already closed; the city looks unusually compact. We arrive at the firm, and Uzzi is waiting at the entrance.

"Did you know that Nathan wants to fire me?" he says right away. "He told me to stay on for the time being and supervise down here, but he's got some bad things planned for me. I have to talk to you, Meir. You'll be able to explain what's what to him. Don't forget to come by on your way out of the meeting." Uzzi escorts

Rachel and me to a small auditorium, not Nathan's usual conference room, but the one he uses for employee meetings and seminars.

As far as I can tell there are no more than ten people present, most of them company directors. It's odd to be meeting here. I'd like to take Rachel to see my new office in the building I'm in charge of, but of course there's no time. People are standing around eating bonbons; I haven't seen so many different kinds of chocolate in a long time. Uzzi comes in and asks what we'd like to drink. Everyone ignores the question and continues talking and eating chocolate.

Nathan walks in (without Dana).

"You may sit down," he says. "Do we have a printed agenda? Could it be that Uzzi has finally organized something around here? Okay, never mind that now. I hope no one has been talking to reporters about the current situation. From now on, Dana will coordinate all statements. She has a good grasp of these things. We'll see if there's a journalist alive who can begrudge such a beautiful woman."

Nathan gets up, calls Uzzi (who is waiting outside), asks him to see why the lights are so dim.

"The heating system isn't worth a damn, either. Didn't I tell you to replace it a long time ago?" He returns to his seat, asks how we like the new chocolate, if everyone can see all right, and whether we want to change the seating arrangement. He glances at me and at Rachel who is sitting at my side.

"I see you've brought your wife along. So you're finally back together." A moment later he continues, without looking at me. "Meir's brought up an interesting idea. Actually, of all the suggestions I received since this afternoon's meeting, his seems the most practical. Now hear me out, Meir, before you start getting excited. The idea is that you should take on all the losses we've incurred. You were at the forefront of the Galilee deal, and Rachel and Hagai have a close relationship." Nathan pauses while his secretary brings in a few letters for him to read and sign. The pages are spread out before him. He leafs through them, quickly signing here and there. He thanks his secretary with a smile and she leaves the room. Again he addresses me, looking at me this time.

"Meir, we're just talking about an idea here, nothing will be finalized without your consent. On the face of it you'll be claiming responsibility for the firm's losses. You'll write a detailed letter of explanation. I mean, really, no one in my company can write the way you do. But the main thing is this: in the meantime you and I will settle everything between ourselves. Even if you have to declare bankruptcy, I will take on your every burden, including your responsibilities to Rachel and Yaron. As a private individual, you'll wind up with even more than you have today." Rachel puts her hand on my knee, and squeezes it in silence. I can't tell what she makes of this. I'm all confused now and I just want to get out of here.

Nathan is informed that Dana's on the phone. He answers loudly from where he sits.

"Worried about your boyfriend? Or maybe you're bored. Take it easy, I told you that Meir is my responsibility." He hangs up and asks two department heads to report on current sales figures. A discussion ensues about the likelihood of the market picking up over the next few months. Nathan looks tired, almost weary, but he never misses the chance to interrupt and paraphrase what everyone says. After about an hour the meeting is adjourned.

Rachel and I get up. She whispers "Goodbye" (it's not clear to whom), and together we leave the room. Again Rachel drives while I compose a brief letter to Dana:

> My dear Dana,
>
> It touched me that you called Nathan during this evening's difficult meeting. Almost no one I know (perhaps I should erase the "almost"; I'll think that over later) is as good and dear to me as you are. I must ask you (as I ask of many) to look out for yourself and to look out for me too. I'm hurt and afraid of Nathan.
>
> Yours, Meir

I'll ask Yaron to deliver the sealed envelope to their house tomorrow morning and hand it to Dana. Rachel doesn't ask what I'm doing and I debate whether to tell her about the letter. No doubt I'll tell her eventually, but why hurry? For the time being I should consult with Rachel about tomorrow: would it be better for me to go to work as usual and tend to the building I've been put in charge of, or to stay home for a couple of days?

40

I STAY HOME. Rachel also suggests that I rest.

"And if you get any calls from the office I simply won't put them through to you."

"That could be a mistake on our part, Rachel." I am alarmed, naturally, but Rachel is firm.

"If you want us to get back to normal life together, it's time to focus on what's happening at home. Yaron's a young man already, but he still needs us, both of us."

"All the same, Nathan may get angry if I don't answer the phone."

"This is something different and important. Forget about Nathan, we're in a big enough mess as it is. Why don't we fix up a cozy little work space for you at home, make a few renovations, maybe even put in a nursery for a new baby?" she says, looking away. I'm surprised at the way Rachel introduced the possibility of our having another child, when physical contact between her and me (ever since my illness and all that transpired afterward) has been limited to an occasional caress.

Two days later Uzzi pays us a call. He says he was concerned when I didn't show up at work.

"Just don't land in the hospital again. We can do very well without your illness," he says, apparently trying to amuse me. "I've brought you some goodies, so Rachel won't have to go to any trouble." From his pocket he takes a large napkin, spreads it out, and arranges a bag of cheese and crackers on it and some new sort of soft drink. ("It's all kosher. Go ahead, check the labels.")

"That letter you wrote to Dana really confused her," Uzzi says to me. "She doesn't know what to answer." I suddenly feel embarrassed, even humiliated. How could I have been so foolishly forward with this woman who may have loved me, whom I loved, the woman who lives in Nathan's home and will soon be his wife? But Uzzi continues talking.

"Forget the letter, Meir. You're getting rattled again about something simple, the way you did when Nathan put you in charge of the company, and I think you also took our stay in the Galilee a little too seriously. But now, to practical matters. I have here in my pocket three letters for you to sign. You really should accept Nathan's offer, you know. Some day you might be rich and secure."

Uzzi takes the letters out of his pocket, hands them to me, and asks me to read them after he leaves.

"Let's not waste our time on letters now. Why don't we focus on something else? For instance, we should try to come up with an original idea on how to celebrate Nathan and Dana's wedding." I am astounded: he shows up in my home, starts criticizing, doesn't even bother to explain why he still has his job (Nathan did say he was firing him), and gives me vague instructions. I look at him and suddenly smile. Uzzi seems surprised.

"Maybe we should talk about what's really important here, Uzzi. The situation and the fact that Nathan and I are close require him to approach me directly. You've chosen a totally inappropriate way to get me to sign. All the same, I suggest you leave the letters here and ask Nathan to contact me later." Uzzi stands up, looking thoroughly bewildered, and walks out. For the first time in my life I have not escorted a guest in my home to the door.

RACHEL, YARON, AND I read the three letters silently to ourselves and then read them aloud. According to two of these letters, I willingly take upon myself all debts and financial obligations resulting from the company's activities in the Galilee, including a brief description of Hagai's involvement, of the expectations, the few achievements, and the big fiasco. In this letter I likewise confirm that I ill-advisedly attempted to bill Nathan's firm for the losses whereas I now freely admit the truth and accept responsibility. The second letter declares that my property shall be placed at the disposal of my creditors, in connection with my upcoming declaration of bankruptcy.

The third letter is a draft in which Uzzi, as acting secretary of the firm—I never knew he'd been appointed—is pleased to inform me that in view of my special contribution to the company, and despite recent setbacks, a major enterprise involving me is being set up abroad. The enterprise, in which I am expected to play a leading role, has a cultural as well as a commercial side. This will require me to stay abroad for several months, with a large budget for the purchase of rare manuscripts and the full backing of the firm. The firm will also consider allowing family members to accompany me. Rachel asks us to be quiet a moment. She rereads the letters and then asks Yaron to read them aloud again. She throws me a strange look.

"We finally get another chance to be a normal family, to bring a new baby into the world, and they have to spoil it all." Her sobbing gets louder and louder. She seems both fierce and vulnerable. She screams at me, uttering peculiar sounds. Yaron looks on, probably trying to decide whether or not to go to his room. Finally he sits down between his mother and me. Rachel cries out again: "You've taken a good, solid family and thrown us to the dogs! What does this man Nathan want from us? Why do you have to earn your living from such a brute?" She falls silent. To my surprise she doesn't leave the room, but asks Yaron if he'd like something to drink. She tries to regain her composure. Everything about her turns rigid, even the little hairs on her face stand out.

Yaron holds the letters in his hands. He takes out a pencil and makes notes on the printed pages.

"Don't worry. You can erase it all later if you want to. Meanwhile I've inserted some important points here." Rachel looks at him in pain and astonishment. "Mom, I think we should reconsider. Maybe we can outwit them. What do we care if Dad takes on other people's debts? They can't take away any more than we have, and that's not much. On the other hand, a move like that could turn everything in our favor. Nathan will have to help us then. He'll be hopelessly dependent on what Dad has to say; he'll be afraid to disappoint us. We'll be able to start something new and dynamic, and to ask Nathan for all sorts of things."

"If that's what you think," whispers Rachel," I'm willing to consider. But there's a terrible risk involved here: even your father can see that now."

"Couldn't Dana help us?" asks Yaron.

"Give her a rest," says Rachel. "We're not interested in Dana at the moment. She's the one who got us in this mess."

"In that case we have to act on our own." Yaron replies. "Maybe I should meet with Shlomo and Shahar; we're on pretty friendly terms these days. Nathan likes me too, he thinks I'm an interesting kid. I can see him at his office, maybe even snatch a few helpful documents there." Rachel lurches at Yaron, and for the first time in his life, hits him hard, on the shoulders. "You will not steal, do you hear me? Your father has involved you with an utterly despicable man, but you will not steal because of him."

"I didn't know it was so important to you," he sobs and wails. "I didn't realize you took it so seriously. Why don't you let me know in advance, each time we're supposed to behave like a decent family?"

42

TO MY SURPRISE I don't join in the conversation. It's possible to become detached from one's possessions, or even from one's wife, so why not from oneself? Let Rachel and Yaron go on talking to each other; I think I'll take a nap or a little vacation somewhere, or maybe I'll go back to the office tomorrow and simply ignore Nathan's proposal.

Over the next few days I stay home, reading and dozing. Yaron brings me books from the municipal library. As a child I seldom availed myself of the public library; I bought my reading matter at the bookstore or else amused myself with my own thoughts. Occasionally Rachel goes off to her doctor's appointments—"At last I've found something that relaxes me and is good for us all"—and Yaron is busy studying for his final exams.

Less than a week later, Uzzi shows up again. Yaron calls me to the door and asks in front of Uzzi whether to let him in or not. I'm surprised, even alarmed, both by Uzzi's arrival and my son's reaction.

"Take it easy, Yaron," says Uzzi, "I'm not your enemy." Then he turns to me. "I'm assuming that with the exception of one or two changes, the letters I brought you are acceptable. Meanwhile Nathan has come up with a few more options, so we may not need your help after all. In any case, here's some material from Nathan that has to do with your possible trip to Europe, should we decide to involve you, that is. I personally have no idea what any of this means, but Nathan says it's the most impressive career move he's ever made either in business or in his cultural life."

"And what about you, Uzzi?" Yaron interrupts. "According to what I've read in the paper over the past few days, there've been some changes at the firm, several new appointments, and you weren't even mentioned." Uzzi turns a little pale.

"So, somebody around here reads the business pages; that's good to know. Don't worry about me, Yaron, there's still plenty I can do for Nathan. You just concentrate on your parents. I think they're totally confused. They should listen to you more often. I always knew you were the reasonable one around here."

"What do you want from me?" Yaron protests. Uzzi puts a hand on his shoulder, either to placate or to patronize him.

"Your father is home most of the time now. This is a good opportunity for you to talk to him. You may finally be able to find out whether your father is really weak and sick, or whether he's quietly planning dangerous things for us all." He removes his hand and quickly departs without waiting for an answer.

For the time being I decide not to study the material Uzzi brought me. Yaron glances at me without a word, strokes my hands in a strange manner and sits down alone. Rachel returns from her errands with a fancy envelope the size of a book. She pulls out a big, colorful invitation to Nathan and Dana's wedding. There is a personal, handwritten greeting added on—in Dana's writing, I'm quite sure a second later—with a request that we "bring Yaron, of course, without whom you are not complete as a family." Rachel immediately asks if I plan to go and I answer that I do. My answer may have come as a disappointment, but it was surely no surprise.

"Naturally you'll go with me, and we can leave as soon as you like. Why should we hurt their feelings on their wedding day by not showing up?"

"It's a good thing people still get married," jokes Yaron, repeating something I often used to say, only all my old sayings have been stifled and I don't feel like joking about Dana's wedding. Yaron says he wants to talk to us. He's thinking of quitting school now ("In any case, I only have a few months to go") and finishing up a few years from now.

"I can see that you need me, more than I thought." Rachel disagrees. She asks him to concentrate on his studies and his friends, to let us handle the problem on our own. "Your Dad and I are in trouble, but we're strong."

"You remind me of the kind of ball that never stops bouncing," answers Yaron. "It just keeps on whether anybody cares or not, whether it was bounced on purpose or just happened to fall off the shelf."

It's strange the way I persistently report various events to myself in writing, yet I feel more and more removed from them. Not just Nathan's office but even my own home seems strange to me. For the first time in my life I feel I am under no obligation to respond to what is said to me, not even to misstatements or evil deeds. Whether or not Rachel is looking after my needs, whether or not my son is loyal to me, I am in no mood to fight, let alone respond.

43

SHLOMO AND SHAHAR are here for a visit. They called yesterday and asked to speak to Yaron in person, and also "with the two of you, if possible." They're both wearing suits—Shlomo, a young man now, and Shahar, already a mature boy. They have brought flowers for Rachel and a gift, a pretty silver dish ("We bought it in London when we were at school there and we've been waiting for a special occasion to give it to you"). They wander around the room a while before settling down on the couch together. They hope they're not intruding, that they haven't spoiled any important plans—an evening stroll perhaps, or a family discussion.

"We know you often have important discussions at home. You're such interesting people," Shlomo declares.

Rachel serves juice and cake (to my surprise she tells them at length about the ingredients). Yaron hasn't joined us yet; maybe he'd rather listen from his room for the time being. I debate whether to start the conversation rolling with a question when Shahar speaks up.

"You all know, of course, that Mother has died, and that Father's business has gone through a rough patch."

"Things are improving though," Shlomo interrupts and promptly falls silent again.

"Now we're facing the matter of Dana and Father. I know there's been some tension between you and him, but you're good friends. You've known Shlomo and me since we were born and Father says the family connection goes back a generation."

"That's why we wanted to spend some time with you, to visit a while," Shlomo interrupts again, and Shahar lets him speak.

I tell them how much I appreciate the visit. How admirable it was of them to make such an effort. I call Yaron in from his room, but he doesn't answer and Rachel asks me not to pressure him.

Shlomo says they can go to Yaron's room, there's no need for him to come out. Shahar says he'll wait here with us, that we haven't really finished our conversation yet.

"Yes, that's right" says Shlomo quietly. "We heard about those letters Uzzi brought you. We're awfully sorry you've been treated so roughly—a good friend like you."

Rachel says there's no need to dwell on this "silly matter" but Shahar blurts out: "The firm's doing better now. Father has learned how to handle Uzzi and Hagai: keep both of them occupied with less dangerous pursuits. Important business decisions should be left to Father."

Rachel points out that the family business is not the topic of this conversation. She asks how preparations for the wedding are coming along. Shlomo hesitates and Shahar says everything is under control. He then informs us that he will soon begin working for the firm, heading one of the departments.

"The army has agreed to keep deferring my service. They probably think they'll be able to get more out of me after a few years of working with Father." Now of all times Yaron decides to come out of his room. Looking rather tired, he walks over to the brothers and speaks to them quietly. Shahar insists that Yaron should attend the wedding, but Shlomo argues that "the wedding isn't that important." Shahar glowers at him and then suggests that they all go out to a newly opened (vegetarian) restaurant. Yaron hesitates a moment, glances at his mother, and finally goes off with them.

44

TODAY IS THE WEDDING DAY. I haven't seen Rachel fuss so much in a long time. She went to have a facial treatment and a new hairdo, and it seems she's bought herself a new white dress. She asks me how she looks and whether she ought to wear jewelry—"or would I look better dressed simply, like a bride?" I encourage her to adorn herself. I'm not sure that pleases her. She wonders whether to take a wrap; the wedding will be held outdoors in the large garden of a hotel, probably the biggest garden in the whole country.

"I want to look beautiful today," says Rachel, and I don't recall ever hearing such words from her lips before.

"Yaron's decided to go later, on his own," she tells me. I am sorry about this. Why shouldn't we all spend more time together? Rachel lays out my clothes and brushes the dust off my trouser cuffs. She discovers that I'm missing a button and hastily sews it on. I don't think Rachel has inspected the state of my clothes in a very long time (if ever). Usually she acts surprised when she finds something amiss, and today she's worried about my appearance.

"We wouldn't want you to cut a sorry figure at this wedding. A lot of folks you haven't seen for a long time will be there and they're bound to look you over." We arrive at the hotel. The whole place partakes of the occasion: neon signs illuminate the balconies, the pathways are festooned with flowers, and decorated automobiles drive around blaring festive music. Finally we join the long queue of guests waiting to congratulate the couple. No one tries to butt in out of turn. Uzzi walks by from time to time to monitor the situation.

"Hello there, Meir," he says to me, "I'm glad that you've come." Hors d'oeuvres are passed around to distract the guests while they wait. There's a special door through which emerge the various entertainers—I discern musicians, clowns, and singers—who will apparently perform during the wedding party. We move forward in line, though at a very slow pace.

Then it stops for a moment or two. They must be allowing some of the guests in directly. VIPs, no doubt, though I don't recognize any of them. The long wait is getting on Rachel's nerves, and she thinks the whole thing is unnecessary.

"Why don't they just let everyone in together, and sort us all out later. Will you say something to them, Meir?" But I prefer not to interfere.

"What's so terrible about our standing here together?"

"Nothing's so terrible, except their lack of respect for the guests."

"We could go home and come back later if you want to."

"No," Rachel says firmly. "If we leave now, there won't be any point to coming back to the wedding."

Around us are mainly employees of the firm and personal friends of Nathan's. I wonder if he thought to invite some of Rina's old chums. Judging by the number of people here, it's hard to imagine that anyone has been left out. Several of the guests take an interest in my health, while others stand apart and whisper cautiously, no doubt updating each other on the state of Nathan's business. I'm not certain they want me in the picture here. All of a sudden, Rachel looks weak to me. She arrived in good form, standing taller than usual, but now something inside her has become weary, as if from disappointed expectation. I try to hold her hand, but her willingness to cooperate is limited. We get to Nathan and Dana. Dana steps forward and gives Rachel a big hug. She asks some photographers to take their picture "so we'll have as many as possible." I approach Dana and shake her hand. She brings her face close to mine and kisses my cheeks.

"I'm willing to kiss you, Meir. You're the one who wanted to settle for a handshake," she laughs aloud. Nathan tugs at her dress (though not very hard) to pull her back into the reception line.

"Congratulations, Nathan. You know we have only the best of wishes for you."

"I know, Meir. I'm glad that you've come. I'm sure you'll enjoy the tasty hotel food. No problem, everything's kosher here, right? We can talk more later, there's still a long line."

We move on. It seems this hall is just for the reception. The wedding itself will take place under the canopy in the garden and the dinner will be held on another floor, in a particularly large area. Rachel is excited again, awake again. Dana's hug made her happy; she's curious to see who they've seated at our table, and she touches my hand a lot. I feel like strolling around the reception hall now, but Rachel would like for us to stay where we are and just look on.

Shahar walks over wearing a dark suit, happy to see us. He says that Shlomo is there too.

"But he's a little nervous, having a rest in one of the hotel rooms." Shahar continues standing nearby and introduces us to most of the people who approach to congratulate him. "Not everyone knows how close you and Father are, and how much my mother liked you. At least tonight I think it's important that they see that." I ask him to go check on his brother, but Rachel and Shahar reply together that Shlomo will do just fine without us. "He can decide for himself how best to relax," Shahar concludes.

Now that the crowd has gone in, the rabbi is here, and the hors d'oeuvres have taken the edge off our appetite, Nathan signals Uzzi and the ceremony can begin. The hotel manager (I assume that's who he is) welcomes the crowd and reads out the evening's program. A number of appearances have been scheduled—several popular bands will perform, one of them featuring a famous European violinist. Anyone with an interesting suggestion to make is invited to see the manager. It may still be possible to work in a few additional performances. Rachel whispers to me that she finds this announcement extremely peculiar.

"What's the connection between all that and the wedding?"

"You're right, Rachel. But we didn't really expect anything else from Nathan."

Now the bride, in a kind of golden chariot, is borne aloft by some of Nathan's employees, possibly with the help of a few hotel waiters. I don't understand why Dana has agreed to make such a strange entrance. On her way in she speaks to the crowd through a hand microphone.

"Tonight Nathan and I are getting married. Thank you for coming. You all know that Nathan was widowed about a year ago.

I'm not forgetting Nathan's two talented and loyal sons by his dear first wife, Rina. Generally speaking this has not been a happy year, except for the love between Nathan and me, and things have become complicated and even difficult. There are so many people and employees to consider—I'm sure Nathan will know what to do. Anyway, tonight everything is going strong, everything is new and loving. Even a shy woman like me can make a speech," she laughs again. "Two more things before I finish. The rabbi's waiting, I know, and the wedding ceremony is what's most important to us now, but first I want to say, Nathan, from now on you will always be healthy and happy, successful and a real winner. You and I together, that's what counts. And another thing: I want to acknowledge our special friends, Meir and Rachel, who some of you know. They are wonderful people. Meir's father was a close friend of Nathan's father's, and Nathan and Meir have been connected ever since. Tonight we are celebrating a new beginning for Meir and Rachel. Things have not been so easy for them either. Sometimes this had to do with us, sometimes it didn't. But tonight they too are gaining in strength and starting over. This will be like a second marriage for them, only with the same partner. When Nathan sanctifies me as his wife tonight, Meir and Rachel will also be joined together. This is what I wish for them. Nathan wishes it very much too."

Dana finishes speaking, a ladder decorated with flowers is brought to her, and she descends to the canopy. Rachel looks down at her own dress, and she seems to be crying. I embrace her shoulders, I don't know what else I can do now.

"Will you marry me?" I ask her, much to my surprise, and again she cries and whispers, "Yes, yes." People eye us with wonder—jealous, perhaps, that Dana mentioned us in her speech. No one else, after all, was mentioned so prominently.

The rabbi performs the ceremony. He does not neglect to mention the other couple present here for whom tonight is a special occasion, "but we won't embarrass you." To my surprise there is not much noise. Some of the guests have stopped talking, some are following the rabbi's speech. Yaron rushes over excitedly.

"I knew Dana was also planning to congratulate you. That's why I only got here now. I figured you should be alone together during the ceremony. I mean, I wasn't with you at your first wedding either, was I? I just wanted you to feel happy today. It's time you two relaxed, try to have a little fun."

"I get it, Yaron," I say. "Thanks, but leave it at that." Rachel glances at me angrily. Maybe I hurt Yaron's feelings, yet he doesn't leave my side. The fine line between staying and going is now marked on my son's face.

At the big dinner we are seated with Yaron, Uzzi, Hagai, and various department heads. We're fairly close to Nathan and Dana's table. The two of them sit close together with the boys facing them. A table for four. The master of ceremonies makes the rounds and asks each table to choose one person to propose a toast, or at least to say something witty. I hope he'll stop before he gets to our table. But if he doesn't, maybe Yaron will agree to represent us.

When he reaches us he heads straight for me.

"I understand you're Meir, the other groom of the evening. Maybe you'd like to sing for us or talk about the Bible. I hear you're an expert." Rachel and Yaron are looking at me in fear and maybe hope. I'm utterly exhausted. I glance over at Nathan, who smiles and starts to wave at me. Dana whispers something in his ear and kisses his forehead the way she used to kiss mine.

My voice is faint. I congratulate my two friends. I say that this is a real celebration.

"Even oddballs like me can find suitable kosher food here." A few people laugh. "My father was fond of Nathan's father. I guess I'm just as fond of Nathan, otherwise I wouldn't have let him marry Dana." Again there is laughter and Rachel covers her face like a blushing bride. "But it's hard for me to say much this evening. Some of the reasons are known to all of you, some are not known even to me." And I hand the microphone back to the comic master of ceremonies who continues moving from table to table.

"Wonderful toast, really a pleasure," Uzzi says, tossing me a compliment. "I knew we should let you do the talking. You have no idea how many people asked to make a speech, but I told Nathan you'd be the best one for our purposes."

"He'd be the best at any number of things," Rachel says to Uzzi, joining animatedly in the conversation. "You had to wait for Nathan's wedding to find out how capable Meir is?" Uzzi looks at her, puts his hand down on her jumpy fingers and Rachel is not pleased.

"Congratulations are in order for you, too," Uzzi says. "I understand that you and Dana planned this big surprise for Meir together, and there are lots of people here who regret not bringing you a present. Tonight marks a new beginning for the two of you."

I think Yaron must be sick of this conversation—why else would he start taunting Uzzi? "And how about you, Uzzi, have you been fired, or what? I thought Nathan got rid of you—or has he found you a job organizing events?" I am quite embarrassed. When did I myself ever speak this way to another person? Rachel looks flushed and satisfied. Uzzi doesn't answer but looks at me with an evil eye and goes away.

"What good was any of this to us?" I ask Yaron.

"They should just drop it. What's between Mom and Dana is no concern of his."

Rachel and Yaron are enjoying the meal. They ask the waiters what's next on the menu and request some changes. This is all very strange to me. How long can you sit at the same table? Besides, I feel unwell, both in my head and in my stomach. Obviously this is not one of my better evenings, with Dana marrying another man. It's true that I myself am not quite alone—I have a wife and a son (and whereas Nathan's sons sometimes get angry with him, Yaron will usually rise to my defense). Now I have to leave the table; Rachel asks me to hurry.

"I don't want to be without you, tonight of all nights." I wander around the big hall and go down to the garden where they set up the wedding canopy, then back to our place in line, and into the room where the reception took place. And again to the garden, where I look at the canopy, which is still standing.

I go back to the dining hall. I glance up at the stage and the show in progress. It's the employees' turn to perform with a popular singer. Nathan and Dana dance together as little girls skitter around them. I can't see Shlomo or Shahar anywhere. Maybe they're busy talking to the other guests. I wouldn't be surprised if we had a quiz show now, followed by party games, maybe even a raffle with expensive prizes. I go to the center of the floor where the bride and groom are dancing. Dana beckons me closer.

"How's the deputy groom getting along?" she roars. "Maybe you should call darling Rachel over so the two of you can dance with us."

"I don't feel like dancing," I answer.

"Come closer, then," Nathan says to me. "Just dance with us a while, and when Rachel sees, she'll probably join in."

Nathan and Dana reach out to me with their free arms and invite me to join them.

"I can't, Nathan. I don't feel well."

"Don't you go collapsing on us again now, hear?" says Dana.

"I feel steady enough, I'd just rather not dance."

"What's the matter? Are you as nervous now as you were at the first wedding?" asks Nathan with a wry smile.

"That's enough, Nathan. Leave me alone. First you insulted me when you tried to make me take on your debts" (I wonder at my daring, calling them "your debts." Normally I wouldn't have been so direct). "Now you're baiting Dana and me. You know tonight is difficult for me."

"Stop it, you guys," Dana comments. "This is starting to get on my nerves. You can talk about it some other time at the office. This evening belongs to me."

"I wasn't trying to do anything."

I look at her and tremble, saying, "And you know I never tried anything with you either, Dana."

"And if you had, would it have gotten you anywhere?" asks Nathan.

"Nathan, leave Meir alone now. You can see that he's ill."

"He's ill and I'm sick and tired of his illness. He should just take it easy."

"Look, I don't want to spoil things for you" (at this point I address them both). "But you, Nathan, are cruel to me."

"Go away, Meir!" Dana screams. "This is the biggest moment

of my life—I'm starting new and important things. Get out! Where's Rachel? Why doesn't she come over here already and take her husband?"

Naturally I leave. To my surprise, I don't even bother looking for Rachel or Yaron. I walk out of the hall, go down to the lobby, and from there I head for home, confused and miserable. I've spoiled Nathan's wedding and I feel uncomfortable about it. Dana's angry with me for sure, and Rachel is probably disappointed—she planned a surprise for me, and all in vain.

Rachel and Yaron are in no hurry to get home. Apparently they're having a good time there. When they finally arrive, they bring me a few fruit tarts, the kind I usually like. Yaron says he has some important things to talk over with me.

"But not tonight." He has to decide about the rest of the school year, "and just how crucial it is for you and Mom to start taking things easy."

I tell them that as far as I'm concerned there's nothing to talk about. Rachel says this is not at all how she planned "our special evening," but that I should go ahead and do whatever I think best.

The day after the wedding Dana calls and says they're postponing their honeymoon in order to take care of some pressing matters.

"There's going to be a total reorganization of the firm and Meir will find his rightful place there too," she promises Rachel. Yaron suggests that I go on vacation, either alone or with Rachel, "whichever is best for you both." He'll get along fine on his own, no problem. He thought about it all night and decided not to quit school.

"Final grades are important to me and there are a couple of things I want to study more deeply now. I can't study the way you do: read a little, talk a little. Either you take our Jewish sources seriously or you leave them behind. Your offhand approach doesn't appeal to me."

45

DANA'S WEDDING affected me more than I expected. How typical of me to behave like a reasonable man while the event is taking place and suffer afterward. By now it's clear to me that I did love Dana, but I was full of inhibitions and anxieties. It seems strange that I lived with her in Nathan's apartment for several months without once trying to kiss her or even caress her face. Maybe I was dumbfounded that a vibrant, free-spirited young woman like Dana hadn't taken the initiative herself, except for the few hints she let drop and the limited overtures she made while we were in the Galilee. But now she's Nathan's wife and Rachel and Yaron are here with me; she's my wife, and he's my son. It's a good thing I can rest a while after all the pressure Nathan was putting on me. The fact that he hasn't mentioned the issue of the letters again is a big relief to me; maybe he really has found other solutions, as I was led to believe by his sons during their visit here.

Yaron asks if I've looked through the additional material Nathan sent over with Uzzi a few weeks ago.

"Remember, he mentioned that in the same breath as his new set-up abroad." We look around for the envelope and it turns out Rachel stuck it in an empty drawer somewhere, hoping I wouldn't come across it. Yaron now opens the envelope and hands me the printed pages.

It sets forth a historical survey of relations between England and France during the Middle Ages. I'm familiar with one or two details I find there, but most of the facts are entirely new to me. Various maps of Europe have been included, and important sites have been indicated on them. I read three pages and put the rest aside. I'm not sure whether this is Nathan's way of preparing me to be his business envoy in England and France, or whether he has some other motive. Rachel is pleased to hear us discussing something educational—"Even though this isn't exactly what I had in mind for you."

I start going to work again in the morning, to oversee the building in my charge. As soon as I arrive I receive written instructions from Nathan about the renovations in progress and the prospects of renting space. I am to send my progress reports to Uzzi. My conversations with various employees seem to indicate that most of the firm's debts have been paid. Nathan was able to borrow money on easy terms from several sources abroad and sold two buildings in the city center. I understand that Hagai himself has undertaken to pay back the various debts he's responsible for by means of some new political activity. Nathan would just like to concentrate on his original business, without anything revolutionary getting in his way. "It's when you take on a new wife that you can go back to old business," I heard he once said at a managers meeting.

Rachel tries to stay home as much as possible. She is becoming conscientious as never before about my clothes and the meals she serves me. I think she meets with Dana from time to time, but she never says so directly. She suggests that we have Nathan and Dana over for dinner some Friday night and I respond with a vague "Hmmm." Shlomo is doing nicely, meanwhile, in his position as department head at the firm; he shows up early, tries to gather a loyal staff, and I wouldn't be surprised if he approached me too. Shahar has returned to London to finish school; I imagine his father is planning an even higher position for him. Our Yaron has completed his matriculation exams and seems rather pleased and quietly content.

With the passing months I notice a new excitement in Rachel. At first I worry that something is the matter, either with her or with Yaron. Then I start hoping it's good news about Yaron. It turns out to be something else entirely: it seems that Dana is in an advanced stage of pregnancy and I've only now been told about it. Rachel is as happy as a child responding to the first clear signs of love from her parents. Again and again she speaks to Dana on the phone, advising her about the right things to do, about avoiding problems, and where to get help. I haven't seen my wife so lively, even happy, you might say, in a very long time. It's no surprise when she suggests that we go visit Nathan and Dana.

"They'll probably be delighted to see you, Meir. You haven't been in touch with them since the wedding. Anyway, Nathan's known you since you were born, and there's no reason why we shouldn't spend a little time together." I agree with Rachel—I may actually feel comfortable around Dana and Nathan again.

Dana greets us, beautiful and happy. Her belly looks big and comfy, while the rest of her is slender and strong. Henri is in the house, serving drinks. Dana asks if we'd like to wait for Nathan, or perhaps she'll show us around the house first.

"Look how we've fixed up the place, Meir. You know the house so well. . . . I wonder if you'll recognize anything. In any case, you won't see the tiger that used to be here. . . . It's a good thing we set him loose in the Galilee. Now we have Henri here. He takes good care of us and is also charming." Her humorous mention of Henri, as a replacement or continuation of the tiger, angers me.

We tour the house. The rooms are bright, and on the walls they've hung pretty pictures and painted mirrors. I've never seen a mirror painting before—that is, a painting on a mirror rather than on canvas. There are also baskets scattered around the rooms, as well as bookshelves in a variety of styles. A number of Nathan's more expensive paintings have been taken down, perhaps moved to his office for a special exhibition. The style of the furniture has also changed quite a bit. Dana urges us to inspect everything—in the kitchen, the dining room, the bedrooms, and the bathrooms.

"I have no secrets from either of you. Look what I've built here in this old house. I want you to be familiar with everything I have."

At a certain point, I find myself concentrating more on Dana's belly than on any object of art. Though her voice still reaches me, her body wins the day. She's carrying Nathan's child, that much is both clear and confusing. A gifted, strong, tough guy like Nathan has succeeded in taking away a woman who might have loved me. Suddenly Dana raises her voice.

"Meir, we're in the kitchen—come see the new corner we installed. Here it is, a kosher kitchen unit for our dear friends, complete with a double sink, and separate dishes for milk and meat. Nathan said I should go all out with this little nook. From now on you'll be able to join us for dinner, even live here if you want to."

Just then Nathan arrives, wearing the usual dark trousers and a short white shirt. Dana slowly and rhythmically caresses his back, places his hand on her belly ("so close to your baby girl"), quickly brings him a drink, suggests that he go change into lighter clothes, asks him if he needs any help. She says she feels fine, happy we're all together in the kitchen.

Nathan shakes my hand, greets Rachel twice, and asks what's new with Yaron.

"You know, you ought to send him abroad to finish his education. Maybe he can team up with my own boys some day." He suggests we have a talk later about how I'm getting on with my work. "Explain to me why it is that I'm paying you a salary," he says with a laugh, and Dana is amused. Maybe I should be too. Now he gives Dana a big bear hug (did he ever hug Rina this way?) and lifts her off the floor.

"That's not healthy for any of us," she says, and Nathan declares that he's perfectly fit.

"I've even lost a little weight, and I enjoy lifting my two sweet girls, the little one and the big one." Dana is happy and asks only that he put it the other way around: "The big one and the little one, that's the suitable order."

Nathan asks what we think of the new furniture.

"I suppose you were especially impressed by the painted mirrors, but the bookshelves are also extraordinary." He asks us to go back to the entrance and pay attention this time to all the new appliances, the window casements and other details. "Meanwhile I'll have a nap, I'm sick of falling asleep in public; I want to be awake." I'm surprised and almost happy to hear this. Nathan goes off, and instead of showing us around the apartment again, Dana takes out some notes and studies them with Rachel. I think they're talking about pregnancy, about what to do with each of the remaining days. There's probably a shopping list there too. From the bookshelf I select an album of early-twentieth-century art and look through it with pleasure.

"Don't let Nathan see those," laughs Dana. "He'll insist on buying every painting in the book and he'll get himself in trouble again."

Nathan returns, calls for Henri, and asks him to bring us some hard drinks "in honor of our expected daughter." I smile for some reason and Dana turns to me:

"Listen, Meir, in a few months I'll give birth to our baby. If there are no hitches, that is."

"What hitches?" asks Nathan, growing irritable.

"You know I like to be careful, and don't interrupt me now; Meir doesn't know what we're about to ask him yet." Nathan falls silent as we all do, until Rachel pipes up:

"I suppose you've already chosen a name for the baby."

"Yes, indeed. We're thinking of calling her Maor." I keep my mouth shut, especially after hearing this unexpected name. I have no doubt it was Dana's idea.

"To make a long story short," Nathan says, interrupting my thoughts, "I have a new wife and a new daughter who will be called Maor. Now all we have to do is make sure that she's as smart and cultured as her mother. And that's where you come in, Meir. As you know, there are few people I respect the way I respect you. You're decent and intelligent. Sometimes you even do pretty well for yourself. And who else, among my friends, has always been faithful to his wife? Let me tell you, in the privacy of my own home, that you're the only man I know who's slept with one woman his entire life." Rachel is embarrassed; it's good she's not walking out. In the past, she would have scolded me for speaking far less brashly. And I have not yet responded, even thought. It's as though my speech is becoming more and more restricted. I prepared a whole essay, I tried to shorten it, I crossed out the repetitions, and what do I have left? I should just shut up now. There isn't anything definite for me to think or say.

Dana hushes Nathan affectionately and kisses him on the mouth, as though trying to soothe the sounds on their way out.

"You know how much Nathan admires you," she says to me. "He doesn't know anyone as special as you and Rachel, and right now we're going to prove it to you." It's wonderful to hear her voice, but at the moment I would prefer to go home with Rachel. Dana won't let up. "We have a request to make, an interesting proposition for the two of you; we would like Rachel and you to help us raise

Maor. Not just as friends of the family, but in a way that only people as dear and precious to us as you are would be able to. We want you actually to spend as much time here as possible, even sleep over sometimes, to take care of Maor night and day—to help and guide us."

I look at Rachel, anticipating her reaction. I can't tell whether I'm closer to screaming with pain or exultation. At last I won't have to go to the office any more, I'll be able to earn my living from Nathan's house and all by taking care of the new baby. What's wrong with that? Still, she isn't my baby. I didn't put her in Dana's belly, and it isn't for me that she'll give birth to her. And now Nathan has a few words to add. He explains that the terms of my employment will not be impaired in any way as a result of this arrangement, in fact they may even improve. Of course, the main burden will fall on me, he adds, since Rachel has the house and Yaron to look after.

"I daresay you'll enjoy yourself," he says in conclusion, "sitting in our luxurious home, fondling and feeding the baby whose name so closely resembles your own."

46

DANA'S PREGNANCY is coming along very nicely. Rachel calls her every morning as soon as she wakes up, even before she fixes hot drinks for Yaron and me. The two of them have a fixed routine and they even have the same laugh now, I think (though the effect on their faces is completely different. Rachel's takes on an embarrassed expression and Dana's gets broader). Nathan's personal assistant calls and offers me "any help you need." She explains the new priorities:

"You'll still be in charge of the renovated building of course, but you'll only come to work when it's convenient for you. Nathan wants you to spend most of your time at his home, looking after Dana's needs and making all necessary preparations for the baby's arrival. He wanted you to hear this from me."

I don't see why the secretary has to be involved in these details, maybe to make sure I'm aware that Nathan considers my new work as deriving entirely from my position with the firm. Rachel has not told me explicitly what she thinks of this new development, but her cooperation with the business of Dana's pregnancy proves where she stands from my point of view. Which is why I begin to show up at Nathan and Dana's every morning. When I get there, Nathan is either still in the bedroom dozing or else in the study, poring over his lists and research notes. By noon each day the firm's new woman driver arrives to take him to the office. Dana wanders around the apartment, awake and happy.

"Here already to pick up the specimens, dear Meir?" she asks me. "Are you sure you have the strength for all these errands? Maybe we should ask Henri to serve us some fruit first?" I usually decline the offer, though sometimes I have a few apples and a cup of tea. Inside the kitchen nook (by the double sink they installed for me to wash the milk and meat dishes separately) there is a small box containing Dana's blood and urine samples. I am supposed to take these to the lab every day, expedite the running up of the results, to deliver them to the appropriate doctor's office, and return to Dana with instructions and written explanations.

"Don't just let them give you a verbal explanation," says Dana. "I want it neatly written in black and white." And she smiles at me and sits down. She herself is always clear in her instructions to me and sees to it that I have cash to cover costs and precise addresses. "You'll see, Meir, this is the easy part. Imagine what it's going to be like when we have to take care of the baby."

Once a day I call home and ask how Rachel's doing, where Yaron is, and when I should be back. Occasionally Rachel asks whether I need her help. ("I haven't forgotten—from the beginning they asked that I be involved, too, though I'm not sure they really meant it.") I answer that I think that for the time being we should concentrate on our independent tasks.

Yaron wants us to study a chapter of the Bible together at least once a week.

"You decide which one, Dad. There's nobody like you when it comes to studying and understanding the Bible. Talmud I have always learned without you, but you really make the Bible come alive." I'm happy about Yaron's initiative—in the past I have perhaps not treated him fairly. I inspired him with a love of the Bible, with the wonder of it, but the truth is that I've confused his life. As for observing the traditions, you make one decision and everything starts to change. Even if your decision is tentative, a flimsy piece of string, it's still more meaningful than anything else. Yet for some reason I wanted Yaron to follow in my peculiar footsteps, to be serious about his faith and at the same time noncommittal.

"The new tradition," he called our religious path in a conversation with Rachel. "But a tradition can't be new, it's always a continuation of something. Dad—and you too, Mom—have totally confused me. Either we're Orthodox or we aren't, one decision changes everything, so long as you keep to it. You expect me to study and feel I'm connected, but you yourselves are always trying out these strange new things." Rachel reported what Yaron said to her, but she didn't tell me what she answered. Maybe she suggested that he talk to me, and ask me about my work and my relationship with Nathan and Dana. I find it surprising that in moments of weakness she still sends him to me.

Yaron and I sit down to study the Book of Samuel. Later I take a nap and talk to Rachel about the day's work. From me she hears about the baby growing in Dana's belly, and how thrilled I am by this, at least to a certain extent. I tell her I wish Nathan would bring me in on office matters too. It's senseless that I should only work at his house. I'd really like to know more about what's going on at the firm. Occasionally he asks if I've made any progress on the historical pamphlets he left for me, and he reminds me that I'd better hurry up, because he has whole books for me to read through. I'm still not sure though whether his growing preoccupation with medieval Europe will have any practical consequences.

The care of a pregnant woman, not to mention the future care of the baby, requires a special sort of hygiene and vitality. These days, however, I often find I have to force myself to bathe and change my clothes. I sometimes fall asleep in my living-room chair right after dinner with Rachel and Yaron. It would be unwise of me to go to Dana's smelly and unclean. Maybe I should ask Yaron to remind me to wash whenever he does. At Nathan's, of course, there are several bathrooms, but it would still be more convenient for me to shower at home.

Rachel gets used to fixing the same meals for Yaron and me. Cheese and tomato sandwiches, a cup of tea. It's all ready for us in the morning. She's never pampered me like this before, or maybe she's calmer now, maybe she's worried about me—I'm not sure why. In any case, I'm less concerned this time with the reason. I wouldn't be surprised if she started laying my clothes out for me in the morning. It could be that someone's suggested that she should take better care of me, or maybe Dana asked her to help me with my tasks.

No one's mentioned the liberated tiger lately. I'm afraid that if I ask about him they'll remember and next thing you know he'll be back. Was it out of consideration for me that they asked Hagai to keep track of him? Anyway, it would be difficult to keep a married couple with a baby girl on the way—and a friend like me who's come to help out—in the same house with a tiger. Not to mention Henri, who is here day and night, strong in body, clear and concise in speech.

"Henri is as strong and beautiful as the tiger," I even heard Nathan whisper to Dana once, "and even more useful to us." They both laughed and then Dana gave him a strong pinch on the cheek.

I understand that the birth is drawing near. I asked Dana if she will mind if I'm not around for the delivery itself. Even if Nathan is busy with some business deal or auction when the time comes, I tell her, I'd rather not fill in for him.

"Don't worry, Meir. We don't want you getting all worked up about it," answers Dana and I'm relieved. Sometimes Nathan phones me (I don't understand why he rarely speaks to me at home and prefers to call me from the office) and asks how Dana's doing.

"You're so knowledgeable about these things," he says, and asks if I have enough cash for expenses. He may expect me to bring up the subject of my salary, but I'd rather not. Rachel claims that my current salary is good enough, considering the sort of work I'm doing.

"You're doing very important work, Meir, but this time you're being fairly paid. I have no complaints against Nathan."

The time has come. Toward morning Henri calls, reports that Dana is going off to the hospital "exactly as planned." I am impressed with Henri's improved accent. Hebrew sounds good from his lips.

"And who's going with her?" I ask.

"Everything's been arranged," he answers. "Nathan didn't go to bed last night—he was looking over a new pamphlet, so now it's perfectly convenient for him to go with Dana. It's a good thing for him that we didn't get to the late morning." I thank Henri for the news and wake Rachel up excitedly. She's happy even though she's half-asleep. She wakes up relatively fast, jumps out of bed, and starts pacing around the house as though in effort to accelerate the baby's birth.

"The most important thing is concentration. Don't forget the things you'll need," says Rachel, grabbing a notebook (it seems to me she's pulled out one of Yaron's). She looks through the checklists she drew up for Dana: what to buy, what to prepare, what to wash, what to take, what to remember. She starts to copy a list of things for me to do on a separate page. "Your help is vital now."

Yaron takes the whole day off (I'm impressed by his organizational skills) and puts himself at my service.

"I don't want you to be alone, Dad. I can drive you around, even give you advice, or talk to anyone who gets on your nerves. I'm sick of people making you angry." We go to a few stores, following Dana and Rachel's checklist. Yaron helps me talk to the sales personnel and carry out the packages. He is about to go in the army yet I've barely paid any attention to his needs. How can a father like me neglect his grown-up son? I only hope Yaron understands how worried I am about little Maor. I have a mission to carry out—Dana and Nathan have chosen me of all people (and Rachel to a certain extent) to be responsible for their child.

We haven't waited so expectantly in a very long time. Rachel consults me (I'm glad she sees fit to ask for my opinion these days) about whether to wait at home or go to Nathan's house with me. The news is liable to sound completely different here and there. It's always important where you happen to be when important news reaches you. Maybe I should ask Rachel to lie down, and I'll wait by the phone. I probably won't fall asleep, though I may doze off for a while. Rachel agrees, lying beside me, having changed already into lighter clothes. She's breathing strangely, like somebody working out. I seem to recall such breaths before Yaron was born. Maybe I'll help her. I hold her hand and every few minutes remind her to keep breathing comfortably.

"You'd think I was the one having a baby," Rachel says to me and almost laughs out loud. "It's so nice of you to worry, Meir. I'm sure Nathan isn't nearly as concerned about Dana as you are, though she's the one having a baby right now, not me."

And finally we get the news. Uzzi calls from the hospital; I wonder what he's doing there. Why did they call him instead of me? Maybe Nathan wanted me to continue with the important preparations.

"Maor has been born," Uzzi announces and waits for our reaction. I congratulate us all. Uzzi reminds me to hurry, "though we're counting on you completely. Anyway, Nathan is all worked up—I haven't seen him like this in ages. Except for when the firm was about to collapse." Of course they can rely on me. I, who ran the entire company in Nathan's place, fought in a war, got his wife back—a man like me is capable of preparing the house for a newborn daughter, which is why Uzzi's remarks are entirely superfluous.

I'd like to ask Rachel a few questions now but I'm too embarrassed. To tell me about Yaron's birth and explain the similarity of smells and the open body. But Yaron is grown up now, Rachel is tired, and I'm in a hurry. I hope to visit Dana later at the hospital. I'm eager to see her face; what could be lovelier than a happy woman with a baby?

Rachel nevertheless gets up out of bed; it might be better for her to rest a while longer after all that exertion. But she wants to be actively involved. What's happened to my sleepy Rachel? I deeply appreciate the way she's helping me now. She's never been so involved in my work before. Why she should be specifically interested in this new job is hard to know, but I don't have to think about that just yet. Rachel is packing boxes of food for me.

"In case you get homesick at Nathan's or if they don't look after you properly."

Again Yaron arrives, this time in order to drive me to Nathan's. He strokes my head and kisses my cheek.

"How are you, Dad? Are you sure you should go over there? You don't have to take on something so difficult." Rachel says good-bye and asks Yaron to look after me.

"You know you have a sensitive and very special father; just don't let Uzzi or any of those other wise guys hurt him." We drive to Nathan's house. On our way similar thoughts run through our minds, at least I hope so; in any case, our silence is the same.

Henri is waiting at the entrance. He helps us bring in our things. Says he's happy to see me in this house.

"Now you're the one who'll make the decisions around here," he says to me quietly. I hope he willingly accepts this. I wouldn't want to get into any argument with Henri. My whole job could be jeopardized at a time like this.

We get the house ready, assemble the baby's crib, air everything out, line up sterilized baby bottles, go out for some last minute shopping. I had no idea I was capable of being so efficient; I have always underestimated my practical skills. Later we drive to the hospital together. I suppose everybody there knows Nathan and Dana. Who else would receive so many good wishes, or be as lovely and touching as Dana?

Henri guides me through the hospital corridors. He must know where the special room they've set up for Dana is. We approach unhindered. Henri says he'll wait outside. I haven't brought a gift; maybe I'll go downstairs and buy something. I wonder why Rachel didn't remind me, or think of buying a gift herself. Maybe she didn't expect me to visit the baby so soon. I walk into the room without knocking. Dana looks directly at me. I'm convinced she's looking at me because there's no one else in the room.

"Hello, dear Meir. How wonderful that you're here."

"Congratulations, Dana! I'm so happy for you. The baby must

be as beautiful as you are. Rachel is thrilled for you too. She wishes you great happiness."

"Thank you, Meir."

"And what more do you have to say to me?"

"I don't know yet. I have nothing new to say, but I do have a new baby," she smiles at me.

"And where's Nathan? Did he have to leave?"

"He's napping in one of the other rooms now. He sat beside me most of the night; I wasn't feeling well."

"Was he actually with you during the birth?"

"The whole time. He wanted to be the first to see the baby."

"We were waiting for the baby at home, too. Rachel lay in bed, breathing as though she were in labor"—I laugh out loud—"and I got everything ready for you."

"What's important is that we'll all be together again. That was a great idea of Nathan's, putting you in charge of Maor. You can show us all your talents at home. Who could ask for anything more?"

I don't know what's happening in Dana's body now and I'm too embarrassed to ask. What's closed, what's torn, what's perhaps healing. Rachel gave birth a long time ago and I had little chance to learn about her body then. And now Dana has a little baby girl, and she is Nathan's wife. This is perfectly clear to me. And I'm in charge of the arrangements at home and the shopping; they might have chosen anyone, but out of all Nathan's employees they chose me.

47

DANA IS COMING HOME with baby Maor this morning and, of course, we're waiting for her. Uzzi was appointed to drive to the hospital and bring her home. Rachel came over to wait with me; Shlomo and Shahar are here; Henri is reading in the kitchen; Nathan is resting in their bedroom. I think it was nice of Rachel to come help me, so the whole burden won't fall on my shoulders. We prepared the house very well and went through every room, making sure everything was in order, just as carefully as I check for crumbs of leaven before Passover. When a new mother comes home with her baby, nothing can be allowed to go wrong. Nathan stayed out of my way and allowed me to look around.

Dana is home. Uzzi is the first one to enter with the suitcase, Henri runs out to the car to help. It's a good thing they don't ask me what to do every minute—they know their duties and are apparently leaving more important things to me. Now Dana is getting out of the car with little Maor wrapped in a blanket, and she approaches us. I run to get Nathan; it wouldn't be right for him to miss the big moment. Besides, Dana's feelings might be hurt. Nathan is sleepy but he says he'll be right out. I hurry off again to greet Dana so that Rachel won't be the only one waiting at the entrance.

Dana walks in with Maor. Nathan appears, hugs them both and Dana asks permission (it's not clear who's supposed to answer) to give us all a kiss now. I don't know whether or not she expects me to respond to this, but I am the one she starts with and I allow her to kiss my forehead. Shlomo and Shahar come up shake her hand almost in unison, and when she embraces them, they start to sob softly. I hope they're experiencing happiness, not just grief for their mother. They couldn't have wished for a woman more adorable than Dana in their home.

And now Rachel. She still hasn't left the sofa to greet the arrivals. Dana comes toward her and then finally Rachel gets up and they embrace like sisters.

"From here on in, you'll be my mentor," Dana says to Rachel. "You have the brains as well as the experience. I still have no idea what I'm doing, but you probably remember every single detail about when Yaron was born, which wasn't that long ago. About eighteen years? I'm sure you and Meir will have more children. Look at Maor and tell me you don't want a whole brood of them right away." Rachel nods and so ends the conversation.

48

AND NOW for the important work ahead: we've drawn up special charts with a list of times and duties. I hope that every task and every hour of the day and night have been accounted for. Yaron helped us out with the charts, using Nathan's sophisticated computer software. He divided up the work with great precision. I stay at Nathan and Dana's, of course, so I'll be ready for anything. Rachel goes home to sleep and usually Yaron is also there. I'm supposed to hear from him soon about his army service; we haven't had a chance to have a long talk about that yet. Maor is a sweet and easy baby. I have no trouble changing her diapers even though she's a girl. I'm also good at feeding her and only with the bathing do I prefer to have help. It's too bad that Maor isn't breast-feeding from Dana, but it's better that I not interfere. I'm not the only person around here exerting himself—the others work hard too, each according to schedule, though I am, of course, looked upon as the one in charge. It's a good thing I'm not responsible for the cooking (aside from Maor's food, that is). Henri and a special cook see to the meals.

Rachel asks when I'm coming home; in other words, when will

my current mission be over? She should understand that I'm going to stay for as long as they need me here. Besides, Nathan hasn't let out any hints about my next assignment. I suddenly like the idea of not having a permanent job with the firm. That way I get to work in every department, which may be how Nathan intends to groom me for something really big.

Tonight they're all going out—for fun and recreation. Nathan requests that Dana also "go out and have a good time" with her girlfriends. Nathan, Maor, and I stay home. Nathan suggests that we sit down to a game of chess. There was a time when I wasn't a bad player, but there's no point now in being defeated by him in a matter of minutes. This being so, he proposes that we order something delicious to eat instead, or simply enjoy ourselves.

"I do enjoy our conversations, Meir. At least you're more reliable than the others."

I consider how to take advantage of this opportunity. Should I tell Nathan that I believe Rachel wants another child? Maybe consult with him about Yaron's future, or ask him for assistance of some kind. I could seize the opportunity to talk about his sons or about one or another of his interests. At this point Maor starts making little noises, and it's Nathan who goes to her. He returns with her in his arms, his body larger and stronger than ever. Baldness has triumphed and now dominates most of his head—as well as his thoughts, no doubt. He tells me he has even begun to see Judaism from a slightly different angle.

"Maybe sometime you could recommend a good book for me to read." I ask him whether he regrets all the years his sons studied abroad, and he says that everything can easily be set to rights.

The baby falls asleep on Nathan's shoulder. I've never seen him with a baby slumbering on him before. Suddenly I'm able to tell him how difficult it is for me.

"Working in your home has been wonderful, but something not so good is happening. I sense a kind of inner turmoil, or whatever it's called." He looks at me with a little smile and then tears come through the smile, or perhaps through his eyes.

"I understand Meir, and Dana and I certainly want to help you. You've been acting a little peculiar, but your duties with Maor should lessen the strain." I'm about to say that I don't desire anything in particular, but my voice sounds muffled.

Nathan gets up with the baby and asks me to hold her. He puts his hands on my shoulders and pats me fondly. He says he feels very close to me—"Even closer than I feel to all the brothers I never had." I understand that he is becoming emotional, but we mustn't get distracted. We must concentrate on Maor and not neglect her. But Nathan continues: "My father never had another friend like your father. Your father was the only one he could count on when it came to his finances, and that's positive proof for me."

But I want to hear something new from Nathan: the real story about his health and about Dana.

"What do you want from Dana?" he asks. "She's got everything she needs and she's happy with me. But you, Meir, you seem to have changed a lot. You're world has shrunk. Outside of Maor's diapers, you have no interests at all."

"That may be so," I reply, "but it's very soothing. And tell me, Nathan, do you ever think of your sons and Rina?"

"What the hell are you talking about?" He is almost angry now. "Some day my sons are going to run the company. And sure I remember Rina. She was a pretty good wife to me."

Again Nathan asks if I'm hungry. "Don't be alarmed. I'm not expecting you to cook dinner. There are limits. Oh dear, what have we done to you, Meir? Dana and I are beginning to worry."

"What's there to worry about, Nathan?"

"Dana is worried that you'll harm yourself."

"Don't exaggerate."

"Even Uzzi asked if it's okay for you to go on writing your reports."

"What do you mean, Nathan?"

"All those reports you keep writing to yourself about us. We know everything turns up there. And in your present mood, maybe it would be better for someone else to do the writing."

"You're really invading my space, Nathan, and there's not much spare room left inside me."

"But Meir, we have to look out for you. Dana is very concerned. I hear that you sometimes even drop letters when you're writing."

"Nathan, have you been sending someone to snoop through my notebooks?" (I scream this. I haven't heard such noise coming out of me in years, and it scares me).

"No shouting, Meir. It's just the two of us here now and there's no call for this. I planned for us to be alone in the house with Maor. Sometimes I think you're too in love with her. You couldn't get anywhere with Dana so now you're clinging to her baby."

"That's mean-spirited, Nathan. If I could count on you, I'd leave you with the baby and go home."

"Enough, Meir, enough. I only said that sometimes a letter gets away from you, or you make spelling mistakes. You need a rest. There's been something peculiar about your reports lately. You write everything in the same style, the same tone. For you there's no distinction between hitting and embracing or between the trivial and the serious. I guess we've worn you out: first there was your illness and then a beautiful girl like Dana came along, plus all your new responsibilities around our house. We've gone too far. It's time for you to move on. Tell me where you want to go, what lovely new destination you want to fly off to. Uzzi will arrange everything."

"Why don't you leave me alone, Nathan? Maybe you should pay more attention to your sons. Look at Shlomo. Shahar may be pleased now, but Shlomo is furious with you."

"You don't understand a thing about my sons. There are other considerations here. My sons are making their way through various stages so that eventually they'll be able to work with me. That's all that matters to them. But you, Meir, you're getting weaker and weaker. And I need you for an important mission to London, a transaction the likes of which we've never carried out before."

I'd better go to sleep. I'm extremely tired. Maor will wake up soon and someone's got to take care of her. Nathan will be occupied with his plans and collections. He can amuse himself, while I have to worry about the baby. Dana's counting on me. They know that, without me around, this whole house would fall apart.

Dana returns in high spirits.

"I missed you. How did you two big guys enjoy yourselves with my tiny little baby?"

"Home so soon, Dana?" asks Nathan without looking at me.

"What's wrong, don't you want me? You both look kind of strange, especially Meir. Even worse than you look in the middle of the night."

"Meir was just planning to take a nap. We talked a while, and now it's my turn to mind Maor. But hey, since you're here already, let's go eat something. We'll explain the rest to you another time, Meir."

In that case I'll go to my room. Nathan and Dana sound happy together. She's even capable of distracting him from his work and getting him to keep her company in the kitchen while she prepares a meal. He's probably watching her as she heats up the food, while he nibbles on nuts and chocolate. Or maybe he's just having a drink, saving his appetite for the special dish she's cooking for him. Or maybe he's planning their vacation, though it's hard to believe they'll take baby Maor with them. I bet they'll ask me to stay here and look after her. If so, it would be best if Rachel joined me. I cannot and need not always get along without her.

49

YARON ARRIVES EARLY in the morning and wakes me up. Seems a little excited. Maybe this has something to do with his upcoming army service. Brings me a hot drink. When was the last time someone awakened me with such affection? My son caresses me.

"Dad, Shlomo called. He wants us to work together." Yaron sounds enthusiastic. Apparently he's already planning what to do after his army service. "Shlomo said we could start working part-time at night. He has all sorts of ideas." Yaron's eagerness astounds me. He knows how much pressure I've been under, and still he wakes me. But I can always sleep. I'm sure there are whole days of sleep ahead for me.

"What does Mom say?" I ask.

"I came straight to you. He only called an hour ago. Said his father thinks the arrangement should continue."

"What arrangement, Yaron?"

"First Grandpa, now you, and next thing you know it will be Shlomo, Shahar, and me."

"Are we talking about friendship?"

"Dad, I think it's a lot more than that. They want us to work together."

"You'll start a new company?"

"No, I'll get a top position with their firm."

"But you have no experience."

"I'll start at the bottom of the ladder and work my way up. Like you."

I feel lousy. Maybe I'll just leave here. There's no way Yaron will work with them. And what's left of the business now? I have no idea what's going on there. I'm completely occupied here with my important mission—staying home with Maor. The office has become secondary. They should leave Yaron alone. Rachel won't like this idea either. (The letters dance around in my thoughts and I struggle with them. Nathan was right. Everything is topsy-turvy inside me; I am not in good order.)

I get out of bed, wash my hands, and drink three glasses of water. I eat a piece of candy and look at Yaron. Maybe he's worried, I don't know. I had better leave the room. Yaron walks after me, calling me. What does he have to tell me? Nothing urgent. I fall—oh right, there are stairs here. I can never remember whether there are two or three of them. I get up. The pain will soon pass. I don't suppose a little noise like that will wake Maor. Last time I put her to sleep at night she looked so peaceful and fell silently into a deep and cozy sleep. I have to think: where is Nathan and Dana's bedroom? They're together at this hour. Why can't I tell which way to go? Maybe there isn't enough light here. Ever since I was in the hospital a kind of dimness has enveloped me. I want more light. I continue down the corridor. Luckily they got rid of the tiger a long time ago. If the tiger were here, I wouldn't be able to manage this. Even a tame tiger would give me no rest. Now to calm down. What's there to worry about? Yaron is here. I find the door to their room. It touches me. Maybe it's been waiting. I strain to hear voices. Perhaps they're talking about me now, or about Maor. She has to be taken for her regular checkup today. No reason to dally. Why must I always dally? Yaron is not beside me. Maybe he's resting a little on his way. I'm sure he can get into any room he chooses. A son like Yaron can find his way around any apartment, even a big one like this. I open the door and walk in. It's dark in there. They're sleeping without a light on. How is that possible? Nathan breathes heavily. I see his big, noisy body. Maybe he didn't take his medicine before going to sleep—sometimes he forgets.

I think he's sleeping in his bathrobe. It's hard to see. He's barefoot. As for me, I usually prefer socks. Dana is hugging her pillow. Something of hers is touching Nathan. I'm really close now and I see. I could start screaming and wake them up, or maybe they'd stay asleep. People don't always wake up when you scream, it depends on what they're dreaming, and how well the scream fits in. What do they want from my son? Nathan, I refuse to let Yaron work either for you or your sons. What are we, servants of the whole world? Leave us alone. I'm doing all I should, and from now on that's enough. Meanwhile I don't seem to be screaming. I must be saying these things in whispers. Do they hear me? That would be easier. They'll understand that I didn't want to disturb them, or even wake them; I merely wanted to say a few words. Yaron is here. He pushes the door with a loud noise. Lately, no matter what he does, he raises a racket. Whether he's sneezing, or even chewing, his body is always big and loud. He is not only taller than I am—he's probably stronger, too. He enters the room, chewing something, I believe. I'm a little anxious. The room is full. What's going to happen now? I stand by the bed, gazing at them. Yaron asks something in a whisper, right in my ear. I think he's asking me what I want, whether I'm angry with Nathan, or have simply come to awaken them. Dana may wake up, and maybe she'll feel embarrassed in front of us. And what now? I look at Yaron and give him my hand, hand in hand. Together we lift one of the plates that are here. We raise it higher and higher, and then together we hurl it at the wall next to the bed. The dish shatters, Nathan stares wide-eyed, Dana whispers something, maybe in her sleep.

"Something just broke, that's all," says Yaron, and leads me away.

50

WE LEAVE Nathan's house. Yaron thinks I should go home and rest. I think he's right. I've seen Dana through the arduous first stage with the baby and there's no longer any need for me to stay. They have regular household help, Henri's always there, and if they need me, I can come right over. Yaron calls Rachel from a phone booth.

"Dad's tired," he informs her. "He's coming home to rest. You'd better wait there, he's feeling a little weak." He hangs up and says to me, "Mom's really glad. I haven't heard her sounding so clear and bright in ages."

When we get home, Rachel is indeed there, waiting to greet us, with a hug for Yaron and a kiss on the cheek for me. We haven't kissed like husband and wife in a long time; maybe that lies ahead. She says she's going shopping and suggests we write her a list.

"You're as much of an expert as I am by now, Meir." She smiles. "Your hard work at Dana's has prepared you for anything and everything. I would never have believed that my Meir could do such a fine job at housework and changing diapers." Yaron gives me a hesitant look, perhaps he's worried that I'll be angry with his mother. I actually believe Rachel is trying to pay me a compliment. Anyway, how much can she hurt a timid person like me, who is always knocking himself out for the sake of others?

Yaron asks Rachel to buy him plenty of treats, "the kind you eat on guard duty in the army."

I ask Rachel to surprise me: "You'll remember what I used to like." She may even think of things I have forgotten. She says I should rest, and meanwhile she has some interesting information for us about Hagai. I was hoping we'd gotten rid of that strange man by now, with his schemes and his spendthrift ways. Yaron joins the conversation and says he doesn't miss Hagai or those "interesting" hikes of his one bit. I am pleased with what Yaron has said but Rachel, surprisingly, doesn't respond. Before she leaves the house I take a good look at her. I think her femininity is dwindling, something there is smaller now. It isn't clear to me whether this has to do with her bosom or whether her figure has changed in other significant ways.

It feels good to lie in my bed. There are many comfortable places to rest, but only in my bed can I rest my feet as well. Did Rachel change something around in our room? Maybe only the pictures on the wall—Yaron now appears in many of them, both as a baby and as a boy. By the mirror on the dressing table there is still a picture of our wedding night, but she's changed the frame. I try to recall which pictures were here before. It's difficult to decide. But there's no need to exert myself. I can always come back to that later; I am not obliged to solve every single question my brain puts forth.

I'm home again, resting alone. I know what smells to expect in the house soon. Lately I've been able to smell things before they arrive, to smell them in advance. The distinct scent of Rachel's body reaches my nostrils, even though she isn't here. Now I have to concentrate on resting. It's time to take a load off my head, and the rest of my body. Let my body pass gently from stage to stage.

Apparently I've fallen asleep. Yaron peeks in from time to time—he likes to look at me. I don't suppose he's actually worried about my welfare, he merely enjoys watching his father. I used to like watching my father in bed when I was his age, too. When I wake up later on I'm hungry. I leave the bedroom and Rachel says she had planned on our eating together but they were famished and didn't want to disturb me. The table is messy. Rachel tries, but no job is ever completed around here. I should ask Dana about this, maybe she can teach Rachel her system. Rachel is now fixing me a cream-cheese omelet. I believe I used to like the combination.

"We have olives, too," says Yaron, and passes them to me. I hope they've noticed that my health has improved; I don't want them worrying about me so much.

"Hagai wants to come over this evening," says Rachel. "He says he really needs us this time, and that it's all been coordinated with

Nathan." Yaron says that Hagai even wrote us a letter, which he can bring me if I like.

"It's next to Mom's bed." How strange that I didn't even realize there was a letter close by while I was resting. But I don't want to show much interest now, and Rachel seems dismayed at Yaron's suggestion.

Nathan calls, Rachel tries to tell him that I'm resting, but he insists on speaking to me.

"Where did you disappear to?" he asks.

"I believe I've already done all I could for you, and then some," I reply. Nathan says that they will let me know if they need me.

"But right now you should take a few weeks to concentrate on Hagai's plans. I'm letting him organize a big public venture—it may even turn out to be political. The main thing is not to let him interfere with my London operation. Give him any assistance he may require, whatever he asks of you, and in your spare time—which is most of the time where you're concerned—keep reading the history books I recommended." I decide not to vent my feeling of being insulted. I only ask him somewhat bitterly whether he has any new plans for Yaron and, with utmost seriousness (it seems to me), he affirms that he has.

If Hagai wants to come over, I don't mind. By now I even find him sort of amusing. No doubt he'll be surprised to find the three of us together again, and he'll especially notice how big and strong Yaron has grown. Rachel says she's glad I'm still hungry and brings me a big sandwich. I haven't eaten such a large quantity of bread in a long time. Maybe it wouldn't be appropriate for Hagai to arrive while I'm eating—that might indicate a certain weakness on my part. But I'm really hungry and Yaron brings me a Bible so we can finally pick up where we left off with the Book of Samuel. I suggest that we (not just Nathan) draw up a list of interesting things together. For instance, the epithets of certain biblical characters and their significance: "Mordechai the Jew," "Nathan the Prophet," "Moses my servant," "Abraham my beloved." I ask Yaron to prepare a chart with rows for names, epithets, and explanations. Once characters have epithets it's hard to relate to them any other way. Rachel seems pleased and asks how about adding a few that became associated with the character in latter years, such as "Joseph the Righteous." Yaron is apparently waiting for me to answer her, but I just keep eating my bread and working on the list for Yaron and me.

Hagai comes up the stairs. I recognize his footsteps. When I see him I'll turn red the way you do when you run into your doctor after recovering from a serious illness. Perhaps I'll go to my room until I calm myself down. Yaron holds my hands tightly to make me stay, but he can't decide whether to go on holding them. Hagai opens the door himself; I'm surprised Rachel didn't lock it.

He enters, looks at me, and approaches Yaron. Sad to say, Yaron stands up to greet him. Hagai studies his face and body; what does he want from my son? Now he turns to Rachel—clearly he came to speak with her and was surprised to find me here as well. What did he think, that I would never come home again? Did he hope I would stay an outsider here forever? No, no, now I'm concentrating on my house and wife. I will not have Hagai coming over and annoying me. I won't have near-strangers barging into my home and giving us funny looks.

Hagai sits down but immediately gets up again to shake my hand. Maybe he's realized he has to behave properly with me.

"It's good to see you here too, Meir," he says. Yaron answers in my stead.

"Leave my dad alone. Anyway, we're not going to participate in your project unless Dad agrees. And what about you, did you ever solve the problem of the huge debts you ran up for Nathan?"

"Relax, Yaron. As for debts, Nathan's decided to help us out and we're doing better. Don't forget that I essentially initiated the whole Galilee project for Nathan. I was just the point man, the expert."

"And I, in my innocence, just wanted to see the Galilee," says Rachel.

"Yes, to ramble around our homeland," I add on, feeling pleased with myself.

"Pretty soon I'll start to think I'm at a meeting of the nature society," Hagai jokes. Only now do I notice his change of style. He's almost elegant compared to the way he used to look, wearing a suit (without a tie) and shiny black loafers.

"I see it's going to be hard to have any fun around here today," says Hagai. "I just wanted to tease Rachel and ask her if the terms 'husband and wife' are applicable in your case. Maybe she and I are more alike than she thinks. But I'll let that go now. What I've found here is a tight-knit family (this makes him burst out laughing). So now let's all have a drink and I'll tell you why I've come."

Though I'm astounded, I sit down in silence (or rather, continue doing so). Rachel serves refreshments, while Hagai drinks with ease and eats enthusiastically. He suggests that I also have a bite and eats some more. He asks Yaron to join him:

"Come on, you're a growing boy, got to build your body," but Yaron gets up, stretches, says he's not hungry and doesn't feel like eating.

"And now, down to business," says Hagai. " Remember that word, 'business'—for us it's the decisive term. What Nathan and I have planned is to set up a new political party. We want to influence everyone—why should we be satisfied with a provincial and fragmentary success? The time has come for Nathan, under my guidance, to turn his enterprise into a national center for action."

"And what does Nathan say about this?" I ask.

"He's a little preoccupied with family matters at the moment. It seems there's some tension between him and his sons about the first anniversary of Rina's death," answers Hagai.

"Well, I was living in their house until this morning and never noticed any tension," I say.

"I'm telling you, there's tension, even when he talks to Shahar on the phone and also when he meets with Shlomo at the office. The boys expected Nathan to erect an impressive memorial to their mother, maybe even a new building. Nathan says the company can't afford to do that at the moment; he has to give priority to what he views as absolutely crucial. The boys were insulted and Shlomo even shouted, 'That's right, you have plenty of money for painted mirrors but none for my mother.' I was just at the office and I heard them at it."

"And what about Dana?" I naturally ask.

"Dana wasn't there. I don't think Nathan wants her involved in any of this."

"I just hope they don't shout in front of Maor. The baby needs to grow up in peace," I say (incensed at his earlier replies).

"Let's come back to ourselves now," says Rachel, her voice calm. "Too many people are fussing over Maor. Somebody should give us a little thought for a change."

"I see Rachel is finally getting stronger," says Hagai, and I begin to feel tense again. Rachel smiles at him with pleasure. There is a new energy about her. She keeps rubbing her hands together as though trying to start a fire.

Hagai suggests that we move to the dining-room table (he just got here, and already he's deciding where we should sit in my house). He rolls out a map of Israel, marks our present location in black, and casually points to the route of our Galilee trip. He then explains the structure of the new party. Preferably it will be based on medium-sized settlements.

"Neither too large nor too small," he says. He shows us a notebook full of stickers and slogans, says that Nathan's financial manager even has the budget plan well under way. Yaron eagerly runs off to fetch some books from his room. He tries to show us a quick way of reckoning population figures and distances. Rachel hurries to the kitchen to bring us more refreshments—we're all looking so hungry. I'm impressed with Yaron's grasp of things, what a shame Nathan isn't here to admire him. Apparently he's giving Hagai a few practical tips.

Someone outside is calling loudly for Hagai. He runs out and returns a moment later with an envelope. He opens it carefully (with a knife, I believe) and takes out a typewritten page.

"Okay, we're in business!" he roars, startling me. "Nathan has confirmed that his company will finance the election campaign. It looks like the company itself will become a political party. We're free to start setting up headquarters now and onward to victory."

At this point I have absolutely no idea what they expect of me. To be involved one way or another in the party, I suppose, maybe even as a central player. From Hagai's explanations to Rachel and Yaron I gather that he's worked out a master plan. He's proposing it as an organizational model for the entire country: various settlements will exchange populations, citizens will be required to participate in daily fitness classes, there will be limits on traffic, and so forth. This is getting scary. But Yaron seems quite interested, asks

Hagai for further explanations, and even contacts a few of his friends who, like him, have some time left before they go into the army. I wouldn't be surprised if they're planning to set up the party headquarters right here in our home.

51

I GO TO BED EARLY. After my exhausting stint with Maor it's reasonable that I need to rest. Maybe tomorrow I'll visit that adorable baby. It seems to me that Rachel, Hagai, and Yaron are still talking, in whispers. It's nice of them not to want to wake me. Eventually I doze off and fall into a deep sleep. I dream of a long conversation with Dana. She is consulting me about new clothes for Maor. I can't understand why the baby needs a new outfit and, if so, what difference it makes where they buy it. I become slightly irritated but Dana smiles at me.

I wake up at about 2 A.M. There's a new smell in the air. Reverberations of the noise suggest that Hagai has recently departed. I wonder whether Yaron is still awake and busy. Rachel is approaching; maybe that good smell is coming from her. She sits down beside me. When was the last time Rachel sat beside me in bed? Maybe she wants to change her clothes here—it may be that this is comfortable for her. Now she's caressing my hand.

"Let's be really really close, Meir," she says weakly. I'm happy. She bends her head down; her hair is uncovered and brighter than I recall. "Something to drink, Meir?" I don't respond, nor does she get up. She kisses me on the forehead. Maybe she was aiming for my nose or mouth, but the kiss definitely landed on my brow. Now her hand is on my back. If I look, I'm sure I'll be able to see it. Rachel gets up to lock our door.

She crosses to her own bed and this time approaches me from there. There can be no doubt that we're embracing and she smells nicer than ever. Over and over she brushes her head against mine. She must have taken off her clothes by now. She's my wife and has come to me. She could have sat up working with Hagai all night. She might have fallen asleep far away, or even pulled the covers up alone in her bed. But instead she came to me, took my hand, caressed my thoughts. I didn't know Rachel could look pretty, too. Why doesn't she try harder? What's the point of looking pretty only now? She should be attractive at all the normal times so that I'll want to sleep with her. Since we're together again now, it hardly matters what she looks like, and yet I do find her pretty. But I mustn't think about that. I have a function to perform here. I too will kiss Rachel. I aim for her mouth, but it's too open for a kiss. She is able to kiss my mouth, while I, strangely enough, cannot for the life of me kiss hers because it's open too wide. And maybe her body is also too open, not just her mouth, and I can't connect with such an open body. It's good that this is what I'm thinking about just now. Nathan and his wives don't interest me in the least. There's a woman here in my bed—my wife, who also bore me Yaron. I know that's what I'm doing here now. For the first time in years I'm sleeping with a woman.

DANA AND I are talking on the telephone. Rachel, sitting beside me, pours me a glass of juice. She wants to hear every word Dana says to me. It's hard to talk like this, or even to listen.

"Meir dear, what's this I hear about an important meeting you had with Hagai?" says Dana sweetly. If I had a daughter, if Yaron had a little sister, it's quite possible she'd have a voice like Dana's. I'm almost convinced of this, but she continues and there's no time to ponder this idea. "I wouldn't be surprised if Nathan winds up giving you a leading role in the new party. I'd rather not go into too many details yet, but you can almost surely expect that it will be a big deal." She is pleased with her play on the phrase "a big deal." This, I have a sneaking impression, is the name Nathan and Hagai have chosen for the party.

"I don't really feel like being a candidate," I tell Dana, and Rachel seems pleased with this.

"Dear Meir, nothing's been decided yet. Don't be in such a hurry to turn down an offer that hasn't even been made," Dana retorts.

"You don't say!" Rachel exclaims. "I think they must be serious, and this time they really need you. You can ask for anything you want." Rachel sits down on my lap a little too heavily, but joy and embarrassment stop me from complaining. She turns her head in my direction. What's left of her old face, and what has changed there, I can't say. "Do you know what you want?" she asks. There are all sorts of pots on the stove warming up things to eat, but I don't believe she was alluding to food.

"You have to understand, Nathan is planning this campaign as a business venture. I wouldn't be surprised if he tried to have the company officially recognized as a political party."

"Is that allowed?" she asks again. Today she has only questions. I myself am not familiar with the law, of course, but Nathan will surely know how to get around it.

People start turning up in our home, several of Nathan's veteran employees. Yaron gets home early as usual. Next comes Uzzi with a number of women drivers.

"They'll be our couriers," he explains. "There's so much material to hand out." Various unfamiliar-looking secretaries arrive, followed by Shahar.

"Shlomo will be staying at the office for now," he informs us as he enters. In the afternoon Dana brings kitchenware, and Henri drags in sacks of apples as well as tea bags. Hagai arrives in the evening with a computer and several monitors, and with a man who stays nearby prompting him with facts and information all the time.

He doesn't stop whispering, but Hagai seems so well practiced that he only has to tune in once an hour. At 10:30 P.M. Nathan shows up looking no worse for wear—more tired than comfortable, more quiet than relaxed, more smiley than cheerful. Dana runs to him and jumps into his arms, then steps back and again jumps into his arms as though trying to set a new high-jump record. Nathan approaches me.

"Hello there, master of the house. We've come to announce the official opening of our campaign headquarters. There is no more appropriate place for us to be than here, in the home of my talented old friend." He may want to kiss me on the cheek, or on both cheeks, but a man's kiss seems strange to me.

Hagai takes out the blueprints and a hush falls over the crowd. I see my house there. Every corner has been labeled: "the response corner," "the rest corner," "the meeting corner," "the information corner," "the party platform corner." Various objects are moved in accordingly, people stand around eating apples, looking pleased, and anyone who's thirsty knows what to do. In this house there's no problem finding water or juice. My Yaron is here again, wearing shorts, which look strange, and dragging around more things than anyone else. We've never had such a big crowd in the house before, even for Yaron's bar mitzvah. Suddenly Dana comes over with a cushion for me.

"Sit down. You have so much to do—rest while you can. Maybe we should ask Rachel to bring you something interesting to read." I stand up, place the cushion between my back and the wall and after a while I sit down on it.

"Finally, a little rest," says Nathan. "Not bad, when you've got everyone else working for you." He's pleased as can be, and those within earshot glance up and smile. "Thanks for letting us use your home, but then it's perfectly reasonable that you should. After all, you are our candidate."

Hagai and Rachel walk over. She seems elated by the honor of this visit. Nathan has never been in our home before, so this is a real first. Hagai glances at me and whispers things to Rachel that she promptly writes down. He asks me to stand up and, using a little pencil, traces around my shoes, my trousers, my shirt, my nose, and my hair, making scarcely any marks, or so I assume, but he never stops listening to the adviser whispering in his ear and dictating orders.

"We'll prepare you like a high priest," he says to me, happy with the simile. "What, you thought I didn't know anything?" I can't understand what he wants from me. Some faint applause is heard, and most of the crowd disappears into the kitchen, where they sit around the table, circles and circles of them, cheering with enthusiasm. All sorts of deliveries are made to the house. I don't believe they're all for me, or for Rachel and Yaron. Whoever sent them must have known that Nathan's party headquarters had been moved here, and so they sent food and papers.

A fresh batch of secretaries arrives on the scene, and Nathan observes them with pleasure and fatigue. Dana covers his eyes in a mock attempt to obstruct his view of other women, and he takes her hand and kisses it, then guides it upward to caress his head, and beckons everyone to gather round for a preliminary briefing. His various businesses are doing reasonably well, he reports, going strong on the whole, but he now wishes to have a broader and more inclusive sphere of influence. Hagai has brought us a practical plan of action, and we've gathered here because we want to win. Our very own Meir will be the party candidate; there's no one worthier (he means me, yet surprisingly enough I'm not embarrassed. Let him say what he likes), but he will need the cooperation of all. If we fail, we'll have only ourselves to blame, because no other party has a candidate like Meir. It's enough for us to tell the world that our candidate has been with the same woman all of his life, has never slept with another woman. Even with his wife—well, no one can guess how it's been between them since their son was born. Nathan has almost finished speaking when Dana gives him a look I find highly peculiar. But to the others everything may seem perfectly normal.

Hagai approaches with a blueprint of our apartment and points out some of the features of the plan.

"There's no need to let you in on all the details. I'd hate to tire you out. Leave being tired to me." He turns to a page with the heading "areas of activity" and explains that I should look for the green line. The red line applies to all party activists and runs right through the apartment, and he shows me the red line his people have drawn along the floor. "What you find on the map is what you'll find in the apartment, exactly the same colors. We've been meticulous about this. And you'll also find a yellow line—the line for messengers." He shows me the yellow line that leads directly from the entrance door to the kitchen, without any unnecessary turns. "And there's a black line for Nathan and me," a special fast route to any spot in the apartment. I had no idea you could get to so many different places in my apartment so swiftly and easily. "Now we come to your green line. You, however, would do better to call it the green zone." Hagai explains that my movements will be limited to a particular area of the apartment: our bedroom, the bathroom, and a certain corridor that leads out to the meeting corner. "That will be plenty. You won't need more space than that and it would be a pity for you to waste your energy and bump into the rest of us. You stay in your room and we'll come to you if necessary." I can't tell whether this is a joke, or whether I have actually been sentenced to confinement in the bedroom of my own home. Hagai now shows me several other markings on the map that correlate with floor markings and is delighted with their lovely colors. I look for Rachel because I want to ask her if she is aware that I have been forbidden to move freely through other areas of the house. Does she realize that I am supposed to remain, almost exclusively, in our bedroom?

DANA VISITS ME in my room.

"How wonderful that we can finally do something with you, me, and Nathan." She looks fresh and lovely. She tells me how happy she is that I'm the one Nathan and the others have chosen as their candidate, and she enumerates the promotional activities and conventions that have been planned for the party. I'm somewhat surprised. Of all people, she ought to realize that Nathan doesn't take politics as seriously as Hagai. For some reason I don't ask her precise intention. If they've decided that I should save my strength and rest in my room most of the time, why should I knock myself out solving complicated problems? I'd do better to ask Dana or Rachel to bring me tasty meals and a new book to read. I ask Dana if she knows to what extent they're planning to limit my movements in the house. She says she doesn't know all the details, but she understands it will be to my advantage to stay in my room.

I ask her to call Rachel into the room and I inform the two of them that from now on everyone will have to pamper me. I am the candidate of choice, and if I must be secluded in this room in order to build up my strength, it is their duty to satisfy my needs and make me happy. I demand that they go all out and provide me with the most fascinating and beautiful books and recordings. As of today, Dana and Rachel will prepare my meals together. It isn't long before I start putting on weight, and for the first time in my life I feel pretty good about this. I tend to eat five full meals a day because the activity outside my room goes on and on and I get worked up about it.

Meanwhile Hagai has written down various suggestions for my campaign speeches and the boys (Yaron and Shahar mostly) bring clothes for me to try on. It doesn't take long to get used to their help; what could be nicer than a father being fitted out with tact and sensitivity by his teenage son? Rachel and Dana ask me to guess which of them prepared my omelet or other dishes, and unfortunately it's pretty easy to tell: when Dana cooks all the ingredients are finely chopped and nothing leaks. Sometimes they send Hagai in to give me "pep talks," as he calls them. He explains how crucial it is that I should remain in my bedroom.

"Only by staying in one room and not wandering around the house can a person develop a tremendous reservoir of power and influence."

But as it happens I am rarely consulted about party issues. When Nathan shows up, as he does fairly often, the meetings go on from morning until night. Sometimes I sneak out for a peak at the blueprints, tables, and slides that are projected onto a wall of the house. Usually I hear distant voices first, and then Rachel or Dana will drop in for a short visit and explain that I'm not missing much. I accept the need to spend a lot of time resting and fortifying my inward self, but it still hurts my feelings that Nathan himself seldom comes to my room to talk to me directly.

Tonight I feel like going to sleep early. Dana brought me a new thriller, but I'll doze off when I want to and read the book tomorrow. All of a sudden somebody wakes me up. There is Nathan at my side and I'm confused. I look up at him and he mumbles something.

"Now you remember me?" I ask.

"There's no time for your remarks, Meir. Come to work immediately."

It seems I have a convenient opportunity to leave my room tonight. I should probably avoid arguing with Nathan and make the most of his offer. I'll just cooperate with him and enjoy what I can. No need to share my thoughts; I'm sick of being so exposed. I get out of bed and decide to dress myself this time. It's kind of nice being helped on with my clothes, but I think Nathan should see that I can still do things for myself. Nathan, who has been sitting aside and waiting, gets up now and starts walking around. He glances at the bookshelves, even picks out a book to read. He's looking very sporty, down to his shoes. I've never seen him dressed like this.

"And Dana's downstairs, waiting for us," he whispers suddenly.

We leave the room together and make our way to the entrance. My house looks different. Most of the walls have been lined with shelves, from the floor half way up to the ceiling. There are work files lying about and some scraggly-looking plants here and there. The rooms are dim; I guess they're careful about not leaving the lights on unnecessarily at night. These changes surprise me. I never heard any noise—smashing, hammering, or builders talking in the house, and yet my home has been transformed.

Nathan is rushing me, tugging at my arm. He seems to be in better shape these days, before he would always huff and puff, even on short walks.

"Move along, Meir," he says, speaking loudly now. "There's no time for all your probing."

"Where's Yaron?" I ask for some reason. And Nathan (happily in a whisper again) tells me there's no reason to worry about my son. "But I miss him and I want to see him right now," I insist to my surprise. Nathan stops, turns red, and then, suddenly softening, plants a kiss on my forehead. I am both touched and frightened.

Outside, someone quietly approaches us. It's Dana.

"I told you to wait in the car," Nathan scolds her.

"But I was scared. After a while I used up all my good thoughts." Dana looks at me and seems to sigh a little.

"Why don't we walk a little?" I suggest. I prefer walking—it's a chance to unwind.

"Why not?" Dana answers with a question, and Nathan leans back against a street lamp. "You look good, Meir," says Dana. "Well done. When someone wakes me up in the middle of the night I'm so groggy I barely have the strength to fall asleep again," she giggles softly, "while you wake up right away like a hungry baby." Nathan throws her a look.

"I can remember one or two occasions when I woke you up and you were ready for anything and knew exactly what to do." Dana turns away, Nathan falls silent, and I feel like an intruder on this conversation between husband and wife.

Henri pulls up in a little car and we all get in. I can't be sure that even Dana knew he was coming. Right away I notice that Henri's Hebrew has become almost fluent.

"And how's our old friend?" he asks me. He seems content, the air is scented with perfumes, and he is sucking on a large piece of candy. "It's nice that we have this opportunity to meet," says Henri with a chuckle. "You of all people, Meir, should appreciate my hard work." I ask Dana what he's talking about and she whispers that Henri wants to convert and is devoting much of his time to studying Judaism. She whispers several more words in my ear and then asks me to turn my head (though this is extremely uncomfortable) so that she can whisper into my other ear. Maybe this is some new game of hers that I don't know yet. Nathan ignores us both and asks how Maor is.

"Don't worry. I left her dry and happy half an hour ago," Henri answers.

We've entered a new neighborhood. Attractive buildings, though they're too tall for my taste. Some people like living in high-rises that turn a street on its side. Henri stops in front of one of the buildings and we get out of the little car ("I've never been in such a little car before," says Nathan). In the trunk are three large cases. Nathan takes one out, Dana takes the second, and Henri, the third. "Maybe I should carry it for you," I offer Dana. But she turns me down, smiling with pleasure. Someone like Dana even knows how to enjoy being hungry.

We enter the building and take the elevator a long way up, though not to the top. I'm certain of this. We enter an apartment—Dana has the key. A new apartment, you can tell at once. It hasn't even been decorated or properly furnished yet.

"Welcome, Meir!" says the big sign on the table.

"So what are you waiting for? Make yourself at home, Meir," Nathan says jubilantly.

"What's the big celebration?" I ask. "Did we win the election or something?" Dana is truly elated with my question.

"How funny you are in the middle of the night," she says. Henri comes in from the kitchen with all kinds of drinks.

"Some election," Nathan says angrily. "Forget Hagai's crazy ideas. This time I'm going to watch out for him. My father didn't set up his investment firm so we could jeopardize it with political conflicts. I'm surrounded by too many weak people like you, Meir, and oddballs like Hagai."

"But this *is* a celebration," Dana reminds her husband, "we agreed that you would show just a little more tolerance." Henri looks at her admiringly, wondering no doubt whether one day he too will have a woman like Dana.

"Everything's okay," says Nathan. "Hagai can continue handling party matters and I'll decide how far he can go. Meanwhile I've got to keep him busy and out of trouble. Now, Meir, come see your room."

"Not one room, but several of them," Dana corrects him. "More than several in fact: the whole apartment is for you," says Nathan. I'm not particularly interested in the apartment at the moment, especially since I can see most of it from here. But they insist on taking me on a tour of the place—shuffling, sniffing around, and even peeling a little paint off to check the workmanship. Soon I'll select a wall for myself (maybe when I find out where my bed is) where I'll drill small holes and glue things. I remember the place in the wall at my parents' home where I constructed all my thinking.

"Everything you need is right here," Nathan reassures me.

"But this isn't my house," I explain. "True, your house is still your house, and this one in fact belongs to me," says Nathan.

"To us," Dana corrects him, and Nathan smoothes back the few shiny strands of hair left on his head and says: "Yes, to us, of course."

"So if it's yours, what's my role here? To make sure no one steals it?" I inquire with a smile.

"Good idea," Henri chimes in and Nathan asks him to leave the room (for some reason I am reminded of the tiger roaming through the house and at once I am ashamed of the thought).

"Meir, this is not a major revolution. We simply need you, that's all," says Dana.

"And what can I do that I haven't done so far?" I ask predictably.

"Whatever you wish. Live your life. We want to let you live according to your beliefs. Nothing specific, so far as we're concerned."

"But why here?" It's irksome to have to ask, but I persist nonetheless. Maybe that last nap at home fortified me.

"Come Meir, sit down here between us," Dana beckons and of course I obey. "Isn't this nice, the three of us together?"

"And what about my house?" I ask again and wonder at my audacity.

"Your house is where it belongs, nobody's trying to cheat you out of it. Rachel can come here too any time she likes," says Dana brightly, and Nathan continues (by now it's difficult to tell which of them is speaking).

"Finally you'll be able to relax, to occupy yourself exclusively with the things you love. We want you all to ourselves, with no waste and no efforts spent on others. Naturally you're a free agent, but you will be our fondest possession. I see you, Meir—please accept this in the nicest possible way—as a kind of property. I must have something stable and expedient around here, and you have been chosen. Personally I had some reservations about you, on account of your weakness over the past few years, but Dana in her usual fashion insisted that 'our Meir is the one.' "

Dana explains how wonderful my situation is.

"You haven't really had a chance to look around yet, but this is one of the most modern and comfortable apartments. You'll never even need to set foot out of the building, you can have anything whatsoever delivered right to your door."

"You can have kosher meals delivered, and even pretty girls," says Nathan with a laugh, and Dana pinches him hard on the leg, in case he's offended me.

"But don't think you're always going to have quiet around here," says Nathan, "Dana and I are planning to go abroad for a couple of months, to explore new places, and this apartment will serve as a permanent rest-haven for my sons, and we'll also come over with Maor sometimes. The place is ours, but you'll take care of it, you'll improve it for us."

"You can even raise it like a child," Dana interrupts.

"We have to make sure," says Nathan, ignoring her, "that in at least one of our residences nothing will ever change. We'll always have somewhere to come back to, just to see your face, just to hear your reports."

Now Nathan sees fit to brief me on other matters. He says he is uncertain who he should appoint as temporary CEO. Shlomo is unsuitable, he says, because he's hypersensitive "and has too many irrelevant thoughts, just like his mother." But a few years from now it may be possible to appoint Shahar, who seems stronger and more interesting. He goes on then to discuss his financial status (and I wonder why he finds it necessary to explain his business to me in such detail).

"I sold most of my antique collections, taking advantage of market trends. I also auctioned off a number of painted mirrors in the style you saw at my house, but I kept the most expensive one. I've allocated funds for Hagai's political venture (I have to keep him busy so he won't get in our way), but the balance is reserved for the British scheme you'll be hearing about."

"My darling Nathan," says Dana suddenly and even I am

moved. "Enough talk, and you shouldn't have sounded off about Rina and Shlomo either. From now on I will position myself on your lap" (she goes to him) "and watch the words you're about to say. If you even come close to uttering a silly remark, I'll scatter it around the room before you have a chance to let it out. . ." And she sits herself down on her husband's knees and watches his mouth intently. "I don't believe Nathan has conveyed how happy we would be if Rachel joined you here. Nathan considers it vitally important to have a respectable family living in this apartment, just a normal family in a home with no major revolutions!" Nathan asks me to come closer, lays his hands on me and says:

"Now you know everything, and you understand just how valuable you are to Dana and me." I hear this and feel bewildered.

"Boys, come have a drink," says Dana, rising abruptly from her husband's lap. She pours something and serves refreshments. The night is almost over. I'm hoping Rachel will get here in the morning and that she'll be pleased. I stretch out on the sofa where we sat, and no one comments. Dana whispers something to Nathan and he takes off my shoes. Either he's concerned about me or he's worried about the couch. I doze a while, and from time to time I look over at Dana or try to imagine Nathan young and slender, his body pale and indistinct. It's hard to fall asleep with them around me, and I wish Yaron and Rachel were here already so they could tell me what they think.

FORTUNATELY YARON ARRIVES EARLY. He kisses me and gives me a big hug. I am blessed with a son who hugs his father even now that he's grown up to be a young man. I wonder where Rachel is. Yaron wants to know every detail. He asks how I got here and whether this could be considered kidnapping. I guess he's trying to make me laugh. He asks what to buy me. He wants to know what this apartment is supposed to be—is it registered in our name? Is it a gift or merely a down payment of sorts? I would rather go on hugging quietly, and then maybe I'd read a new book—or we could read together, or each on his own. I'm not interested in the legalities of this apartment. My situation may seem peculiar, but alternatively I could be viewed as someone who has merely worked very hard over the years for Nathan and his wives and has finally been rewarded. I ask where Rachel is.

"Mom will be here soon," Yaron says. "She wanted to make herself beautiful for you and she also wants to bring you some special treats."

Nathan and Dana left the apartment some time ago. As I understand it, they're flying to Europe today or tomorrow and will be away for several months. Yaron says he'll find out for sure from Shlomo and Shahar. He has the impression that things will be simpler from now on.

"They're starting to loosen up," he observes, and I'm impressed by how articulate he's become. Meanwhile a courier brings me a letter marked urgent and asks me to sign for it. Yaron is wary, but I sign. I'm no longer afraid each time I have to write my name. Yaron opens the letter and we read together.

> Good morning, Meir.
>
> We took off quietly so as not to disturb you. Let me reiterate, in writing this time, just how important you are to us, and tell you that I may be needing you in ways you'd never suspect. Dana too has great admiration for you. I only hope she won't fall in love with you again. Believe it or not, I'm truly in love with her. Last night I slept for only one hour and in that short interval I managed to dream about her—that we were kissing like a couple of teenagers. Can you imagine that, Meir, a man like me having such an innocent dream? I, who have touched the bodies of so many women, aroused by a dream of a single kiss? See how sentimental your rich, fat, old Nathan is getting? You, I'm sure, could never kiss her properly. Oh, one last thing: I'll be sending you some extraordinary historical material in the near future that I want you to look after and study carefully.

Yours, Nathan

P.S. Let's be clear about this, Meir. There will be no direct contact between you and Dana—everything must go through me. I trust no one.

"What does he think, Dad?" asks Yaron. "That Dana is in love with you? Can't he see that you and Mom are always together? What's he so worked up about? I guess even Nathan has reached the point of really falling for a woman."

"I don't know, Yaron. I'm a little confused. But you and I are here now and soon Mom will be here too."

Yaron looks at me strangely. He picks up the letter again. He sneezes full blast, and seems to have sprayed the letter. He lays it down on the kitchen table and pours us both a drink. Rachel is outside shouting up to us. When did she learn to holler like that? We go to the window. She waves at us excitedly, points at a little white car. I realize that Yaron and Rachel have a surprise for me: they've bought a new car. To my amazement Rachel blows me a kiss, and I call back affectionate words. There's so much to think about, but why don't I put off my thinking until later tonight?

55

LIFE IN THE NEW APARTMENT is relaxed. Rachel, Yaron, and I eat a pleasant supper together every evening. I have never before enjoyed eating so much. Also, in the past I didn't consume most of my food at mealtimes like this, but ate little snacks throughout the day. Now I feel perfectly comfortable sitting for long stretches at a time, wondering what Rachel has prepared for supper, and daring to taste new styles of cooking. I think I'm getting fatter, but Yaron says that soon we'll start working out together, with a personal trainer who will come to the house. I'm very much impressed with his store of information—he knows more people and places than I ever did.

More often than not, Yaron prefers to stay with us after supper. He calls up his friends, but in the end he decides to stay home. We all read (sometimes from the same book) and doze in the comfortable armchairs Nathan and Dana chose for us. Rachel suggests that we take a nap; I lie down on the big sofa with Rachel on one side and Yaron on the other. Rachel hugs my stomach and lays her head on me. Yaron pats my shoulder and kisses my forehead. I never thought I would have enough strength for two grown people. I guess I didn't realize how important it is to eat large, regular meals, like a nursing mother. Were it not for this improvement in my physical condition I would be unable to be a pillar to my wife and son. Presumably Nathan and Dana take an interest in my body too, though of course I'm only thinking this in jest. It's time for me to start joking around at home—I think Rachel expects that.

Three months go by before we hear anything from Nathan and Dana. Nathan is the one who calls. He asks if we've seen his sons lately. Says he expected Shlomo and Shahar to visit us sometimes.

"We've left you a roomy enough apartment so you could all be comfortable together. I wanted my sons to be able to go there and relax." I say I would be only too happy to oblige. Rachel takes the receiver from me and says that we can't be made responsible for his sons as well. Nathan is silent. Now Dana takes the phone and tells us about a marvelous trip through little villages in China. "Not the usual places people visit."

Rachel calls Yaron in and asks him whether there are any little villages in China. I insist on speaking to Dana about other things. I ask when they will be returning, and whether they need anything from us. "No, no," says Dana, "just stay a happy family, together in our apartment."

The conversation is a little hard on me. Rachel asks if there's any way to help.

"It's a rotten shame they called. Why don't they just leave us alone?" Yaron suggests that we call Shlomo and Shahar, or at least one of them. Maybe they're too shy to come over without an invitation.

"Oh sure, go on, invite them," whispers Rachel. "As if we had enough quiet around here. . ." Yaron looks at Rachel but he doesn't seem angry or even insulted. He telephones Uzzi and asks him how to find the boys. Uzzi says he isn't in touch with them regularly.

"Anyway, there's not much going on at the Israeli branch of the firm. It's possible that Nathan is developing some new enterprise in Europe, but I wouldn't know anything about that." Yaron asks Uzzi about salaries. "Two or three of us receive a salary of sorts for reporting to Nathan about our end of things or if we have ideas or suggestions to offer. Let me just say, Yaron, that one of our duties is to report on your parents."

"What's there to report about Mom and Dad?"

"A lot more than you think, but less than Nathan hoped for," says Uzzi. With that, apparently, he ends the conversation.

Rachel wants to sleep. I should probably also go to sleep. Yaron wishes us a pleasant sleep and tells us that he may go out for a while—and try to locate Shlomo and Shahar (or at least one of them). We go into the bedroom. Rachel seems very tired. There are different smells emanating from her, but it's hard to tell which of them she put on and which are inside her. I close the door.

"Shouldn't we lock it?" Rachel asks. I try to but the lock keeps popping out again.

"You can see that this door has rarely been locked," I say, and Rachel looks at me strangely. Yaron comes in to ask if we need any help. He heard banging sounds and didn't know what it was.

"So now he can do that for us too," says Rachel, and Yaron doesn't understand, or at least he doesn't respond. He fixes the knob with a little jackknife (since when has he had a jackknife?) and wishes us a good night.

Again I try to lock the door and succeed. I go to Rachel and kiss her body in various places. Her smell has changed—one element has overcome the others. Less variety, more clarity. My body is in a different state. Anything I think—however disgusting, silly, or remote—merely intensifies my passion. Now Rachel's smell is in her voice, and there's no difference between now and the moment when she gave birth to Yaron some nineteen years ago. There's no difference in her voice, in her smell, or in the way she lies down.

PART THREE

RACHEL

56

BY MORNING Nathan's sons are with us, amiable and happy. They weren't aware they could come here. They didn't want to bother us. Didn't understand their father's plan and were afraid that visiting us might get in the way of his intentions somehow. They're so happy to see us all.

"And especially to see how you've recovered. Meir." It seems Nathan talks to them more than I realized. But he hasn't let them know when he's coming back yet either.

"I don't know what's holding them up anymore," says Shahar.

"What are you implying?" asks Shlomo.

"You know as well as I do that Father would like to come back now but Dana has other plans," Shahar says. "She says this is her big chance to see all of those places." Now, from what the boys say, something new emerges. It seems that Dana and Nathan are not always together in the same place at the same time. Dana goes off to see various exhibitions and actually prefers to be on her own. As she explained to Shlomo, that way it's easier to concentrate on what she sees.

"You don't really imagine I could stand being stuck with your father every minute of the day, do you?" she asked Shlomo a few weeks ago. "Suppose I feel like running from one place to another? Your father is so big and so heavy, despite all the diets I found him. And besides, he's been nearly everywhere, and I'm not interested in going anywhere new with a person who's already been there. It's very annoying."

The situation is, I realize, rather complicated. Dana wants Nathan to return to Israel and his sons while she goes on traveling and studying a few months longer. She takes their daughter along wherever she goes, day or night. Doesn't want anyone's help with the child.

"She sits on my knee and learns to see"—this is the little rhyme she has composed and recites to anyone who'll listen. Sometimes she teases Nathan about his lifestyle and the peculiarity of his business affairs.

"One wife dead, two sons sad and distant. Meir, your one real friend, cooped up in the apartment. And as for your business ventures, or what's left of them, I don't understand anything anymore." I wouldn't be surprised if Dana started calling me and asking my advice. My opinions, it seems, are more respected than I realized, unjustifiably so in my opinion. Shlomo and Shahar continue to fill us in. They explain that their father refuses to give up.

"He's stubborn and he knows how to succeed." He's waiting for Dana, follows her from country to country, supplies her with a vast amount of material to study, and is her guide in every area and language.

"Father's really in love," says Shahar, and he and Shlomo laugh nervously, or just a little strangely. Yaron tries to change the subject. His motive is fairly clear. He talks about the new business ventures, about the level of education in Israel. He suggests that Shlomo and Shahar start a company together.

"That way we can divide the hours between the three of us, so that we can work and study simultaneously." They seem to like the idea.

"Why shouldn't we continue the family tradition?"

"And we don't have to decide who gets what position yet," declares Shlomo. "We'll just start off together and see. Maybe you'll be our chief executive and maybe we'll all be partners." I want to interrupt but Yaron signals me to keep quiet. Their proposals don't seem to bother him. Later they talk about doing their army service. Yaron says his deferment has run out and now he'll probably be a pencil pusher somewhere near home.

"Where I can keep an eye on Mom and Dad," he says, and

winks at us. Interesting that he didn't tell me about any of this. I imagine Rachel knows more about it than I do. Shlomo and Shahar ignore Yaron's questions about their own army service.

Rachel calls me to the kitchen and asks me to help her with a heavy tray. She suggests we leave the boys to their talk and refreshments while we go to sleep. Maybe she wants another child but won't say so directly. A few hours later, Yaron calls from behind our bedroom door. It seems to me that Rachel would rather pretend to be asleep. I go to Yaron and hear that Dana called a little while ago with the details of her arrival. She's coming with Maor and asks that we be "ready and beautiful." Rachel overhears this and gets out of bed. She seems as excited as a schoolgirl who's just heard there's going to be a test in her favorite subject. What needs to be done in the next few hours is as clear as the lack of variety in our refrigerator. Yaron goes out to do the shopping, Rachel cooks, and the three of us organize the rooms—planning where everyone will sleep, bearing in mind that Maor will need a crib. I'm glad I haven't left the apartment even once. Luckily Nathan and Dana never showed up while I was out.

57

I'M EXCITED that Dana will be coming home shortly, several months after her departure. She tells us her estimated flight arrival time and requests that we all come to meet her. Rachel thinks this is a good sign.

"She could have asked you to come by yourself, but she's invited Yaron and me as well." After a long interlude without them I have to start taking tranquilizers again. I used to worry about that, but now I prefer to take medication before the pressure in my belly becomes unbearable.

Yaron can't figure out why Dana is hurrying back now. Only yesterday we heard that she was determined to continue traveling on her own, something she was never able to do in her childhood and early youth. Rachel thinks Dana wants to consult us about something ("especially Dad"), and then she'll leave again. I don't feel I have anything to contribute to their conversation. On the day of Dana's return we set off together (earlier than necessary) to meet her plane, with Yaron in the driver's seat, Rachel beside him (she feels more comfortable in front) and me in the back. We've all brought gifts for Dana and have decided not to tell each other what they are. I bought her a historical novel, Rachel probably found her something unexpected, and Yaron is likely to give her a fancy box of chocolate.

On the way to the airport, I remember Dana's face and figure. Yaron asks if I find it easy to see Nathan in my mind's eye, and I admit that I don't. Rachel takes out a lovely bouquet of flowers and fusses around with them. It occurs to me that I never said specifically whether I prefer to sit with Yaron or in the back, but there's no point changing seats now, we'll be there any minute.

We wait about half an hour before Dana emerges, pushing a luggage cart (with Maor inside) and trailing a suitcase on wheels. Everything inside and around her is sealed and orderly. Except for her hair, I don't believe she's changed, put on weight, gotten taller or anything. Only her hair seems different, dyed a lighter shade. She chatters as she approaches, presumably in the belief that we can hear her. Now I see it's really Dana. That's her smell all right, that's her face. She's come to us with her daughter. And though there's something unfamiliar there, her smile wins out.

It takes me only a minute to get used to seeing Dana again.

"Hello Meir, and hello to all of you. It's so wonderful to be with you again." Kisses all around and a special hug for Rachel, who seems to blush, while she explains something in a whisper and gropes for a question. "Hey, I'm back," she continues. "Look how Maor has grown." Maor is stepping carefully beside her, clutching some gadget that makes sounds I can't work out. "Nathan sends many compliments, many for him, that is. I'll tell you all about our trip and the plans for the next phase later, but now Maor and I are tired and hungry." Rachel whispers in my ear that maybe we should go to a restaurant, and I say aloud that we'll hurry home together now. Yaron brings the car around, loads the baggage, and drives off carefully. Since we're on our way we have to talk, especially Rachel and Dana, who bubble over with excitement. Or maybe only Rachel is excited and Dana is merely sharing the emotion, and they're both feeling wonderful. We park outside our building. Maor has fallen asleep and I volunteer to carry her up. Yaron asks where he should drive next and Rachel tells him he's confused; all of us are home now. We enter our charming apartment. I have not found out yet who's registered as owner, but I could still check, maybe even make amendments. Dana wants to know whether her key to the apartment still works and Rachel says we haven't changed the locks.

"Locked or open, everything's the same as it was." Then we walk in and Yaron asks where to put the baggage. Dana glances at Rachel and leads Yaron (who's hauling her suitcases) to the far room with the adjoining bathroom. Even here in the apartment Dana's hair looks strange to me. I don't understand why she changed it. Maybe the new color helped her somehow on the long journey. She is as beautiful as ever, though less clear to me.

The territorial division of the apartment is fast becoming evident.

"Nathan will get here whenever he gets here," says Dana, and this sounds quite clever to me. "Until we know what his plans are, I'd like to live with you." Yaron leaves the room, perhaps in order to phone Shlomo and Shahar. I, who never expected to have another woman to myself, and certainly not a married woman, am now a member of a big, happy menage.

Tonight I'll go to bed early. I have to plan ahead. It's impossible to know when Nathan will be back with new instructions for me and I must be prepared. From the bedroom I hear Rachel and Dana speaking animatedly, and also Yaron talking to Shlomo on the phone.

"What's the big deal?" Rachel and Dana ask each other. "Separate bedrooms, separate bathrooms, when we feel like it we'll eat together, read together, and talk to Meir and Yaron. Several generations under a single roof, two close and happy families. No dangerous mingling, just mutual friendship." I for one am not convinced that this is all there is to Dana's return. But since she hasn't changed her appearance (outside of the hairdo) or way of talking, and since she says she's happy living with us, I have no objection. She can do what she likes so long as Rachel agrees.

I wake up after a few hours' sleep and see that Rachel hasn't come to bed yet. I go to look for her and find her and Dana dozing in their armchairs in the living room. They must have talked a lot and fallen asleep. I wish we could go on living cozily like this. Nathan probably wonders how we're doing and will send us some sort of salary, but in any case all five of us (including Yaron and Maor) are getting along fine.

Dana stirs, perhaps because I've been watching her. She points at the slumbering Rachel, to hush me. I would have been quiet in any case, but she may have wanted to express her concern for Rachel. Now she comes to me, with barely a trace of sleep on her face, and whispers:

"It's so good to be here with you, with all of you. It was such a wonderful trip, especially the times Nathan let me go off on my own with Maor. He's a lot tenser than you realize, Meir, and it isn't easy to enjoy beautiful places like that. Well, you can see why he would be nervous, with everything he owns on the line this time. You'll hear all the details in time. I've returned earlier than expected to fill you in and prepare you for what will be required. I have here a photocopy of some rare historical material that Nathan got hold of, and you're supposed to study it carefully. But leave all that hard work for later; let's be carefree now and enjoy ourselves." She brushes her lips over my cheeks, glances at sleeping Rachel, squeezes my hand, and goes to the room we fixed up for her.

58

RACHEL TELLS ME she's pregnant and I'm excited and happy. When was the last time I was so sure of my happiness? Of course there are some things that worry me. I'm not sure how capable I am of being a father to another child. Not every child is as mature and easygoing as Yaron. This time I'll have to be more involved in raising the baby from the moment of birth; I'll have to do more than see to Rachel (and Dana) and her demands. When Rachel tells Yaron she's pregnant he kisses her with great emotion.

"I really wanted a brother or sister, but I didn't think there was any hope," he says with a laugh, then comes over to hug me. He squeezes me tighter, lifts me off the floor, and says he won't let me down again until I swear I'll "stay the wonderful dad you are today."

Rachel and Dana have a lot to talk about, either in whispers or loudly, from one room to the next. I don't remember noisy conversations like this in the old apartment, maybe the new apartment is conducive to loud noise. Sometimes I find Rachel lying on the living-room sofa with Dana beside her sitting on a big cushion; they're talking, reading together, or even muttering strangely. Dana is becoming ever more involved in household matters and it could hardly be said that she's confining herself to the room we assigned her. Often she's the one who does the cooking for all of us, and sometimes she even asks me what I need.

"You don't mind if I fuss over you a little, do you, Meir? You deserve it. You've welcomed me into your home and you're about to bring a new child into the world. You amaze me, Meir. Look at the way our big strong Nathan has disappeared, and look at you, the one who stayed. Our faithful Meir, taking care of us, two families that need you and depend on you. I'd like to hug you, but Yaron warned me not to start anything. He claims you might fall in love with me all over again. Well, maybe I'm teasing you a little, but you're very lucky to have a wife like Rachel and a son like Yaron. Hey, why am I talking so much? I only wanted to ask you what you need. Rachel's a little under the weather, and we all have to pitch in, so I'm at your service most of the day. The rest of the time I'll be busy with Maor."

I don't have to plan everything now. Let's see what develops with Rachel's pregnancy. Yaron wants to talk to me. He says it's time we started studying seriously.

"I want a whole year to learn about Judaism from the one person who knows how to teach. That's the whole point: to learn from someone who knows." Yaron apparently means me, though I know far less than people think. "Later on I can make up my mind about what I want to do with my life," he adds. "Shlomo and Shahar's enterprising ideas can wait. It's high time for at least one person in our family to study Torah seriously. There's no way I'm going to wind up like Mom and especially you, Dad. The home you raised me in was so mixed up." Maybe Yaron is right, and of course I won't prevent him from studying.

Dana and Rachel seem to enjoy each other's company. I rarely disturb them. They like to go shopping together, especially for food, and maybe even for fun. Rachel is amazed at Dana's financial options.

"Did you see that, Meir? She has a credit card and she can buy anything she wants. It's unbelievable—Nathan letting his wife go out and spend like that. He's always been so worried about other people's spending. Remember the way he would ask Rina for weekly reports?" And then I hear her talking directly to Dana: "You mean to say you can buy anything you want? Just walk in and sign? I guess Nathan is more in love with you than I thought."

Perhaps Dana is expecting more help from me with Maor. Maor is undoubtedly a very sweet and lovely child. Sometimes she seems to be smiling a deep and knowing smile at me. Not just when I act funny or when we play. It could be a smile of shared thoughts, though I'm not sure Maor really needs me. And a little nap wouldn't hurt me. I don't always have to be doing something, working within a clear-cut framework. I could just sit peacefully in my chair and watch the city from up here. I could rest a lot more, and not always have to listen or answer the questions they ask me. I'm in the mood to relax in one room or another. If they want, I'll move to another room; if they want, I'll go rest in the corner. It's perfectly clear now that there's no need for me to get involved in what's going on in this big apartment.

This evening Dana is all excited when I find her, and then Rachel hurries in too.

"Nathan's on the phone, he misses me," Dana tells Rachel, who blushes with pleasure. "He wants to know how you're doing and when Maor will start to learn new things."

"And what does he say about me?" asks Rachel (and I'm surprised).

"He says *mazel tov* on your pregnancy," Dana replies.

Yaron comes in and asks if I would also like to talk to Nathan. This doesn't seem necessary so I mumble something in reply and leave the room. Suddenly Dana comes after me and asks that I come to the phone right away.

"Listen to Nathan's voice. He sounds awfully strange to me. You've known his voice longer than any of us—please tell me what's going on." I pick up the receiver and listen. He sounds a little weary, and a little distant. For as long back as I can remember, he always was a heavy breather.

"The time has come for you to join me," he says. "When was the last time you took a trip abroad? You don't have anything really important going on over there, do you?" This is pretty exciting. Nathan desires my presence. It'll be an exhausting trip no doubt, but I'll ask if Yaron can come along.

"Could Yaron join us, perhaps? That would make all the difference to me," I say and Nathan agrees.

"Great idea, both of you can visit me in London. Dana will see to your plane tickets and a little foreign currency for you. You'd better hurry, though. I may soon put a limit on her credit cards to cut expenses."

Yaron is happy. He says this will be his last chance to travel before he's busy with his pencil-pushing army job or his religious studies.

"And we can be back before Mom gives birth. I don't know about you, Dad, but I want to be here the week the baby's due. I'm so excited." He hugs me, and once again it seems that he's lifted me off the ground. "What a beautiful apartment you've given us. Thanks to you, Dad, everything's wonderful!"

I tell Rachel about the trip.

"You know that some day I'd like for us to go together. But it wouldn't hurt Yaron to have some time alone with you, especially now. For the few weeks you're away, Dana and I will raise the two babies, the one already born and the one that's due." And she laughs merrily at her own joke.

DANA SAYS it's time to study the material she brought me.

"Actually, Nathan asked me to stay with you so I can make sure you arrive well prepared and in top condition. I agreed, of course. I enjoy being with you, even when there's no special purpose."

She unlocks her briefcase and shows me a file. Nathan, she says, insisted that I read it before she does.

"Here you'll find a photocopy of one of Europe's most valuable manuscripts. Nathan will fill you in on all the details. It's a sort of memoir written by the king of France while he was imprisoned in England in the fourteenth century. For some reason, that period of time the king spent in prison is very exciting to Nathan. He believes this will lead him to a revolutionary, new interpretation of the last two hundred years. It contains the essence of the complex Anglo-French relations—and, as you know, only what happens in these two countries really arouses his curiosity."

I listen to Dana and wonder why I'm not bewildered. It's true that Nathan alluded several times to a historical trend that had preoccupied him, but I had no idea he was investigating a rare manuscript written by the king of France himself. Dana says I should take a few hours to sit and concentrate on the photocopies.

"I know you're not used to this anymore. Don't take offense, Meir, I'm only following Nathan's instructions. Just think, this is only a small part of a very large manuscript. If you like, we can ask Rachel to join us, so she won't suspect we're whispering secrets about her or her pregnancy." Suddenly she's smiling at me again.

We rouse Rachel from her nap and she asks us to call Yaron and wait for him to get here. I can't understand why she's so worked up. Maybe she's worried that Nathan is about to change something in our convenient situation. An hour or so later Yaron arrives and Dana spreads out the numbered pages (to facilitate the reading). She explains that Nathan hired a famous scholar to translate the king's medieval French text into Hebrew. She will read the Hebrew translation out to us.

"I myself have been taking French lessons, but Nathan said you were never particularly good at foreign languages, Meir."

From the Diary of the King of France, Interned on English Soil

I saved Paris and forfeited my honor. The English have not yet fathomed my method. For them, a king is victorious, he dies, or else he stays home with his women instead of going off to war. I understood we would lose the battle this time—and if so, I thought, why not lose forthwith? Who needs the conflagrations and the corpses and the ruin of stately homes? I prevented their destruction by simply surrendering. Like a banquet that ends with the guests on their feet, like a crown prince who will never be king. And what will they fight for, now that they have me? With the king in their hands, they need not conquer his land.

I have never liked fighting, and it is not at all clear to me why people expect their kings to fight. I am obliged only to plan the battles, not to know the details. But the English prince enjoys every minute of the fray. "The Black Prince," they call him, and there is nothing more interesting to him than winning a battle. But what he really wants from me, I still don't know. His father, the English king, does not understand him very well. He could never conquer France. A castle, perhaps, and then another castle, but even if he sets a whole region on fire, France will remain as indifferent to him as to my own barely acceptable sovereignty.

There is another possibility. Perhaps their entire military campaign was designed merely for the purpose of capturing me. They knew in advance that I would fight in the company of my sons in order to give our soldiers the pleasure of watching us. And the English wanted to capture me and humiliate our army and our knights. They know that a genuine monarchy exists in France alone. This is their greatest source of envy, for in England the king is no longer a full-fledged monarch. He must consider the motley representatives of the people. They planned to take me to London as a reminder of how a real monarch behaves. They wanted to parade an unmistakable king through their streets in order to tempt the English people back to a strong monarchy.

How will our ensuing battles look? (The other kings of Europe are fearful that we shall stop the war and turn against them instead.) I decided to understand the English from within. From here I believed I could learn at last why they wish to conquer France, or at least how I can defeat them once and for all. But I have been in England these seven months and have made little progress. Every morning one of the English courtiers comes in to bring me news, how much ransom money my son, the prince, has managed to collect so far, and how the parleying between our two armies proceeds. Why all this talk between the English and those of my servants who remained in France? For I am here, am I not? Only talks with me may be considered talks with France. France has moved to England with me, and they do not understand this yet.

I am rarely invited to visit the English king. He has appointed a reasonable staff for me; they even do their best to prepare tasty food (although they don't know how to blend aromas or cut their bread and legumes properly. Anything to do with knives or sharpness is somewhat bewildering to them). The king refrains from seeing me, so far as possible. Perhaps he expects me to initiate a meeting, but I am his guest after all, his prisoner, and the obligation to invite me rests on him. Perhaps he despises me. It is because of me, after all, that his son has gone off to war. Or perhaps he fears me, for it is no simple matter for England to sustain two kings. I see clearly that a few more years of prison will enable me to claim that I too have sovereign rights here—not merely English rights in France, but also French rights in London.

I have spoiled everything for them. I surrendered before the war had even started in earnest. I gave them many a battle but no major war. I imagine that most of my French subjects despise me for surrendering. They would have preferred for me to die in battle. They do not realize that my surrender saved many of them and limited the destruction. But the question persists, in what respect am I still their king? In that I saved them? In that they must purchase my freedom at an exorbitant price? Or in that they besiege me with requests and consultations? Or in that I was once their king?

And what does a king like me do in captivity? He eats less than one would expect, takes pleasure in his daily promenade, sleeps only toward dawn, argues much with memory, speaks with the English advisers appointed to me. I spoiled the war for them and in revenge they have spoiled the detention, rendered my exile a strange ennui, a minor humiliating shame, a banal life for a king. They refuse me nothing: neither meetings with anyone I wish to see (except for the English king himself, though I daresay he too will one day change his ways), nor special foods from France, nor women, nor even the letters sent to me by my sons. Perhaps they hope I will remain here permanently—or on the contrary, perhaps, they are afraid my captivity has failed and desire me to quit here at once.

A few hours of the week I spend writing my thoughts down. I imagine they will leave them here forever, as a strange proof of their victory. I retell my present occupations, for myself; I summarize the years of my reign, and I plan the remainder of my kingship in France and my victory in war. I shall be victorious by dint of this diary. There are simple men who keep diaries and dream of one day being king, and there are kings such as I who learn to rule through their memoirs. I realize now that what I am writing here is of the utmost consequence, for everything I note will become an official memory of France. Every battle will be taught according to my description thereof, every law will be interpreted according to my words. There is enough in my meager accomplishments to sanction a long reign, and I can write a great many words about a small number of deeds.

It is not clear to me how long Europe will remain unique in the world. If the French and English fail to make ready, other forces are liable to arrive on the scene. One day we may set off to conquer new lands and discover that they are conquering us instead. I wish to prepare myself for this. Apart from the king of England and I (and a few others possibly), no one can put Europe in readiness. I am amused at talk of "development" and "advisers." A handful of individuals (two or three kings at most, a small number of others) embody all thought and all development.

I am fed up. It bores me to think about my accomplishments. I shall ask the English to introduce me to more interesting types, they have a few such thinkers here. Perhaps they will even allow me to journey to the Holy Land. I want to learn about places everywhere. Meanwhile, I am a little melancholy: my country is getting along perfectly well without me, and the English are indifferent to my presence here. If I returned today, it would be difficult for me to reign. Why must I, of all people, build and decide? Most people shrink from making decisions and I have to make them every day—yet it is no longer clear to me how one decides. . . . It would be better for me to concentrate on my release. I must conserve my strength. The main thing is, who to bribe, who to mislead. And those who fail must be destroyed. This time I will not surrender. Those who oppose me in France shall be put to death.

I shall urge the English king to prepare a master plan. Henceforth this diary will be devoted to sweeping suggestions: How to divide Europe anew. What the limitations on future wars will be (it may be determined, for instance, that in no case will fighting persist for a period exceeding half a year). What attitude toward the Jews is proper. What is the rightful seat of the papacy. Perhaps a common school will be established for the princes of various realms. Why shouldn't they be educated together? We kings are not inclined to spend much time with our sons.

They have just informed me that tomorrow there will be news. The king's adviser is coming to bring me up to date. They urge me to rest well, as there will be difficult decisions to make. They ask what I wish to eat for supper and if I wish to take my evening promenade. They tell me that messages from my palace have been received and will be delivered to me once they have been perused. They hint that my face looks gaunt, that I am not fastidious about my toilette. They say they are very fond of me, that they will always be grateful for my surrender. What they fail to see is that I will defeat them from here. They took Paris away from me and are making me forget my palace, but if they keep me here a few more years all will be confounded. Just as I spoiled the war for them by surrendering, I shall spoil my captivity with this dangerous writing.

I'm fed up. They were right, those who doubted my sovereignty and called me weak. Enough of this. From now on there is no reason why I should not be, even in captivity, preoccupied with myself. Yes, if the French wish it, I shall continue as their king, but only as a man preoccupied with himself, I am sick of everyone else. They have spoiled my diary now. The English asked me to let them go over it page by page.

"We will copy it out for you in a fair hand. Your royal script is unclear," they say to me. "We have special scribes here to copy the words of a king." I oblige them, of course, and when they return the pages to me for proofing, and I always find at least one mistake. Like a secretary who is afraid to complete his copying lest he be dismissed, or like a woman in love who fears her solitude, they transcribe the pages of my diary with a few mistakes each time, a line skipped or even a changed word or two. At first I believed they wanted to torture me, humiliate me, force me to stop writing my memoirs. But now I think otherwise: the scribe is worried that I shall finish too soon. He always wants to leave himself more work to do, to increase my dependence on him. This is the only way he knows to underscore his service to me, and who wouldn't wish to serve a king such as I?

But they fear other things as well. What if my memoirs should turn out to be a unique historical document? Ultimately, of the long war they have won thus far, only the words that I have penned will survive, and this is what counts. Not victory, territory, or soldiers—only the written word. This I learned from the Jews. For them, it is not territory that matters; I know about their commentators who have settled in my country and live at home in an independent and completely separate world of written words.

Who knows how much longer kings like me will reign in the world: beware, there will be weaker and crueler ones. One day when no one else was around, that tutor Father stuck me with said: "Power you will have in any case. Let me teach you weakness. There is so much of it in all of us that, if I acquaint you with only a small part, your reign will long endure." I was surprised, of course, even astounded. But what has he to do with me, or with this diary I am trying to write now? I cannot dismiss one servant without regret, not an hour goes by without pining for my Paris. It is well that I have a new way of thinking, which I learned here in England. According to it, I alone can drive myself mad. Things happen, and I, strange king that I am, imagine myself to be both acting and reacting, making a difference and influencing the course of events. Like a leaf on a tree, that either clings or falls, or a tune that is forgotten or noted down, or the sea which either drowns you in a vortex or lies becalmed, so is man in this life, and all else is fancy. Just as a leaf may (or may not) fall, so things occur in the world and I in my folly attempt to grasp my part in them.

But enough of this. I must not lose my sanity. Something in me is through with writing for today, and besides, I am loath to overwork the English scribe. My writing will astound them—wait until they come upon my discourse on women, my meditation on whether I have any interest in them. Meanwhile I should rest. Perhaps the king of England will invite me to the hunt, to a game of chess, to go walking, or to endure some torture. Only now does he begin to understand that France has not been defeated; only now does he realize that I am here alone, like an anonymous song everyone is humming.

We shall be king again one day: we shall speak in the plural, prepare our lists of traitors, and levy new taxes on all the misers of the realm. I know these things, but one problem remains—a problem of medical diagnosis, I would call it. But how shall we carry out this diagnosis? I know that the world is afflicted with a disease of the heart, but I cannot tell when it overtook me. I know that there is treason in my country, but not when I was made its target. I know that catastrophes befall us but not if my present circumstance is one of them. I know history tells of a king who lost his country but not if I am he.

It is fortunate that France is so dispersed, with its many villages, feuds, forces, foods, and shores. Who are these English, who believe they will defeat us, or me? Beware of new ideas, and of the attempt to muster forces. I love dispersed countries, which do not come to an end so quickly. Other madmen will prefer to concentrate everything into a single city, a single street, or even one house. They will invent a kind of mechanism—so vast that it really will be possible to vanquish an entire country. When the populace leaves the open spaces for the swarming cities, it will be possible to overwhelm and close down an entire nation.

I alone of all the kings of Europe am a captive. They sit on their thrones while I am a stranger in a strange city. But from this moment on everything will change. They cannot hurt any more: once they are rid of me, I will be impervious to threats. I believe that at last the English have lost their will to go out and conquer France. Having captured me, what more can they hope to find there? So I must tend to my own affairs, my royal responsibilities. I keep health records, ascertain which foods suit me and which do not, while I think ahead to other times, other ways of educating my pampered sons. I concern myself with rest, with my digestion, with the witty writers of Paris, and with soothing music. There is much to do in my present circumstances, and there are so many plans and notes to prepare. Because I alone have been deposed and I alone remain. And now, my dear strange English people, as you read these notes you will understand that our war has just begun. You will find me and I will find you, we will marry and fight and kill and kiss, and one day your island will be joined to our land.

60

DANA READ ALOUD to us from the memoirs of the king of France for several hours uninterrupted. From time to time Yaron would pick up a page and stare at it in amazement, while Rachel stared at her belly and I watched Dana's face for a clue.

Rachel is the first to respond:

"I'm a little worried about this. Nathan has gone too far. He wants to interfere in historical processes that have nothing to do with us." But Dana only smiles and starts pacing around the room to release the strain and oppression.

"Believe me, Rachel, getting pregnant at your age isn't any less radical than this project of Nathan's. He only wants to possess a particular manuscript, and to feel he is the owner of the most precious thing that one can imagine." Dana goes to Rachel and strokes her hair. "Where did you ever find such a sensitive woman?" she asks, indicating Rachel. "Do you have any idea how wonderful she is?" I hear her but am hard pressed to understand what she means. Rachel is excited, she takes Dana's hand (which is busy stroking her hair), and she clasps it with some fervor. They seem more intimate than I realized. I am surprised, especially since Rachel does not usually let anyone stroke her hair or touch her in general.

"One thing is clear," says Yaron. "This time we're talking about a plan Nathan has been working on for some years without our knowledge. He diverted our attention to other matters, while he went ahead with his secret plans. So what do you say, Dad?" he says, turning to me. "Do we go? Nathan invited us both, but it depends on you." For some reason the three of them are looking at me now and I answer in an almost normal voice that, if I agreed to join Nathan in London before, why should I change my mind now that I've heard more of the details? Meanwhile, I think I should rest—maybe I'll read Nathan's precious manuscript over myself this time.

Yaron helps me choose suits for the trip and it seems I've put on more weight than I thought. He takes me out to shop for a matching tie, but I'd rather not. He makes lists of what to pack and what we'd do better to buy in London. He asks Rachel (and Dana too, I believe) what they want us to bring them, and he promises a surprise for Maor. He shows me a map of London but then remembers that I have difficulty orienting myself with maps. Yaron has a store of information about food and kosher restaurants. He asks if we should tell anyone about the trip, and whether there's anything important that he should know.

"It's time you confided in me. There are matters I should be aware of before we leave. Like your health, Dad, or Mom's, or even mine. Maybe you have debts you're afraid to mention. And of course any details about Nathan that might help us. I don't believe he invited us there just to show us around London."

"I think you know everything I do, Yaron," I answer with a measure of truthfulness. "No area of this apartment is unknown to you, and there are very few conversations you haven't heard."

Dana and Rachel read to each other the night before our departure. Rachel pulls my head down to her belly, asks me to remember what's inside it, and to be careful. Dana asks Yaron if she can kiss him, but he prefers not. Both of them have prepared little going-away presents for us. Dana also gives me an envelope full of letters to deliver to Nathan.

"All the letters I wrote him but was too lazy to mail. Now he'll get them all at once. I bet Nathan will love my innovation."

Yaron and I fly to London. He falls asleep on the plane and I doze. Then we play Twenty Questions and reminisce about Yaron's childhood. Now I think he wants me to tell him about that interesting trip to the Galilee, and if possible about the time I was seriously ill, but I find it difficult to answer and prefer to glance around without the memories.

The moment we land, Yaron's plans are set in motion: we know where to go, how to get there, and at which hotel we have reservations.

"I know, Dad, it takes you time to get used to new places—Mom told me. That's why I made a list of everything we'd need." I wonder if we have an appointment with Nathan yet, but I'll probably find out about that soon enough. I used to find it difficult to fall asleep when plans were left up in the air, but nowadays I concentrate on the pillow beneath my head. It isn't necessary to look at the person you're talking to. It isn't necessary to answer every time someone asks a question. It isn't necessary to correct their every mistake. It isn't necessary to relax in order to fall asleep. I know these things.

Nathan's apartment is on a pleasant street with a large park nearby, I believe. The trees in London are unfamiliar and I ask Yaron to stop from time to time so we can look at them. I used to believe each tree had one trunk, but now I see they each have several trunks, and some don't even reach the ground.

It is Henri who opens the door for us. I didn't realize Nathan had brought him along. Henri hugs Yaron, shakes my hand, and smiles amiably.

"Everything's ready for you," he says, and I clearly have no idea what he means. He leads me to a large room where Nathan is standing. "Look who's here," he says in a booming voice. "My two friends." He squeezes our hands with much warmth and stares into my eyes, maybe he'll find a few tears there. He looks pretty good in that old bathrobe, (I think it used to belong to his father). He smells nice too, like another piece of furniture in this impressive room. He leads us in, draws the curtains, and displays a magnificent mirror.

"This is the greatest treasure I have left. The most expensive painted mirror in all of Europe! I've checked with the connoisseurs and there can be no doubt about it. They're going to verify it for me formally. See what's been painted on this mirror, a woman lifting a baby, and they both keep changing. First the woman looks big and the baby is tiny and then the baby gets big and the woman shrinks. You can't tell where their limbs are—it's simply astounding!"

Henri joins us. Then he goes out and comes back with refreshments and fruit, some juice, and biscuits in an unopened packet.

"How's Dana? Does she miss me or is she doing okay with the two of you?" Nathan says suddenly and surprises us. Yaron blushes and looks at me. "Is someone around here still in love with her?" Nathan turns to me directly, and in response I emit a strange sound from my throat, or maybe from my brain.

"Getting down to business so soon, Nathan?" I answer. "You know we're not concerned with new love now."

"I have no idea what you mean," Nathan hastens to reply, "But I don't have to understand to enjoy talking with you."

We sit down. I'm a little cold and Yaron asks whether he should get my coat. Nathan says this is the only weather that suits this place. He asks Henri to fetch us an old album. He beckons us closer,

"Sit on either side of me, I won't hurt you." He looks older, like someone with an impending disease who is losing his vitality. With trembling hands he opens the album, points to a family picture. "This is my father when he was studying abroad. Snazzy dresser, wasn't he? And here I am playing with him. Soon you'll see Mother—I probably resemble her more than you imagined. And here's one of Rina as a young girl. Did you think I forgot her? She's the woman who bore my two sons, and a fairly interesting woman. How funny that I have a picture of Rina as a young girl here—I guess she just pasted it unobtrusively in the album. You never knew with her. And that's me playing something, I don't know what. Here I'm grown up. And that's me as a student at the world's finest university. Notice the details, see how similar I look to myself today. And those clothes, I've always had good taste." He leafs through the album, explaining everything with Henri's assistance, and checking on us to make sure we look and listen attentively. It's strange to have arrived in London only to look at Nathan's photo album and listen to Henri prompting him on various details. How many times did he hear Nathan's descriptions before he attained so much knowledge? It would be interesting to know, but I'll think about it later. Nathan leans over the pictures and renders a detailed account of who the photographer was, who was there but not included in the picture, and what they were talking about. Yaron seems to be dozing off and I too need rest, so I ask Nathan if we can continue a little later, maybe tomorrow. Henri hurries over, to help with our coats, and orders a cab for us.

At the hotel I start wondering if I miss Rachel, or maybe Dana and Maor as well, so I quickly call them. Rachel sounds cheerful and energetic. She initiates some questions, doesn't complain, says she's happy about our trip, states that "it's important for the two of you to spend time together," and talks about her pregnancy.

"See, you're not the only one who's alone with one of our children," she says. Now Yaron speaks to Rachel. He reports a few details about our trip, tells Dana about Nathan and says the situation "appears unclear." I worry about statements like this. But Yaron said it, and I won't interfere.

Yaron prefers to eat what we brought from home in our hotel room. He is not eager to "sit among all those people eating strange food." I hope I get over my confusion so I'll be able to concentrate on the purpose of the trip. Henri calls to ask when we'll be back, and Yaron says we've barely had a chance to rest. They make an appointment for our next visit. Yaron lies down, reads a book, and falls asleep as I look on lovingly. This is my son, before my eyes, I have no doubt.

61

WE SET OUT for Nathan's again. I thought we might walk there, but Yaron said maybe next time. Nathan opens the door himself.

"Hello, hello," he says, "it's about time." Nathan invites us into his cluttered study. He asks what we know about European history, and about French history in particular. I try to recall a few facts. Before I can answer him Nathan takes out a variety of journals, books, pictures, and diagrams. "We're talking about the fourteenth century," he says," when wars were interesting. Wars that lasted for decades or longer, with all the paraphernalia that went with them. Not like the cold destructive warfare of our day." Yaron is not pleased. He tells Nathan that war is a curse however it is fought, acceptable only when there's no other option, and even then it's difficult. Nathan listens attentively, but says there's no time to argue now, we have to get back to business.

"You haven't come to London for your education. I'm going to focus on what's essential: in the mid-fourteenth century, as usual, France is beset with internal struggles. Enemies of the king turn to the English, who land in Cherbourg. The heroic "Black Prince" sets off on a campaign of conquest from Bordeaux to the French heartland. The ultimate battle takes place in the region of Poitiers. The bloodshed is immense, the organizational principle fails, and at a certain point the English soldiers come upon King Jean of France. He has no choice but to surrender alongside many of his officers, who are either killed or taken captive. But as you already know, my main interest is in this king of France. He was captured and sent to England, where he was imprisoned at several sites. The English demanded a huge sum of money for his ransom, and colossal efforts were made to raise it. King Jean even sold his daughter as a bride for a handsome price to the family of the viscount of Milan. His exile lasted four years, and this is the period that fascinates me. It seems that the king kept a diary during this period. My most important goal is to get that diary."

Now Nathan looks at us—though more at Yaron, it seems to me. Henri runs and brings in sweets for us; Yaron glances at them but doesn't take any yet.

"Don't worry, don't worry," Henri whispers to me. "Nathan has no bad intentions." Nathan gazes at him with emotion, possibly having overheard.

"I always wanted to be best at something," he explains in a loud voice. "It didn't matter what. The best pianist in the world, the best opera singer, even the best chef. But people always got in my way or else I got in my own way. That's why I've been preparing myself for something different these past few years: I am going to buy the most fascinating manuscript in existence. Do you understand the significance of a captive king? Do you realize what it means to engage in war when the king is no longer in command and has been captured by his greatest enemy? Like music to deaf ears, like a country without territory, like me now that most of my property is gone."

He turns practical again and takes out the sales regulations, saying that this is privileged information, something only a few people know about—scholars and political leaders. He demands that we first sign a secrecy clause and considers asking Henri to sign even though he's already signed once. He reads the regulations to us and translates them word for word in case we don't understand. His English is excellent, although he has a peculiar accent. I am excited because it seems that something exceptional is required of us here. I never thought it would come to this. Yaron wants to know the facts and isn't interested in interpretations. Nathan is pleased with his approach. During most of the conversation he looks more at Yaron than at me. Henri says Dana is on the phone, but Nathan says he can't speak to her now. He goes through the regulations, clause by clause, and looks up facts in several encyclopedias and other books. It seems he has been busy buying books about the history of France, the wars between England and France, medieval Europe, the discovery of manuscripts, the traditions of the monarchy, and so forth. Henri runs around bringing in more information. Nathan uses a sophisticated computer to access all the major European libraries.

"So what do you think, Meir? Are we partners again?" says Nathan with a happy grin. "I have a chart here and on it are our plans with time slots for dinner breaks, a sufficient amount of sleep, and the names of two kosher restaurants that will deliver meals. If Yaron agrees, we can arrange for him and Henri to go out for a few hours and see a good soccer game." I still don't understand why Nathan needs me here. Not for my knowledge of history and languages, and certainly not for my wit, because he's superior in all those departments.

"And don't forget to check out of your hotel tomorrow. It's a waste of money. There are two comfortable couches here, so we'll be able to talk and work during the night as well. I'm hoping you two will come up with some bright ideas."

Now we come to the personal clauses: who is eligible to participate in the auction of the manuscript and what is required of every candidate. I feel a great deal of tension and am almost convinced that I'm going to get sick again. Nathan continues reading: "Every candidate must give proof of marital fidelity. Preference will be shown to contenders who are married and have children. References from spouses are advisable. Contact with children is imperative." He reads the words again, once in a whisper and then vociferously.

"What do they want?" he shouts. "Why is it any of their business?" He gets up, sweating profusely, and Henri hurries over with the cold water and lemon Nathan likes. He quickly calms down, then scrutinizes me closely, and I'm afraid. "Now you see what I want from you. A strange fellow like you, for some reason, fits their bill. Fortunately, I have you here to represent me. All I care about is succeeding. We'll prepare you really well and check every detail."

Yaron comes closer. He doesn't know whether to be angry or excited. He asks to read the auction regulations over himself. For the first time since we arrived in London I notice a change in Nathan's face. The top of his head is completely bald, all that's left is a round black fringe. He looks much more like his father than I remembered, though he's a lot bigger. Henri brings in the account books, but Nathan is annoyed.

"Not now. We're not ready for the money business yet. They

haven't even accepted us as potential buyers and you want to pay them." Henri looks at Nathan, starts to say something but thinks the better of it, and sits down in an armchair beside us, firmly and perhaps stubbornly. "Now you understand my scheme," Nathan addresses me. "All that time I let you spend in my apartment, the salary I paid you for doing nothing. I knew that one day I would need a man like you to stand up to their difficult and unreasonable criteria. A man who's never had another wife and is sure who his son is and who he isn't. A man who has slept with only one woman his whole life. If they ask you to talk about your life, the biblical passages you know by heart, and the foods you're not allowed to eat, all this will be extremely advantageous to me. I will be responsible for the remaining practical and financial matters. With most of the money I had left, I bought that painted mirror you saw—it's worth a whole lot more than you'd guess. I'm sure it will maintain its value until I exchange it for the manuscript of the king of France."

Henri is listening with intense concentration. He seems to be making mental notes. Maybe he's one of Nathan's official assistants now, or even his secretary. At this rate he's liable to make Henri manager of one of his businesses. Yaron asks permission for us to step out of the room a moment. He wants to talk to me in private. Nathan calls after him with a laugh.

"Just don't scare your father away. For once in my life I really need him." Yaron suggests that we go sit in the comfortable arm chairs. He asks if I understand Nathan's scheme and adds that in his opinion we're talking about a long procedure that could take months.

"I was planning to study, and Mom might give birth meanwhile." I look at my son and listen. Maybe I should keep quiet and let him do what he thinks best, but Nathan needs me very much now. Meanwhile we're informed that Dana's on the phone and wants to speak to me.

"Dear sweet Meir, how are you? I'm so glad you know everything now. At last you understand how important you are to Nathan. I'm sure you'll help him. Rachel and I can wait; we have plenty of patience. What you're doing is important and special, perfect for you, and no one in the world is more deserving." I ask her how everyone is, Maor mumbles a few words on the phone (as though I were her father), and with a shout Rachel sends kisses. She's resting in the bedroom now. Yaron says goodbye to Dana and returns to concentrate on me and my overdue reply.

Henri has fixed up a comfortable room for us in the apartment. It has a couch for Yaron and a couch for me, some books we may enjoy, and precooked meals. There's no need for us to stay at the hotel. Because everything we need is right here, it would be a waste of time and energy to leave now. We go to bed and I fall asleep easily with Yaron's thin, strong hand in mine. I hope to have a peaceful night dreaming of Rachel and Dana blithely smiling at me.

Early in the morning Henri calls us and brings in some photocopied pages of the manuscript.

"You can go over these until Nathan wakes up. They were distributed to prospective buyers so we would know what we're talking about." The photocopies are in French and I have difficulty reading them. Henri says he and Nathan have begun translating them and shows me what they've done so far. Yaron and I sit down on the carpet and read the first page together. In it the king of France describes his circumstances in captivity: the scarcity of servants, his meetings with the English king (and the heir apparent), his tours around London, and his opinion of the city and of the people's fashions. He speaks about the books he has been reading, the special dinners served to him, and his attendant physician. There's no reference here to France, to Paris, to the ransom money, or to his defeat in the war.

DURING THE NIGHT, Nathan wakens me in a whisper and asks me to come to his room. He wants to talk to me in private—to explain just how much everything depends on me, and how he intends to prevent me from taking advantage of this. I am astounded by his suspicions, of course, but he seems extremely agitated, whether because Dana is so far away, or because he's worried about his children. Or maybe it's because his holdings have diminished to such an extent and the most valuable possession left him is a work of art he will have to sell in order to purchase the diary of the king of France.

Nathan's room is filled with books and classical music is playing in the background. I recognize several machines that used to be in his office.

"There are fools in this world who dream of composing a masterpiece. I, in a single tour de force, am about to purchase what experts agree is the most important manuscript of the past millennium. We're talking about an uncanny analysis of French history, of the development of Europe with its various systems of government, the mystique of the monarchy, the church, and so forth. You find inspiration in the Bible, Meir, but I have the chance to acquire a unique understanding of modern history. So far as I am concerned, everything significant in the world today has its roots in European history. I'll reach the foundation of all the antiques, paintings, and musical compositions I ever collected. I will hold in my hand the key to modern man."

I'm prepared to agree quietly (he's worried that Henri will wake up now and walk in) that our goal is truly fascinating. Nonetheless, I have to ask him whether he thinks it was worthwhile risking all his property, and he responds with a dismissive wave of the hand.

"The important thing is for you to understand your special role in this, Meir. The British government has decided to put this diary up for sale. Their motive in so doing I believe is to convey the atmosphere of European unification, while signaling the debasement of those monarchies still in existence. News of the sale has not yet been made public, and only the leading collectors (like me) have been notified about it. But the English are a strange lot. They've decided that the manuscript is of national importance and should reach what they term 'worthy hands.' Since they prefer private collectors, each candidate has to demonstrate the highest moral standards, or at least what appears as such to their eyes."

He now takes a large sheet of white paper from his pocket and explains that this is his "victory list." On it he has itemized the advantages he will present to the sales committee. With great fervor, his face sweaty and worn, he declares that he'll show the British his proven record as an excellent collector.

"My antiques collection was quite impressive, my set of painted mirrors was unique, and I am currently in possession of the most valuable painted mirror in the world. Not to mention the more common collections (stamps, paintings, etc.) which have passed through my hands. Let them test me on any subject and I'll prove how much I know. No one is more knowledgeable than I about art and history." He proceeds to the next item on his "victory list":

"I am a skilled businessman and can boast of many financial triumphs. Moreover, I have a demonstrable knack of getting out of monetary crises, even the danger of bankruptcy. Why did I let Hagai involve me in the Galilee mess? So that I could bring the evidence here and show the royal commission how good I am at dealing with acute failure."

This time even I am astounded. I know that the people around me think nothing fazes me anymore, but Nathan's disclosure of his former strategies really infuriates me. I don't know if it would be a greater failure on my part to leave now or to stick with Nathan.

"And just wait, Meir," he says to me, "we'll come around to you soon and then you'll see how very important you are in all this. And now to my next advantage," he continues. "There are few private collectors who can point to such a public and political success. You may not know this, Meir, but the party I set up for you—with headquarters in your old apartment—is really doing well. I'm letting Hagai run things for now, but we'll see when the time is right to quit or make changes. You have no idea what a pleasant surprise I had from this stupid project. It kept Hagai too busy to interfere with my preliminary arrangements for purchasing the manuscript, and the English are utterly amazed by my political prowess.

"And now we come to the really crucial points. As I told you earlier, the English have decided on additional personal demands. A huge amount of money and my professional advantages are not enough for them. Even my vast historical knowledge won't satisfy them. They will weigh various characteristics, some of them totally absurd if you ask me. So here's the list I drew up for them. He points to a certain section on the page and reads aloud, tracing the words with his fleshy forefinger, carefully enunciating every letter:

> I have a pretty young wife.
>
> I have children and even a baby (Maor).
>
> I am capable of deceiving others, but I don't overdo it.
>
> I have no exaggerated loyalties either to people or ideas.
>
> I am reasonably benevolent to those who are close to me.
>
> I know how to enlist and foster the abilities of a primitive person (Henri).
>
> I can completely dominate another person (Meir).
>
> I am capable of loving a woman without succumbing to confusion (Dana).
>
> I have a faithful and virtuous friend (Meir).
>
> I know a man who has slept with only one woman (Meir).

He reads the words out slowly. I have never heard him speak at this tempo before. He is so worked up that I don't know if he can stand it, especially without Dana here. A moment ago I saw, with my own two eyes, my role defined on paper—and now I don't know how to respond, if at all. Anyone else would just beat him up and leave. But I am not convinced that Nathan's using me like this has been injurious. Of course I'll have to consult with Yaron, and maybe with

Rachel, too. It's vitally important that I know whatever Dana knows. I never thought someone like me, who merely wishes to rest, could become a means to an end. Nathan looks at me finally, smiles, and reaches for my hand, but I don't respond.

"You're one of a kind," he says. I can't help wondering why Nathan should find a couple of British experts so formidable; for me, this is mildly amusing.

63

HAVING SLEPT barely at all, we set off for our meeting with the royal commission. Nathan, Yaron, Henri, and I climb into a taxicab. From time to time, Nathan utters some explanatory words about buildings we pass on our way. I think he ate a relatively small breakfast this morning. Yaron and I just had something to drink.

The commission building is an impressive, grand old house that has recently been restored and painted a glorious white. At the entrance we are met by a representative of the commission, who leads us to an elegant and well-heated room that is illuminated by a single lamp. Several armchairs face the small desk of the three-member commission. Drinks are served and the meeting begins. Nathan himself is escorted to the middle chair and the rest of us can sit either next to him or behind him.

After a few preliminary questions about Nathan's education, his qualities, and so forth, he is asked to talk about his wives (the commissioners say "Dana" and "Rina" with an almost Hebrew ring) and his children. When they get to Rina, the three commissioners take their time. They want to know about her life, her achievements. Is it absolutely certain that she died a natural death, and can Nathan prove as much? They ask if he mourned her adequately, when and how Dana appeared on the scene, and whether there was ever tension between the two women. Nathan replies in great detail, his English fluent though heavily accented. To my surprise he blushes now and then, yet he never fails to be witty or to find analogies between his own life and the lives of the more fascinating figures in European history. At this stage he asks the commissioners to tell him a little bit about themselves (aside from their names and titles, which appear on the little name plaques on the desk). The chairperson represents the British royal family, the second man is an Oxford don, a distinguished professor of history (his field of expertise is of course the Middle Ages), and the third is a member of Parliament.

Two hours later the clerk, who met us at the entrance, walks in and announces that we will adjourn for a brief recess. Refreshments and hot drinks are served on a nearby table, and we (including the commissioners) partake of them together. The chairman chats with Yaron. He asks him about his favorite childhood games and what he thinks of English soccer. Yaron is quite knowledgeable about these things, unlike us, and seems to impress the commissioner. I speak very little but only drink a few cups of tea and feel the tension mounting in my stomach and my head.

Again we sit down, in exactly the same order as before, and this time they question Henri. They ask him about where he's from, the terms of his employment with Nathan, and whether he is treated with respect. Henri confirms everything with great seriousness and glances at us with satisfaction. Suddenly, at his own initiative, he asks the commissioners if they realize how knowledgeable Nathan is and what an exciting life he leads.

"Once I even kept a tiger in my home." The commissioners look at each other, then down at their notes, and they seem reassured to find this bit of information there.

When Henri has finished, Nathan asks permission to speak again. He stands up and inquires whether the commissioners know the full extent of his education in the United States and England. He asks whether they've heard about the priceless mirror he purchased, and whether they know any collector more knowledgeable and diversified than he. The commissioners are reluctant to answer and they ask that he sit down. Henri pats Nathan on the knee and tries to calm him. Nathan gets up again, crosses to the table to pour himself a drink of water, returns to his seat, and quietly puts his head in his hands. I have never seen him like this before and I wouldn't be surprised if he burst out crying. I appreciate how nervous he is, and my feelings of anger toward him have mellowed into empathy and friendship. The chairman now suggests that we adjourn until the same time tomorrow, and he requests that we bring several missing documents with us when we return.

"Now do you see how important this is?" Nathan asks me in the taxicab. "Whoever owns the manuscript will understand the history of Europe, and that's the only history that interests me. There is no combination more fascinating than the cultural blend of the English with the French. Every painting, antique, and political development will come alive for me. And I alone will have the privilege of deciding who may peruse the manuscript."

"Fine, Nathan, I understand what you're saying," I answer quietly.

"No, you don't understand," he shouts at me. "For the first time in my life nothing else matters to me, not even sleeping with a beautiful woman. At last I know what is important to me, everything is crystal clear—and just when this happens, I have to put up with the peculiar demands of this commission. Why do they care about my family life? Why should it be any of their business whether I'm a murderer, a rapist, or simply a liar? They should just sell me the manuscript and be done with it. I have the money and the education. Why are they torturing me? You understand this better than I do. Explain it to me, what's their motive? This psychological poking around is better suited to you, Meir, and to those notes you keep about us. Maybe you can finally be of some help to me."

Back at the apartment, Nathan goes into his room and probably passes the time playing chess with himself. When he emerges later, he eats huge quantities of the food Henri has prepared for him, barely using his fork and mainly helping himself to the food with his hands. Then he gazes a while at the painted mirror and suddenly asks if anyone wants to go out for a walk with him. Yaron is game, but I would rather stay home and phone Rachel. She seems happy to hear my voice, interested in what I say, and also fairly up to date on our doings here. She asks about Yaron and laughs softly at my vivid descriptions of the commission. After the conversation I fall asleep with my clothes on and have a nightmare that has something to do with a crime I apparently knew about but failed to report.

IN THE MORNING we reconvene for the negotiations, and Nathan uncharacteristically arrives on time again. I doubt that he slept much last night, but he looks reasonably good and gives off pleasant, unfamiliar odors. This time the commission treats us to a full breakfast, and there are even vegetarian dishes for Yaron and me. The commissioners eat and drink in moderation and I have a hunch they're scrutinizing Nathan's table manners. They ask us if we want to stay for the deliberations, because anyone who isn't testifying this morning is free to go out for a walk in the park nearby.

The chairman escorts us back to our seats and tells Nathan that there's been an important development.

"Your wife Dana is due to arrive at any moment. We asked her to fly here from Israel yesterday. It seems to us that you'll be more relaxed and do better with your wife beside you. Moreover, we're interested in hearing some details directly from her lips."

Nathan glances at me and, all at once, his weaknesses burst forth on his face: his obesity, his somnolence, his increased tendency to sweat, his shortness of breath, and some irksome, unfamiliar pain. When we hear a short knock on the door we know who's there. Dana enters, bright and happy. She kisses Nathan on the head and shakes my hand. She smiles at Yaron and says hello to Henri. The commissioners stand up and hurry to bring a comfortable chair for her, tripping over each other in their alacrity. Dana sits down, smiling pleasantly at them, and says she's ready for anything. The historian asks if she would prefer that any of us leave the room while she's testifying.

"Embarrassing information may come to light," he says, but Dana answers that she's perfectly comfortable with all of us here.

"Everyone I love is here, except for my daughter Maor and my friend Rachel. I have nothing to hide from them."

The questions start: In your judgment, does Nathan understand the importance of the manuscript in question? Is he capable of safeguarding it? Of never trading it? Does he really devote as much time to its study as he claims? How easily is he seduced by money and beautiful women? I listen to these questions in a state of suspense. I'd prefer to leave the room now; this inquiry is making me ill. Nathan looks at me sternly, for he clearly wants me to stay. Dana meanwhile answers the questions succinctly and with a smile.

"My Nathan has done everything possible to buy this manuscript from you. Whatever he lacks in trustworthiness or sensitivity, Meir and I can fill in for him," she says, glancing at Nathan and even winking at him.

Now the commissioners ask Dana about herself. Did she contrive to marry Nathan? Is this why she came to work for him? What was her relationship to Rina? Is Meir thoroughly resigned to her marriage? Dana responds in reasonable English. This time her answers are even more succinct, but they seem a little ambiguous to me. The chairman suggests that we adjourn until tomorrow. He cautions Dana to speak with us as little as possible tonight—"We recommend that you sleep at a hotel rather than your apartment though we don't wish to make things difficult for you"—in order to be free of undue pressure and influence.

When we leave the building this time I feel quite cold, and Yaron's arm around me barely helps at all. Dana suggests that we stop at a restaurant on our way. Yaron offers me some honey candies for strength. Dana kisses his face with a new intimacy. Henri asks Nathan what we should do and Nathan ponders quietly. He's wearing a heavy gray coat (he usually dresses more lightly, even when the weather turns cold).

"Tell me, what are they hiding there? What did this king of France write that they're so afraid of exposing? Maybe he's proven the futility of war. Or demonstrated that nothing is achieved even by capturing a king. I must have the manuscript. Only from this can one fathom the meaning of absolute triumph and total domination."

Henri remembers to say that, on his way out, the commissioners handed him two additional pages. Instantly Nathan grabs them from his hands.

"What are you good for if you forget the important things?" He steps into a nearby café (followed by the rest of us), sits down, shouts at Dana to order him "a few main courses," turns to the pages before him, and begins to read. Suddenly he chuckles. "This should interest you, Meir," he says. "Even here your religious Jews have an influence. The king of France talks about the survival of the Jewish People without a government or territory. He says they take their sovereignty wherever they go, rolled up in parchment scrolls. That's exactly what it says here, and this they give me to read? I don't understand what they want from me."

This evening we all stay home. Dana calls us to the dinner table and once again her fragrance rules the apartment and my consciousness. Nathan comes to the table bathed and groomed, and he smiles at us with affection.

"Meir, you know I've got some complaints against you. Many things in your life are enigmatic to me, even absurd. But this time, there's no doubt about it, you've shown your worth at last."

"Thanks a lot, Nathan," I reply, uncertain whether indignity or satisfaction dictates my response. But Nathan continues.

"And if you're still a little bit in love with my Dana, don't worry. Some day we can work that out, too." He then takes his place at the head of the table, and Dana, without uttering a word, peers strangely first at him and then at me. Henri's deep black eyes bulge and Yaron sits down in the empty chair beside me.

We start to eat and Dana, perking up, tells us what's been happening in Israel since we left. Maor is getting bigger and Rachel is wonderful.

"You have a wonderful wife, Meir," she says to me. Later, when dessert is served, she says it's time she too learned something about history and the Bible. Nathan asks her if she's ready for her testimony before the commission tomorrow and orders us all to get ready right away.

When we arrive at the commission the next morning, Dana insists that we stay in the waiting room while she goes in alone. Nathan, surprisingly, doesn't object (maybe he's afraid to make her angry right before she testifies) and tells her to call him in if necessary. Dana enters the room, Nathan sits down, dozes intermittently, and browses through some scholarly journals he brought along.

Three hours later they call us in. Dana smiles at us from her seat next to the commissioners' table. The chairman informs us that I will be the next to testify and that they have agreed to let Dana do the questioning.

"We understand there is a special closeness between the two of you and that you are a rather sensitive and vulnerable man, Meir. We have no objection to Dana's examining you, although, if necessary, we shall fill in the gaps with questions of our own." They ask me in which language I wish to answer (English or Hebrew) and Nathan whispers that I should answer in English.

"I prefer your mistakes to the translator's distortions. I don't trust him."

Dana opens with an overview touching on my family, Rachel and Yaron, and what she's heard from Nathan and others about my childhood, my upbringing, my studies, and the relationship between Nathan's father and my own. She duly mentions my bout of illness, the Galilee trip, and of course, various tasks I have carried out on Nathan's behalf "in matters of business, family, friendship, and even the excellent care of our baby." I assume that matters more closely related to her and Nathan, like Rina and the tiger, have been fully covered in her own testimony. She now addresses me and asks me to answer in brief:

Are you loyal to Nathan?

Yes.

Is it true that you fell in love with me but have gotten over it for the sake of your wife Rachel?

Yes it is.

Did you bring your son Yaron up to be decent?

I hope so (for the first time there's a smile on my face as well as a slight trembling in my knees).

What will you do if we get the manuscript?

Try to make sure Nathan doesn't sell it and also see that every major scholar has access to it.

Are you yourself interested in the manuscript?

Only a little. I prefer to read other things.

Such as?

Nothing very unusual. Just the Bible or *Midrashim* (I say the word in Hebrew, and for the benefit of the commission it is translated as "commentaries").

Is it your opinion—as the one who knows him best—that Nathan can be relied upon to keep his word?

Nathan can be expected to keep his promises when it is in his best interest to do so—a case in point being his present determination to acquire the manuscript by the king of France. (I am pleased with my cautious phrasing).

Will you stay with your wife and children forever?

That is my wish.

And why, in your opinion, are we asking you all these questions?

Perhaps in order to amuse yourselves with a funny little fellow like me (I say this somewhat facetiously).

Suddenly Dana stops questioning me. They bring light refreshments of sandwiches, fruit, and juice. I eat only a banana. I feel the need to call Rachel. I ask the chairman if I may, he deliberates a moment and then consents. Rachel isn't home, but one of Nathan's sons (I can't tell which) answers.

"Rachel's fine. We're looking after her and little Maor and waiting to hear good news from you."

When we return to the apartment we hardly speak. It seems to me that Henri's dressed a little outlandishly (a part of him has reverted to those early days at Nathan's, when he was charged with minding the tiger), and he keeps jumping all over the place. Nathan says my testimony wasn't half bad, and that maybe we can hope for a bit of progress.

"I'm sick of being interrogated. Believe me, I'd snatch that manuscript out of their hands and bolt, if I could, though naturally I'd send them the money later."

Yaron and I retire to our room, sit down on the bed, and read from the Book of Judges. I feel a chill so I ask Yaron to shut the window all the way and cover me (the way I used to cover him when he was small) and to make me a cup of tea. Both my location and my thoughts seem very strange to me. Dana walks in (dressed to go out though it's the middle of the night).

"I just wanted to say that you're both sweethearts, and don't let Nathan's irritability upset you. He's determined not to botch things up this time, so I'm sure he won't do anything silly in front of the commission." I fall asleep and dream about some obscure but terrible crime to which I am an accomplice, and this, I am clearly aware, means that my life has come to an end.

65

BEFORE DAWN Dana wakes me in a whisper. She helps me dress, and I tremble all over just as I did when I was ten years old and my parents cast doubt on my trustworthiness. Dana rubs a pleasant ointment on the back of my neck, combs my hair (something I don't usually do), takes my hand and leads me to the bathroom. She finds my electric razor and shaves my face carefully and thoroughly. Her own face is beautiful and hard now. We leave the apartment unobserved by other eyes. A car is waiting for us below, and we get in the back together and the driver whisks us away. It's morning but the cold and the confusion still affect how I feel. We arrive at the commission (I recognize the building relatively fast for me). Dana leads me through a maze of corridors into a large library where several people are sitting at a table (among them at least two members of the commission) drinking and reading.

Suddenly I see Rachel there too. Conspicuously pregnant by now, she stands up with effort to greet me,. We embrace a moment and she whispers that she's come to stand beside me at this crucial time in my life. The chairman asks me to sit down and says he'd like to introduce me to the larger panel of experts and officials. For their sake he will repeat some of the questions regarding personal matters that were raised yesterday. Another member poses some general questions about Israel and then asks to what extent my knowledge of other fields ("including Judaism, of course," he says) is professional and thorough. I admit that my education is fairly limited but here Dana interrupts and says there is no one more cautious and loving than I.

Before our eyes the panel votes and the chairman announces the decision.

"Meir appears to be a perfectly nice man, faithful to his wife and family by and large, though we had expected to see more strength in him, something on the order of Nathan's libido without the dissipation. Nathan himself is both wealthy and capable and we feel we can recommend the transfer of the manuscript into his caretaking, with certain restrictions. We shall draw up a list of these and send them to you as soon as possible. It is clear, for example, that Nathan will have to obtain Meir's approval before he can put the manuscript to any use whatsoever. Nathan will be required, likewise, to send us annual reports about the progress of his research on the manuscript."

The British men rise, followed by Dana, Rachel, and me. The chairman kisses Dana on the cheek and shakes our hands. An envoy of the commission escorts us to the car. Nathan, Henri, and Yaron await us at the apartment. They are fully awake by now, though it's still early. I think Yaron has been crying (maybe he was worried to find me gone), Nathan is leafing through an art book, and Henri is polishing the painted mirror. Dana reports briefly on the events of the morning. Yaron embraces me (though he's still angry about my absence), Nathan folds his hands over his belly, reflects a moment, sits down, and says he wants to think in private.

"Great idea," Rachel says. "At long last Meir will have some peace."

Rachel, Yaron, and I leave the room together. I embrace Rachel and kiss her on the mouth, and she holds her hand out to me somewhat lethargically (maybe she's still fatigued after the long trip from Israel).

"See, Meir? We're all here. I missed you and Yaron, and I also wanted you to see my gigantic belly." Her voice is calm and sweet.

Yaron suggests that we leave the apartment and I agree, though I'm not sure about the weather—the temperature, or even the light. We put on our coats, Yaron suggests that I wear a scarf, and then the three of us go out for coffee. When Yaron suggests that we smoke a cigarette, I agree though I'm afraid I'll get a headache, and Rachel is not pleased but says nothing. Suddenly she asks how Nathan would have reacted if the commission had refused.

"Do you think he and Henri would have been capable of stealing the manuscript?" Yaron asks.

"And what would you have done, if so?" Rachel asks. I tell them I have been asked too many questions in the past few days and I'd like to drop the subject, and Rachel says we have to hurry if we want to get back to Israel in time.

"That much, at least, is clear to the three of us."

After a brief silence, we recall the charms of London and Rachel tells us all about childbirth.

"Do you remember anything about Yaron's birth, Meir?" she wonders aloud. Yaron says he's homesick and that he can't wait to begin his formal studies. It seems the army has granted him another deferral so that he can start school now, and he's decided he'll join an infantry unit when the time comes. It's strange to hear him talking about this so casually.

We return to Nathan's apartment. Dana rushes in to show us the official document that has arrived from the commission, containing the full terms of the agreement. Dana points me to the final paragraphs and asks me to read them.

> The Commission hereby entrusts the manuscript into the hands of the petitioner (Nathan I assume) for a period of no longer than ten years, according to these terms: The manuscript shall be supervised professionally. It shall be Meir's duty to inform the Commission of any changes, breaches of agreement, or dangers to the manuscript. Meir is eligible to receive a monthly salary from Nathan in return for said services and interventions. After a

period of ten years, the British government will have the right to demand the return of the manuscript.

"Scoundrels!" says Nathan. "They want me to pay almost everything I have left from my father and from my own accounts, while they maintain all the rights." He huffs and puffs and gulps down a glass of water with lemon slices. But Dana hops up and down with excitement:

"You've won, Nathan! At long last we can go home together with the manuscript." Nathan scowls and smiles simultaneously. Rachel approaches me, presses my hand (I feel there is something a little strange about this), and tells me we're flying home tonight.

"Nathan and Dana will probably have to stay on a while until the manuscript is delivered," says Rachel. "We'll go home, take care of Maor, and wait for our baby."

It seems the suitcases are ready to go: everything's been packed for me, even my dirty clothes in a separate pile. Yaron says that soon they will come to take us to the airport, and he wants to start taking the luggage down. Dana hugs Rachel, and Yaron joins them before he leaves the flat. Dana asks Rachel for permission to kiss me. Rachel watches and is happy. Dana snuggles up, says she always wanted me more than I wanted her, that she always admired me more than I admire myself.

66

WE'RE HOME; or rather, in the apartment Nathan put at our disposal some months ago. The rooms feel strange to me, but it's good to be back. Shlomo and Shahar met us at the airport in a nice-looking car. They were both dressed in pale suits and were not very talkative. They asked a few questions about their father and about Dana. They were especially eager to know whether there's any chance of wrapping things up quickly with the British so their father can return. At the door we said goodbye and they told us we should call if we need anything.

"We're at your service," they say, and give Maor a hug to remind her that they're her loving brothers.

Rachel says we have two important missions ahead. One is the expected birth, and the other is Yaron's education.

"But there's one more important mission," I respond.

"And what's that?" she asks with a tired smile.

"It's time you figured that out for yourself. Your mission is to look after me now—someone's got to." Rachel blushes, but maybe this time she's pleased and not insulted. A few days later Yaron begins his regular Bible and Talmud studies in Jerusalem. He promises to come home at least once a week, but Rachel tells him not to wear himself out.

"Dad and I will miss you quietly here while you concentrate on your studies." I would have encouraged Yaron to come home more often, of course, but we'll just leave that for the time being.

This evening Dana calls from London and says she misses me already.

"It's awful here without you," she says to me. "There's so much red tape here, and Nathan is really nervous and getting fat again." I tell Dana I'm sure they'll be back in no time, and that Rachel and I have to prepare for the baby.

"Rachel's uncomfortable already."

"You and your baby," she laughs, and her voice sounds a little bitter to me. "Anyone would think it was your first child."

A few more days go by. Shlomo drops by and asks me to contact his father. But Dana answers the phone and says she's about to leave for Israel.

"I'm sick of waiting here. Henri can stay with Nathan." Now Nathan grabs the phone.

"How's my apartment? Enjoying it, as usual?" he asks, with a snicker perhaps. He then wants to know whether I've been in regular contact with his boys, and how Maor is. "Don't go putting any of those strange ideas of yours into her childish head." Then he has a coughing fit and Henri rushes over with his medication (or so it sounds from this end). Suddenly he raises his voice—I don't know if his words are aimed at Dana or at me on the phone.

"And what if it's all just an illusion? Dana's luscious body, the painted mirror I sold, and the manuscript I'm about to acquire—what if it's all a strange and arbitrary figment of my imagination?" he ends the conversation, and I'm afraid. Suddenly a thought occurs to me. Why is it that when you're in a room with someone, you look at their eyes? I mean, there are so many other places to look. Dana takes the phone again and asks to speak to me. She says she's coming back soon and would like to live with us for a while, if possible.

"I miss you, Meir." I quickly tell Rachel and she answers that someone around here is being totally ridiculous.

A few days later Dana arrives and comes straight here, carrying a small suitcase and a rather large toy for Maor. She embraces Rachel and caresses my face.

"So, Meir, you must be pleased with yourself: you've beaten everyone. Our shy and vulnerable Meir. You know that I'm in love with you, don't you? Maybe I don't love you, but I am in love with you. Rachel can explain the difference. I need a little rest from Nathan—he's wearing me out. I don't think I'm really sick of him yet, but I need a rest and I also want to be near you both. So here I am, Meir, the way you always wanted. I didn't come here to spoil anything for you and Rachel. I just want to be close." Rachel, turning pale, stares at her in mortification and leaves the room. I watch as Dana draws closer to embrace me. "Come back, Rachel, come back," she calls aloud. "See for yourself, I'm embracing Meir very carefully—there's no temptation here, nothing immoral." She laughs strangely on my shoulder.

Rachel doesn't appear and doesn't answer. Dana picks Maor up asks me to carry her suitcase down. She says she'll go to her own apartment and leave us alone for a few days. Then she asks if I can help her get organized the first few days and tells me that Nathan is not in good health. I quickly carry her suitcase down to the street, and am back upstairs even before her taxi arrives. Rachel sits waiting for me in tears, though I'd hoped somehow that she would jump up and greet me joyfully.

A few hours later Dana calls, tells us how tired she is and that she has a stomachache. She asks first Rachel and then me what she should do. Says she'll stay at the apartment only if I promise to come visit her there. Then suddenly she says again:

"Okay, Meir. You win. I get the message, and I want to be near you, like you always wanted me to be." I'm speechless. She's making this very hard for me, her voice is grating, unrelenting, I ask her to stop, and she whispers that I must now look after her as well. "You can't just win the day and disappear. *Noblesse oblige,* Meir." I answer that I know nothing about winning, that I've never fought a war, that Rachel is about to give birth, and that I have to get ready. Dana's voice sounds calmer suddenly and she says that we can work it out. "We'll make sure Nathan takes care of all our finances. I'm not willing to go without money again, that's my big fear." Again she laughs in a strange, lamenting voice, and says: "So, Meir, I guess we hate the things Nathan does, but we love the man himself."

67

A FEW HOURS LATER Rachel tells me it's time to go to the hospital. I'm frightened but am able to calm down more quickly than usual. Rachel kisses my face and says that from this moment on she'll have to concentrate on her body. Again Dana calls (what does she want in the middle of the night?) and says she's been thinking a lot about the two of us and has a solution for every problem. I tell her Rachel's in labor and she says she'll meet us at the hospital right away. I say nothing in reply for fear of insulting her or angering Rachel, who is listening to the conversation.

We drive to the hospital and for the first time in quite a while I am behind the wheel. Not Rachel, not Yaron, and not a stranger! I'm glad we got back in time for the birth and Rachel is happy that the two of us are alone. I reflect on the child about to be born—I haven't asked Rachel the baby's sex, though it seems to me she hinted it was a girl—and how different its world will be from all that came before.

At the hospital Rachel is admitted for a preliminary check up. The nurse comes out and says there's still time. Half an hour later Rachel comes out and says we should leave for a few hours. Just then Dana arrives. Looking tired and distracted, she strokes Rachel's hair and kisses my cheeks. Dana says that if I'd like to sleep, she'll stay with Rachel and notify me when the time comes. Rachel is silent and I remain. The three of us go out to the car and I drive to the beach so we can get a breath of fresh air and watch the night. Dana tries to amuse us with anecdotes about London, how they dressed her up, how the commissioners tried to flirt with her, and then she reconstructs some jokes she didn't understand. I'm not sure it's right for the three of us to be hanging around together when Rachel is about to give birth.

Dana goes off to buy Rachel a drink and brings us all sweet snacks. Rachel leans on me, Dana walks silently and then suddenly laughs. She says she remembers our first meeting, the day she walked into our house as Nathan's messenger. She admits that she has never met anyone as clever as Nathan. He forgets nothing and there's nothing he doesn't understand.

"Except other people. He doesn't understand them very well," I say, to raise a laugh, but the two women beside me don't respond.

"Hey, Meir," Dana suddenly says, "you'll be there to enjoy the new baby from the very first day."

"From the very first minute," laughs Rachel. From this I deduce that she wants me to stay with her throughout the birth. I try to be witty again and say that I finally understand which came first, the chicken or the egg. They stand still and look at me, and I say that obviously the chicken came first, and the egg came from the chicken.

"Okay," says Rachel, "I think it's really time now."

Back at the hospital Shlomo and Shahar are waiting and that

seems strange to me, but Dana says she felt it was important to notify everyone. Shlomo approaches us, holds his hand out to me and I reach mine out to him, but we don't manage to shake hands. Again I reach out and though he intends to take my hand we don't quite connect. The hospital people take Rachel away and say they'll call me when they're ready. We go out to the waiting room. Shlomo and Shahar both talk together and are silent together, and it seems to me that they're playing chess. Dana wanders around and I pace. Finally she suggests that we sit down.

"Nathan may call you in the next few minutes," she says, "He'll probably be needing the apartment back as soon as he arrives." I contemplate the meaning of this bit of news and tell Dana that we're perfectly willing to return to our old apartment.

"I think Rachel will even be glad." Shahar comes up and says that we need to talk.

"All of us know by now that you're much stronger than we thought, Meir, stronger than you made yourself out to be, and it's time for us to start working together." I tell him that what I'm interested in at the moment is the birth. Rachel is having contractions and our new baby is right there. Suddenly Shahar punches me in the face. For a second I can't see anything and then a little blood seems to trickle down. He screams that everything's ruined because of me. "Father's wasting his time in London, the business is falling to pieces, and Dana is not being entirely faithful to Father, while you go on pretending to be unfazed." Shlomo jumps up to silence him, Shahar bursts into tears, and Shlomo takes him aside and comforts him. Dana says it's only a temporary upset and that nobody could be closer than we are. Shlomo says he's glad he has a chance to prove that he's the older brother for a change.

Just then the nurse calls me and I hurry, even run, to Rachel. I'm not sure there's an entrance from this direction, but I'm afraid to start looking for a different way in, so I push past the people in the direction of the doors and bump into them.

Rachel is crying happily, holding the baby. She says she waited, because she wanted me to be the first one to see her in the birthing room.

"But never mind, from this moment on the baby belongs to

you and me and nobody else, and we belong to her and to Yaron." I too start crying and caress my daughter's head. I decide that I will be with her forever, keeping a precise and continuous record of her life. Dana's at the door and Nathan's sons peek out behind her. I ask Rachel's permission and she agrees to let them all in for a moment, "and then tell them to leave us alone." Dana enters meekly, looks at the baby, hugs Rachel and wants to hug me, too. Shlomo runs in, says his father is on the phone, and hands me the receiver. Nathan congratulates me, tells me this is a cause for celebration, and reports that he'll be arriving in a few days and will thank me to vacate the apartment. I willingly agree. He suggests that I find myself another part-time job.

"With a wife and two kids and all your strange ideas you'll be needing more money, and you can't expect me to provide it all."

Shahar apologizes for the punch and the outburst. He asks if we have any baby names in mind. Rachel says that, if I agree, we'll call the baby after the boys' mother, Rina. They stare at us, so alone in the world they seem to be looking for their minds. Shlomo asks how to thank us. It's possible their father will not be able to provide me with a full-time job. Dana says she's sure I'll manage and wouldn't it be a wonderful idea for us all to visit Rina's grave in the village one of these days. Shlomo insists on knowing how to thank me. Shahar says maybe they could work for us and help around the house with little Rina, "the way you helped us when Maor was born." Shlomo says in jest that he'd even be willing to shave me every morning. Shahar rebukes him and I say there's nothing wrong in what he said. I'm amazed at the way people know how to get close to me and still make me angry.

Rachel and I go back to our original apartment. I carry little Rina and Yaron greets us at the door like someone who really knows how to be happy. Now that we're home I have to think how I'm going to handle the rest of my reports about Nathan and his wives. I can't go on using the old system now that we have a baby in the house. I'm determined to keep a running record of her every moment (or at least a few lines in summary), and I can't afford to be distracted at this point. Nathan will just have to find somebody else to chronicle his life and achievements, and if he can't, Rachel says, that's not my problem.

A few weeks later Dana comes to visit wearing shorts and sunglasses. She carries Maor in her arms and kisses the top of her head every few minutes. She looks at little Rina and probably remembers the Rina who lived and died. She talks to Rachel and barely looks at me. She adjusts her shorts when they hike up, as though she'd started out wanting to look modest but then forgot. She asks how Rachel is getting along in our small apartment.

"I mean, it got a little run down over the past few months." Rachel asks if I could make her a drink and reminds me that there are some delicious cookies in the kitchen that Yaron brought home from Jerusalem. I go off to prepare what they have ordered. I'm not sure what each of them wanted, but the important thing is to serve the drinks to them in reasonable fashion.

When I enter I find Maor looking at little Rina, and Dana looking at Rachel. Suddenly Dana looks in my eyes and says she's happy to be with us.

"I'm hearing such good things from Rachel—you two are like an old couple in love."

"There's a sweet poetic image," Rachel looks at me and says. She tells Dana that I have been giving private lessons and even lecturing large audiences. "He's becoming well known, more and more people are inviting him," she says.

"That really does suit Meir," Dana agrees.

"In any case, he does better staying home most of the time," Rachel says, and concludes: "When there's too much activity going on, you never know what might happen. Meir is a man of surprising powers, and I wouldn't want him to get us in trouble again."

From this I deduce that Rachel would prefer that I stay home. Maybe we should agree at the outset which part of the apartment I'll stay in most of the day. Though I prefer roaming around in big houses, I should be able to manage here. Nathan will soon be back, he'll need my help, and I'll have to send reports to the commission from time to time, in accordance with their specifications.

Rachel and Dana go on talking; I think they're making a date to meet. Before she leaves, Dana comes over, puts her hand on my shoulder, and looks at me. She says I'd better not make any other women fall for me or get confused by my behavior. She says I have a beautiful family and that she has to hurry home to find out if Nathan's left any messages about his return.

As soon as she leaves Nathan calls and asks where Dana is and whether we're looking after her properly. He says he's happy to hear my voice and that he'll be back in Israel by the end of the week.

"Don't think I've forgotten a certain service you provided, Meir. Sometimes, a man's friend can be even closer than his wife. Once, in my office, when we were arguing about the meaning of idolatry, you used a verse from the Book of Deuteronomy to prove that the greatest temptation to idolatry may actually stem from a person's closest friend." Then he coughs and I'm alarmed at the way he came up with this example out of the blue. As soon as he returns, he says, he will ask me to advise him how to proceed with the manuscript.

I say goodbye and, somewhat excited, I wish him a safe journey. This evening, I think, I'll try to work out with Rachel which room I should stay in for most of the day—and when, in spite of everything, I should visit Yaron in Jerusalem.

Miron C. Izakson, born in 1956, is the author of seven books of poetry and two novels. His poems have been translated into several languages. *Nathan and His Wives,* first published in Hebrew (1998), subsequently appeared in French translation (2001). Izakson received the President of Israel Literature Award in 2001. He is the chairman of the Literature Department of the Israel Art and Culture Council. He is married and a father to seven children.

Betsy Rosenberg has translated the work of many Israeli authors, including David Grossman and Aharon Appelfeld. She won the British Comparative Literature Association Prize (1994–95) and the Marsh Award for Children's Literature in Translation (1999–2000).

Ken Frieden holds the B. G. Rudolph Chair in Judaic Studies and is a full professor in the Department of English, Literature, and Religion at Syracuse University. His books include *Classic Yiddish Fiction: Abramovitsh, Sholem Aleichem, and Peretz* (1995) and the forthcoming anthology *Classic Yiddish Stories.*